BROKEN LULLABIES

RYAN T. SMITH

ISBN-13 Number: 978-0692275344
ISBN-10 Number: 0692275347

"The truth is rarely pure and never simple."

-Oscar Wilde, The Importance of Being Ernest

Prologue

They say an egg will fry on the hood of a car during a Missouri heat wave. Once the heat index goes over 115 degrees Fahrenheit it'll fry something like some bacon and eggs on a Sunday morning after church. When Milton Hawkins's head made its way all over the hood of his car no one would have mistaken it for a fried egg. It could have passed for one of those so called edible somethings next to the chicken sold at the gas station in town, not the crispy finger foods of course. It was more like those gizzards in the sauce, definitely the ones in the sauce.

Six minutes before his head would come to resemble a gas station appetizer Hawkins heard the first set of tires throwing gravel from his driveway. Milton looked to the sky as the birds flew the coop of his private forest home, most certainly sensing his ill-fated future. Any car that would make the turn onto his driveway would warrant a closer look. If anyone made it up the three hundred yard drive, and past the rusted out three-wheeled school bus, the house surely turned them away, not even the door-to-door steak salesman bothered once they saw the 65-year-old farmhouse with a wrap- around porch that no longer wrapped around. Milton listened to the second, third, and fourth car pull onto the drive. After four he stopped counting. He was busted. Cars were still heard turning onto his gravel road when the lead Impala came into view. They'd sent the cavalry, he knew they would.

The cars quickly formed a barricade around the detached garage Milton had been working outside of, working to transform his tan Cutlass into a blue get away car. He could see three different colored Impalas. He made out the cars; State, County, and City squad cars. They knew who he was, and he knew the score. Milton had three options, and 7 seconds to pick one.

He could turn himself in, and go back to jail. That was number one, not really an option.

He could make a run for. He guessed the number of officers to be about forty-five, and knowing they were smack dab in the center of 12 acres didn't make this a viable option. Even if he wanted to take out a few cops he wouldn't get far, but that wasn't his kind of thing. It was a no on option two.

That left number 3. Milton always thought three was a bad luck number. Criminals were superstitious that way. Put a one if front of that three and you're left with unlucky 13. In the end it was his only option, and he didn't need seven seconds to make any kind of decision. He knew the outcome long before he heard any tires spitting rock across the driveway. It was a fate he had chosen from the cold emptiness of his cell. The fate he sealed in his last couple of days in this world.

Milton walked to the driver's side door of the 1986 Cutlass Sierra. The hood of the car remained a sun-faded tan, almost white. The rest of the car had been painted navy blue by Milton. Once his sketch appeared on the previous evening news it was only a matter of time till someone called in to put a name to his face. This was his last known address. It didn't take long. Milton thought to himself how maybe he didn't want to get away. Then he saw the ambulance off to the side of the brigade, maybe there never was an option one. No, no way.

The just under six foot, and just over a buck fifty ex- con reached into the driver's window of the car. He grabbed the revolver off the cracked leather seat. Milton stood up and looked at the rear driver's side window. He smiled at his reflection one last time, and admired his newly bleached hair. He rubbed his bare chin, wondering if even his oldest friends would recognize him without the goatee, and long dark hair.

Milton ignored the screaming officers, unfazed by the Captain with the bullhorn. He reached to the back of his neck for his chain. It had been around his neck as long as he could remember. The chain carried a medallion of St. Nicholas, the Patron Saint of Children. In the fifth grade when he forgot to wear it his mother showed up before school's first bell to put it back in its rightful place. Since then it was only removed to check into prison, and even that was temporary. It had been a part of Milton's life until last night.

The shadows of the trees started to close in. A small ray of sun burst through the trees, and reflected off of his new hair color. He smiled at the glow around his head and thought of his childhood trailer home. So this is what flashes in front of your eyes before death, he thought to himself. Milton looked down and ran his hand across his chest one last time, feeling lost, naked without the medallion. It was better off now, he told himself. This time Saint Nicholas would complete his task at hand. Milton looked to the firing squad as they waited for him to announce his end. A silence overtook his world. The standoff had come to its finale, time to choose his inevitable fate. Option three.

The screaming approached paranoia as he dropped his hands from his chest. He walked to the front of the Cutlass. Milton looked at the broken down home. It had to have been thirty years since it was painted. He didn't know if the garage was ever painted. The bullhorn sounded like the Captain was sitting right on the hood of Milton's car. It was so loud he couldn't make out what was being said or didn't care. He remembered when he first saw the ad for this property in the paper.

Farmhouse in need of some TLC, 12 Acres, Mostly wooded.

It was a sorry ad that was still better than the house, which was in need of much more than "some TLC." He watched the line of officers facing him. He could hear the screaming, the bullhorn, even the helicopter above him. He looked back to the house, so much to do. The bullhorn went silent, as did the helicopter. Milton watched the chaos, saw it unfold, he heard nothing. He smiled to the bullhorn. The gun rose. The birds were now gone, silence.

Then six seconds of continuous gunfire filled the quiet forest. Calm smoke cut into the air. Milton's body slid down the once tan hood of the once tan Cutlass Sierra. His body buckled over in front of the car then slowly rolled until it stopped under the front of the hood. The hood Milton didn't have time to paint. The hood that was now streaked red with a resemblance of the grilled somethings they sell with fried chicken.

The heat index was one hundred and seventeen degrees. The metal of the car was over 140 degrees to the touch, hot enough to fry an egg.

Chapter 1

"I'm going to need a urine sample." The Assistant Principal was precise and direct. Cammy stared into the vomit filled trashcan as one of her superiors continued the order, "Before you leave today."

Assistant Principal Savard was one of five bosses Cameron Hart had to answer to. The High School had four assistant principals, and one main principal. Last year the school district cut ten percent of the faculty and staff from Franklin High. All four assistant principals and the school's Head Principal received a measly five percent pay increase. They felt they still deserved the full seven and a half percent a year increase because they had been counting on it.

Cammy was THE guidance counselor at the high school. The year before the school had two women doing her job, which was cut down from three the year before that. Cammy was a year removed from receiving her Master's so she was willing to work hard. So now Franklin High had one hard working counselor making the minimum salary while the town had two more families struggling to make ends meet. Budget cuts.

Cammy wiped the puke off her chin. She was about to speak when she lost what was left of her morning bagel. It was the third week of school, third straight week of morning sickness, and still only nine in the morning. She felt like each day was worse than the previous, and longer. Cammy couldn't remember throwing up this much since college when Gatorade and Advil cured all.

There were a total of eight faculty and staff members who lost their jobs last year. Six were due to the ever-decreasing amount of money given to the district by the state. The other two were not asked back when their side-jobs as meth cooks resulted in a couple of exploding homes, and future court dates. Cammy figured the random drug test would become more isolated once she was found kneeling in front of a trash can every morning. She could tell Savard the truth, but it didn't matter. She'd still need that urine.

The assistant principal started to leave, but turned back with a smile.

"Oh, and before I forget, we are celebrating for Hannah Cross in the faculty lounge. If you feel better come down for some cake." Savard smiled at Cammy, then waddled her pink pantsuit out of the office.

Walking wasn't an option at the time for Cammy so she'd have to rely on gossip for any breaking details. Hannah Cross was the story of the year in Franklin County, and the first time Cammy's new town was heard of by anyone on the other side of the Missouri state line.

Chapter 2

The toilet was disgusting. Just looking at it could make me puke. Apparently this year's janitor was as productive as last year's tweaker. I listened to the two cheerleaders putting on make-up at the sink. They didn't help my situation. The current predicament I found myself in was trying to vomit, silently, while appearing to take a monster shit. My ass was over the back of the toilet as I held my face over the seat, using the seat. A talent made possible by a lonesome childhood of self- taught gymnastics. The last thing I wanted was these two gossip bitches putting my biz on Facebook. Fucking Facebook.

"I'm glad they shot the sicko," one of them said. "I mean what a perv." This was just minutes after bragging about having two different dicks in her mouth over the past weekend. I'd put that on Facebook, but most likely, she already did.

I held my ass in the air, and face over the toilet for a couple more seconds before I gave up. If I was going to vomit my bathroom yoga had prevented anything from leaving my stomach. I stood up straight to stretch out, flushed the toilet, and walked out of the stall. There were three sinks in the girls' bathroom. The cheerleaders occupied the two outside ones. I walked up to the middle sink. They both stopped talking. I didn't look at either one of them. In the mirror I stared at my pale reflection, beads of sweat had bubbled on my forehead. I wiped it into my hair, what a sweaty mess. I turned the water on and splashed my face a couple of times, then swished some water into my mouth. I could feel the cheerleaders both watching me, waiting for me to leave. Finally I gave the blow job queen my best F- off look as I spit the water back into the sink, most certainly getting some on her purse and make- up bag. I walked out of the bathroom, trying not to smile as I heard them resume talking. I really didn't give a shit if they liked me or not. I had no friends my freshman year, and was in no rush to make friends as a sophomore either.

"What a freaking freak," Queen BJ said.

"For real," said Cheerleader number two. What an insightful addition to the conversation.

Chapter 3

It had been 72 hours since all of Missouri, and most of the Midwest had learned the name Hannah Cross. The first grade girl was walking to school with a neighbor when she fell behind. Her older neighbor's observant fifth grade recollection would ultimately lead to a manhunt for the recently released convict Milton Hawkins, and the rescue of the little girl.

The fifth grader Jasmine relayed all the details of the morning walk to the police. Hannah was bending over to pick up a dead orchid along the sidewalk. She shook the brown dust left by passing cars off the flower, and continued to walk behind her friend. Well, behind her neighbor. It wasn't Jasmine's idea to walk Hannah to school every morning, her mother made her do it. She made her do it not as a favor to the girl's parents even though she had never even spoken to them. Jasmine's mother made her walk with Hannah because she always feared something would happen to the little girl with no supervision. She was often outside after dark and walking around the neighborhood alone. The girl was always alone. Jasmine's mother had never even seen the mother till the little girl went missing. The father worked nights, she believed, his truck was there in the day. The parents never came out of the house.

Jasmine recalled the morning walk to the police. She periodically looked back at the little girl, who would continue to fall further behind as she examined the dying flowers. Jasmine yelled to her whenever Hannah fell too far back.

The morning breeze was cool for the scorcher that arrived later that morning, when the sun would demand the full attention of all Missouri. The further the girls walked the heavier Jasmine's feet got, and the less she looked back on her job assignment. Then she heard the man. Jasmine saw him talking to Hannah, who just nodded her head and took the man's hand. She was led to the passenger door by a skinny guy with long dark hair, and a long dark goatee. Jasmine ran toward her, but was too late. The tan Cutlass Sierra peeled out, and before Jasmine knew what was happening Hannah was gone. That was the story Jasmine relayed to the Franklin County P.D.

An APB was put out on a mid 80's tan Oldsmobile Cutlass Sierra. Jasmine was able to describe the assailant in detail. He was a white male with shoulder length dark hair, and a dark mustache and goatee. Despite the long hair and facial hair he had noticeably high cheek bones to go along with the long banana seat face. He was believed to be around thirty years old, and able to tip a scale to 150 pounds on a full stomach.

The next seventy hours were tense in the County. Cammy joined other faculty members in the school district to distribute fliers with Hannah's photo. A police sketch of the kidnapper created from Jasmine's description was taken to local businesses to learn of any recent purchases or habits.

Cammy knew from her research like obsession with true life crime shows that the odds of finding Hannah greatly decreased after 48 hours. One of her favorite shows was even titled from this fact. She wanted to be in the faculty lounge learning about Hannah and what had taken place in the last few hours. Maybe the cake and other sweets would help her- probably not. She would have to continue to hide in her office until ten, that's when the morning sickness subsided.

Chapter 4

My third hour class was Art II, best class of the day by far. Not that I was a great artist or anything, after the first assignments were displayed I realized I may have been the worst in the class. I did the work though, and that's really all these teachers cared about. My other classes were easy. Spanish II was my toughest, but I managed an 88% on the first test. I'll take that.

Art Class was kind of fun because there wasn't a lot of thinking, just doing. The other students were pretty cool for the most part. There were a couple football players and their cum-dumpster cheerleaders, but all four sat in a corner by themselves. They pretty much messed around on their phones the whole time, the other students were either the Artsy type, or loners. I would classify myself as part of the latter group, but some these loners tried to be friends with anyone. Like I said though, most weren't bad to talk to. It was just today I wasn't in the mood for anyone. I tried to bury my face in a charcoal drawing of a tree in the middle of a river. It wasn't really the typical drawing of one of us loners. It lacked all teen angst, death, or destruction.

"Macie, hey Macie whatcha scribbling there?" asked Cooper Lawson. Cooper was a kid who tried much too hard to be part of any group.

This would lead to his time in high school as being classified a Career Loner.

"What's up Coop?" I asked but really just said. I wasn't looking for any kind of detailed answer. We live in the same trailer park, and had been in class together since kindergarten so I'd known him since forever. I did my best to be nice, but whenever I talked to him too much he ended up with the wrong impression.

"What's that picture there?" he asked. He kept talking without waiting for a reply. "Hey, you see they shot that kidnapper this morning, thirty-some cops took him down, I heard they blew his shit all over the place."

"How would I not hear, it's all anyone in this school is talking about."

"Yeah," he said. One thing about Cooper was he was smart enough to know when I didn't feel like talking to him. "Girl's safe, that's good," he said. It was his way to get out of the conversation.

"It is?" I asked him. I was kind of annoyed with all of it by now. "It's good there's a little girl who's going to be pretty fucked up for the rest of her life, and we got a bunch of people who are so de-sensitized to violence that they all have hard- ons over a man getting his brain blown all over Franklin God Damn County. It's a real feel-good story Cooper."

"OK, forget it. The girl's safe is all I'm saying."

"Well, I think the whole thing is pretty fucked up and sad really, all of it. The little girl, her poor mom, the dead guy, it's all pretty sad. But Cooper you wanna know what I find to be

14

the most depressing part of this whole happening?"

"Hmm?" he asked. Already half turned back around in his desk.

"Kidnapping, drugs, death all over the TV's, newspapers, our phones, and in the end everyone is just looking at it as something to use to make conversation, but never something they really talk about," I said. He gave me a blank stare, not really sure what it was I was saying. I wasn't really too sure myself, but I had an idea. No one did talk about the people, just the event. This usually led back to talking about themselves, and some fucked up story in their life, which was something I didn't care about. I don't go crying about my shit life to you, so don't come telling me about yours.

The dejected loner gave me a half smile. He mumbled something to himself as he turned back around to continue his drawing of a Zombie milking a cow. Sometimes I felt bad for treating him like shit, but most the time he just kind of creeped me out.

Chapter 5

Fifteen minutes after Assistant Principal Savard demanded Cammy's body waste there was a knock at the door. The door swung open and Pete Wellman smiled at Cammy before she could answer. He held a piece of chocolate cake. Pete was the Home Economics, Show Choir, and Acting teacher. If a modeling agency ever crossed his path he could be a star within a year. His surfer good looks in middle of nowhere Missouri worked as blinders to the rest of the female faculty to his true physical desires.

"How about some cake Princess?" Pete sang as he waltzed into her office. "How're we doing this morning?"

"Same as every morning, shitty," Cammy complained. Pete was the only person at the school Cammy had told she was pregnant. She actually never told him, he figured it out, like he never really told her that he slept in a different room than his wife. Pete came in every morning after second hour for their morning chats. These chats inspired rumors among faculty and students alike of a passionate love affair between the two. It would make sense if you looked at the two together. Pete's surfer good looks would be perfectly matched with Cammy's olive skin and dark hair. It was her green eyes that usually stole the attention of the fathers who would talk to her about their children. If the concerned dads weren't focused on her eyes they would find some body part to try to sneak a peek at. Cammy was a cheerleader in college and still held that small framed fit body. It didn't help deter the gawkers that she was perfectly proportioned in every way. Compared with the pasty skin and cigarette stained fingers of most woman in town, Cammy was the closest thing to pure beauty they knew. The rumors still made Cammy laugh since Pete was the one man in town she knew she could never seduce.

No new information had come out since the initial press release detailing the recovery of Hannah Cross.

A young couple had stumbled across her path while they were cutting through a car wash parking lot at three in the morning. Hannah was hiding in a car bay when she called out to the couple. The little girl's hair had been cut like a boy. She had been dressed in a red tank top, and red basketball shorts. The intoxicated co-ed somehow managed to see through the little boy masquerade and recognized the missing girl from three days of constant media coverage. The only other information released was that Hannah was completely healthy and unharmed. Not a scratch on her body.

Chapter 6

Pete put an elbow up on Cammy's desk to move closer. This was the way he crossed over into conversation they weren't supposed to have. Cammy smiled, "What do ya got?"

"Do you know Macie Jennings, or have you heard of her family?" he asked. He got up and closed the office blinds.

Cammy shook her head to let him know she never heard of the girl or her family.

"Six years ago her sister was found dead on the banks of the river. You haven't heard the story of J.C. Jennings?"

"They're Macie and Jacie?" Cammy asked.

"J.C. was Jaclyn Christina I think, that doesn't matter. She was an addict, like most of the Jennings Clan. Only thing more shocking than her death was the lack of an investigation."

"What's to investigate? Cops know an O.D." Cammy snapped so he'd be clear on her lack of compassion for addicts. Cammy had a brother who was addicted to meth. His addiction left her with a firsthand experience of what it did to families- what it did to her family. Her lack of sympathy for users was a product of her brother's sickness, but 'sickness' was not how she would describe addiction. She fought for ten years to get him help, but he convinced her family he had it under control. Cammy

18

ultimately demanded he attend rehab. Her parents took his side, so she left. That was four years ago.

"They felt the same. My personal opinion was there wasn't much of an autopsy either," he said. Pete was the one person who may have been even more criminally educated by television than Cammy.

"Why should they? County's broke, let'em all kill themselves," she snapped back. Cammy's lack of sympathy baffled the Home Ec teacher. She was supposed to be on his side. Part of their job was to be optimists in education.

"Well, she was pregnant," Pete waited for a reaction. Cammy failed to appease him.

"Half these girls are knocked up," she said. "You think because I'm pregnant I'm going to care? I don't."

"For the third time."

"How old?"

"Seventeen," he said. Pete leaned forward before he delivered his final tidbit of info. "No babies, she was never a mother."

"Go on," Cammy insisted. He had finally managed to garner some interest from the counselor. Pete told Cammy how J.C. Jennings was pregnant in each of her first three years of High School. The first two pregnancies ended in miscarriage, both during the third trimester, and both within days of being full term. "What about the third pregnancy?" Cammy asked.

"Never would admit it, denied the pregnancy for eight and a half months," Pete said. "At one point she was telling people she had a cyst growing in her stomach."

"Maybe she did."

"Girl, I do have two kids. I know what a pregnant woman looks like," Pete reminded her.

"Do you know what a pregnant woman looks like?" Cammy asked. "In the flesh?" she smirked.

"I'm ignoring you because this brings us to what I want to talk to you about. Macie, Jaclyn Christina's little baby sister, seems she brought back a bit of a baby bump from summer break. I'm guessing she's about five to six months."

"I told you they're all pregnant. Every week I get another one. That's actually a fact, it's the third week of school and she makes the third candidate for next season's Teen Mom," Cammy said. "Should I call MTV?"

"Ask her," Pete said.

"Why don't you? You're the one who's concerned. They won't tell me anything till they need to anyway," Cammy said.

"I can't ask a fifteen year old girl if she's pregnant. What if she's not? I could lose my job. You know how emotional they are," Pete said.

"I can?" Cammy asked. She stood up, and shook her head. She knew Pete was right, he couldn't ask. You could offend anyone by saying anything these days, especially discussing something as sensitive as a teen girl's body. Pete Wellman talking to a sixteen year old girl about anything other than sewing, cooking, and hitting a high C- note could be grounds for termination. Franklin County had enough unemployed parents with their back alley divorce lawyers on speed dial, all who would love a shot at holding the school district ransom for a few extra bucks.

Macie was a sophomore so Cammy could call her in to go over her Four- Year Plan. The plan was a tool used by the school to make sure the students would graduate in four years. Macie didn't have her plan set in the computer. She wasn't on pace to graduate in four years either, so a meeting would be needed. Cammy looked up from her computer.

"I need to meet with her anyway. She managed six of eight credits as a freshman," Cammy shook her head. Students complete eight credits a year. Thirty- two credits were needed to graduate. "I'll have her mom come in too."

"Ha, you're so new, even after seven months," Pete said.

"What's that mean?" she asked.

"Mom was Donovan Elliott's number one cook," he said. Pete spread his hands wide in the air. "Then," he paused for effect, "ka-boom."

Chapter 7

Fourth hour was movie hour every Friday. The reason being the twenty- four year-old first year English teacher was typically hung over. He liked to frequent the local bars on Thursdays, usually starting right at 3:30 when he left school. I knew this because my 'boyfriend' Angel washed the dishes at the Mexican restaurant where Mr. Danzel was a Happy Hour fixture. The potent aroma of Cool Water cologne and Altoids I smell from the third row every Friday always confirmed the hangover. This Friday's movie was another Shakespeare remake, this one with Leonardo DiCaprio. We didn't even read any Shakespeare, according to HIS syllabus. I'm sure he figured we'd like it because it was cool when he was in high school, probably touched his first tit when he saw it or something.

I wondered this because that's what was going on in the front row. Some couple sitting right in front of him was into some heavy petting, I think the guy actually tried to get his hand into her jeans. He looked like a five year old boy digging for earthworms. Good luck with that buddy.

I wouldn't say I'm annoyed when I see these couples pulling some serious PDA. I'm not even disgusted or upset or anything like that. It's not like I'm some bible thumper, or a virgin for that matter. I guess I'm just kind of bitter. The bitterness is most likely a direct result of my love life, or maybe the start of it.

The large hand sat on the little girl's upper thigh, I was seven- I was that little girl. I didn't know who the man was. I had never seen him before, and there had been plenty of men who came in and out of our trailer when I was little. This guy was different, he didn't go into the bedroom with my mother right away, he wanted to sit and talk in the kitchen- with me- he told my mom.

"What is this? What happened to yer blue jeans?" he asked me. I remember silence. I couldn't answer, or didn't want to.

"Macie Marie," my mother stuttered. "Answer the man, answer Mr. C." I asked her to help me with a look, a look she ignored. "You answer him now."

He leaned close enough so I could smell the muddle of tobacco and whiskey on his breath. His fingers slid under my cut off blue jeans, "Ya heard yer mama, answer me girl."

I remember the heat on my cheeks and the cool I felt from my tears. I still don't know if I was crying because of him, or my mother. "They ain't blue jeans," I stammered. He raised his eyebrows and looked into my lap. His fingers crawled higher.

"Sure look like blue jeans."

"I cut'em, they're shorts."

He smiled to my mother, then turned back to me. His laughter was followed by a booming voice that yelled, "Aah, there ya go, that's my girl. She can talk." I shuttered as he clawed at me. I looked to my mother, she had turned around. I watched her walk out the trailer.

You could say I was born alone, I say it. I don't know a damn thing about my mother actually. When I was three she fell off the wagon, and went back to meth. It was her only true love in life that she had abandoned after the birth of my sister, so the story goes. That was the last time I ever saw that woman. After her revamped taste of ice she was a different person. I was lucky though, I had my sister to look after me, for a little while anyway. My sister knew she had to get me out of there, or I would end up like that woman, or my sister. When J.C. asked for our birth certificates the crack head said she lost my original. She eventually started to cook meth in the shed out back. She did this so she could provide for my sister and me, so she said. It didn't last long. J.C. used to tell me our mother wasn't a smart woman to begin with, the drugs sure never helped. So she claimed to have lost all of our paperwork, there's really no reason not to believe it. Addicts pretty much lose everything, and then they're dead. If it is meth and they're cooking, death usually comes by fire. That was how she met her demise, a big exploding trailer.

My sister was the closest thing I ever had to a real mother. She was my only mother. My sister passed when I was ten years old, so then it was a life of state provided foster care. It's safe to say I learned to fend for myself at an early age, eventually leaving last year when I turned sixteen. The last lady could have called the police to get me back, she didn't.

Broken Lullabies

I went to live with a guy, the dishwasher. Most people think he's my boyfriend, I'm pretty sure he does. I don't think I ever loved him, but I don't hate him. He's a good guy, it works in the end.

Chapter 8

Two trucks sat side by side at the entrance to the trailer park. They were facing opposite ways so the drivers could talk, but really so they could make the deal. Neither of these two ass holes seemed to care about the four little kids throwing rocks at each other twenty feet away. They only cared about their business deal. The dealer cared about money, the addict about his fix, and neither gave a shit about anything else in the world.

I pedaled my purple Schwinn past the two men, and I made sure they saw me stare at them the whole time. My bike was really a status symbol in Franklin County among sixteen- year-old girls. Maybe it wasn't, but kind of, it cleared up any questions of my social status: loser. I had gotten over all that, and had learned to embrace my bike. It was a brilliant purple with a purple basket on front. The basket might sound childish, but it came in pretty handy when going back and forth to school. Plus I figured my main mode of transportation was a bike, it didn't really matter if the bike appeared to belong to a fifth grade girl or me- it was a fucking bike. I even added a little bell about a year ago. The bell was a nice tool to ring as an F- You when people gave me looks I didn't like.

The addict quickly turned away when he noticed me looking at him, and looked into his lap. The dealer held eye contact with me as I watched him. He is that type of guy who feels like he can intimidate and frighten people just from his menacing stare. Like I would cower and look away from his big bad self. I'm sure he recognized me. I recognized him. He was a Vandal, the local biker gang, and supplier of whatever it is you were addicted to in Franklin County.

The biker selling was Vampire Eddy. Not his real name, of course. Eddy was a lifer who grew up in Franklin County. The rumor was he had a brother who lived here in the park. About a month ago the two hoosiers got in a fist fight in front of his brother's trailer. The fight was over money or drugs, I'd guess. Eddy suffered a broken nose. He fared better than his little brother who ended up with two broken ribs and thirty- seven stitches from his shoulder across his back courtesy of a broken beer bottle that was lying under the steps. Like I said the rumor was it was his brother, I stay out of this trailer park bullshit, so I couldn't say for certain.

I rode past the brother of the year candidate and stopped my bike at our row of mailboxes. Two women sat on the bench along the road. They were both rail thin, pale as the teeth they used to have, and had thin stringy hair that looked like it would fall out if they did decide to shower. The only difference between the two was one had red hair, and the other was a brunette.

"How's it going?" I asked. Neither acknowledged me. Why should they? They didn't seem to notice their children were throwing rocks at each other right next to an obvious drug deal. I wasn't going to get them to acknowledge me. They were lost in whatever it was they both saw in the sky. The brunette may have been sleeping. I didn't stick around long enough to get a good look. I threw the mail in the basket, and hopped back on the bike.

I rode along the road in the gravel through the trailer park. It always amazed me when I saw someone driving through here like they were in a race to get somewhere special and managed to not kill anyone. I stopped at the bottom of our double- wide stairs, and grabbed my bag and mail from the basket. A large manila envelope with my name written across the center was at the bottom of my basket. Did I pull it out of the mailbox? It was missing my address and a return address. I ripped open the envelope while I was still straddled over the seat. What would be hand delivered to me? I pulled a black notebook from the envelope, and flipped the cover over to reveal the first page. I read *My Dearest Macie,* and thumbed through the pages till I got to the last page of writing. Holy Shit! It was him.

Chapter 9

The News Channel 4 Helicopter was still perched two hundred yards over the Hawkins' property when Cammy drove home. All traffic was detoured from the crime scene to Main Street, which was less than two miles from where Hannah was held captive, while over three hundred volunteers had combed the entire town for any sign of the missing girl.

Cammy turned the television to the nightly news as soon as she walked in the door. She never got the internet since she had free access at school; the only problem was many websites were restricted on the school's server. Cammy grabbed a jar of peanut butter, spoon, diet soda, and parked herself in front of the TV for the night.

The coverage alternated between the criminal history of Milton Hawkins, and the local police triumphantly handing over Hannah to her father. Her mother was not in the clip, which lasted a total of fifteen seconds. It was played throughout the night, well over sixty times.

Chapter 10

The notebook in the mail would not go over well with Angel. I think it's safe to say he would have flipped his Latin lid if he found out, so I would be sure he didn't. The good thing for me was he pretty much left me alone most the time, and I knew where he'd be when I walked in the door. I put the envelope containing the notebook in my book bag while I was still at the bottom of the steps. I locked up my bike, and walked inside the trailer.

"Hey," Angel mumbled from the couch. I looked to my left, nodded, and walked to the bedroom on the right. The bedroom of the trailer was small, as you might guess. It was big enough for a queen size bed, with maybe an eighteen inch path around the bed to walk. It wasn't quite high end living. I climbed over a pile of Angel's dirty clothes and went to the far side of the room, my side of the bed. I threw my bag on the bed, unzipped it, and took the envelope out. Angel was walking around now, probably trying to stretch his legs because I'm sure he'd been sitting there all damn day. His sliding feet got closer. I heard his feet at the tile floor in the kitchen. I quickly picked up the mattress and threw the envelope between the mattress and box spring.

"No Hello?" he asked. I froze for a second before I turned to him. I stared at the six foot, two hundred and fifty pound Angel who took up the entire doorway to the room.

"What? I said hi," I said.

"No you didn't, what's up?"

"Well I nodded, that's pretty much the same thing," I said back to him. Did he see me? How long was he there, I know I heard him walking, but was the door open? It's a doorway, with some kind of hanging beads that act as a door, either way, if they're pulled shut you can't see through them. Not clearly at least.

"Suit yourself," he said. He didn't really care if I said shit to him or not. I know him, he was just worried I was up to something since I didn't drop my bag and head to the fridge. My typical routine when I get in. "So what are you doing?" he asked. He emphasized the word are, which proved my point he was just being nosy.

"Nothing, I just have a lot of shit to do, thought I'd get started." I nodded to him, he just nodded back. Felt like we sat there nodding for thirty seconds- minimum. I raised my eyebrows to him as I rolled my eyes toward my bag. He got the hint.

"K," he said and started to walk away. He took two steps and turned back around. Ugh, what does he want now? "Did you hear about the thing? For the girl?" The 'thing,' was a big show planned for the Mayor and other local Politicians and police officers to get a chance to present themselves on TV with Hannah and her family. One of those giant kiss our ass events, not my thing really, at all.

"How could I not?"

"Well a heads up, I'm probably expected to be there," he said. I just nodded. He knew I didn't give a shit where he was expected to be. I didn't say anything. "So you should probably go too," he said. He didn't want to go, that's why he said it more as a question than statement. I know he wanted me to say I wasn't going to go; he wanted an excuse not to go. He had already annoyed me by being nosy and up in my shit so I didn't give him the satisfaction. He stood there for another minute, neither of us spoke, finally he turned and walked away.

What did he see me do? What'd he think I was doing? Who cares really? If he knew, or found it he wouldn't do anything, he worshipped the ground I walked on. It is kind of nice having someone like that, probably why I was still there. He could read it and it wouldn't have changed a thing, I was pretty sure. I was very sure that I had to get away, I needed to read that notebook.

Chapter 11

Cammy watched the news for three hours. She waited to see more on the kidnapper's personal life, maybe even his early life. She knew he grew up in Franklin County, but that was really all they said about his life outside of crime. Is someone born a monster? Was he molested himself? His criminal history was deficient of any crimes against children, so how does a drug addict become a child predator?

Hawkins had been arrested multiple times for possession of illegal narcotics, and possession with intent to sell. The most he had ever spent in jail was thirty days. That was, until the last six year stint which ended just five days earlier.

Cammy watched all night. She thought of the entrance at the Wal- Mart in town. The wall between the two sets of doors, opposite the shopping carts, was a giant milk carton of missing children. The wall always had about twenty young faces, the faces were always smiling which Cammy felt were their last smiles of childhood. The faces were always changing. Changing to new smiling faces, left on the shopping center wall, then replaced by another. Hannah did not end up on that wall. She got to go home, she got to hug her parents, and everyone got to watch.

Just before mid- night Cammy decided she had seen enough, or seen the same clips enough times.   She walked across the one bedroom apartment and into her room. Cammy kneeled at the nightstand, to the picture of Russell in his Marine Uniform, and kissed it.

"Goodnight my love, hold you soon," she said. Cammy closed her eyes as her head landed on the pillow.

Chapter 12

Macie Jennings was late for school, she was late every day. In the school's attempt to rectify the problem she was transferred to a first hour study hall in second semester of her freshmen year. She could now be late, and the school could now look the other way. She continued to open each day with study hall sophomore year, she also continued with an unfailing ability to arrive after the first bell had already rung. The tardiness was ignored because she did show up, so she did count for attendance, and attendance was the magic number when it came to the state's cash flow into the district.

"Someone wants to see me?" Macie asked more than stated. The sixteen year-old-girl wore a long sleeve undersized button up with chewed up spit soaked sleeves. The white tank top underneath was so thin Cammy could see that Macie's bra was pink, together it was an amateur attempt to hide the little bump above her jeans.

"I remember you, Miss Hart, right?" she asked. Cammy remembered Macie too. It was hard to forget the little girl with curly hair that was so blond white may actually be the better way to describe it. An overbearing numbness overtook Cam's body when she met the girl, for the second time. Cammy was pretty sure Macie was pregnant, most likely in or near her third trimester.

Macie had come down at the end of the school year to talk with Cammy. She wanted to know how easy it was to get emancipated from the state. Cammy gave her the usual information, Macie wasn't the first high school kid in Franklin County to believe she could live on her own. Cammy re-called the first meeting in her head as she went over Macie's four- year plan, the reason she told her she had called her down in the first place.

Macie entered Cammy's office that previous April morning like a countless number of the ninth grade girls living anywhere in the Country. She didn't like school, being told what to do, and couldn't get along with her foster mother. Cammy remembered Macie had stormed in, unscheduled, and started asking questions before her presence was acknowledged. She was more abrasive than expected of a girl with such a frail, delicate frame. Then again Cammy had been learning in that first year the smaller the student often meant the stronger and louder the personality. Macie not only wanted to know how to get her freedom, but how a pregnant friend would go about getting Medicaid.

The storming in and line of questions gave Cammy an immediate distaste for Macie in that first meeting. She knew the pregnant friend was her, it always was. That previous April Cammy was trying to get over her second miscarriage, and her maternal failure was amplified whenever one of the young fertile students came in to seek advice for the pregnant friend. The words pregnant friend never failed to plunge into Cammy's stomach, to twist and tear at her hollow womb. She had resented the ungrateful teens that seemed fertile enough to get pregnant every time they gave some fifteen year old boy a thirty second hand job. Cammy smiled at Macie, and pretended to care.

"Slow down, which is it? Emancipation or Medicaid, one thing at a time," Cammy said.

"I need Medicaid, for a friend," replied Macie.

"Of course."

"I'm not pregnant," claimed Macie.

"I didn't say you were. Why would I think that?" Cammy asked. She then watched Macie watch her.

Macie decided to try her second question. "Well, how would I get the state off my back?"

"How old are you?" asked Cammy. She was already digging through the cabinet behind her looking for the pamphlets on Medicaid. Cammy kept them handy. It seemed most of the girls who ended up pregnant and turned to her were not covered by their parents insurance, because the parents didn't have any. She knew she was probably stereotyping, or at least making a generalization, but more often than not it was true. So she handed Macie the pamphlets on Medicaid as the girl explained why she wanted to get out of the state's care. Macie ran through a number of horrors she had experienced in different homes over the years. Cammy couldn't tell what was true and what was bullshit. She finished with the current home.

"She has sex with her boyfriend and I can hear it from my room," Macie said.

"That doesn't seem horrible," Cammy responded. Maybe it was a little disturbing, she thought, but didn't say. She had trouble comprehending this reason, seeing that it came from a knocked up sixteen year old. "Is that it, does she hit you? Does he?"

Macie was quiet for a moment before she looked up. She told Cammy the woman and the boyfriend did it while she babysat for a friend, with the baby in the bedroom. The baby was just over three months old she told Cammy.

"I'm going to be honest," said Cammy. "I really don't see this as reason for emancipation. "She's not breaking the law," Cammy said. "Maybe you should just let them know how you feel, or even talk to the baby's mother."

"I can't."

"Why not? I thought you said she babysat for the baby?" asked Cammy.

"She does it with my five year old brother in there too," said Macie. Cammy looked at the girl and scratched her head. She wasn't sure if the girl was telling the truth at all.

"Well, that may be categorized as sexual abuse. These are very damaging accusations. Does the guy-" Cammy stopped as she read Macie's file. "Do you have a brother Macie?" According to her file Macie's only family were a deceased sister and mother. The foster family had no boys in their care.

The girl was silent for a second. She ignored Cammy's question, "What about the Medicaid? Am I covered if I leave these people and state care?"

Cammy had sent Macie home advising her to talk to the woman about the problem. In the end she had a feeling Macie had already left. The family probably didn't say anything because they continued to receive their check. Cammy had meant to look more into the situation, but it was a file she never went back to. According to school records Macie had been with four families in the last six years. She was pretty sure the girl had already left and was just trying to see if the state knew. Macie was smart enough to know she still needed Medicaid, now that she was pregnant.

In the second meeting Macie denied the questions or receiving the info on Medicaid from their first encounter. Macie was now aware that since she was a ward of the state she would receive Medicaid until she was eighteen. She implied this was an obvious fact she had always known, Cammy knew otherwise. She said she remembered coming into her office, but it was to change a class. Cammy could tell the girl didn't want to discuss her predicament, but she decided to pry anyway.

"Does your foster mother still have the same boyfriend?" asked Cammy.

"She's never had a boyfriend, not since I could remember."

"How about the babysitting, is she still babysitting?"

"There wasn't a baby. Who told you that?" Macie was halfway out the door. She wanted nothing else to do with the nosy counselor.

Cammy yelled to the girl just before the door closed. "Have you told anyone you're pregnant?" Macie froze, and came back into the office. She closed the door.

"I'm not pregnant, how could you say that to me?" Macie asked as she pulled her shirt down over the bump above her belt. Cammy leaned back from the desk, and pulled her shirt tight to her stomach.

"That excessive air freshner you smell, it's to hide my morning sickness. I've already lost two babies, I'm trying to keep this quiet till we're in the clear."

"Two? When are you due?" asked Macie. The young girl momentarily lost her shell of protection when she heard this. Her head turned as she leaned a sympathetic ear toward Cammy.

"First trimester, long road still," Cammy said. She had the girl's attention now, so she gave another push. "I lost my second at thirty two weeks," Cammy said. She was silent for a moment. "How about you, when are you due?"

"Me? I'm, I'm not pregnant," Macie hesitated. She opened her mouth, only silence followed. Macie wanted a companion, but Cammy was an authority figure, someone she couldn't trust, not yet. Cammy was an outsider too, not even from around these parts.

Macie knew she was cornered. "I didn't come down here last spring."

"You didn't need Medicaid. That was for a friend, you needed to get emancipated from the state and foster care. That's how it went."

"I'm not pregnant." Macie walked out of the office.

Chapter 13

What the fuck just happened? That's all that ran through my head over and over as I walked out the school to my car. What did I just do? I let the counselor know I was pregnant, what was I thinking?

I remembered going to her before school got out, but all I did was tell her a bunch of bullshit. What was I thinking asking about emancipation? Who the fuck was she to judge me and what I wanted anyway. She had no idea what I had been through. She didn't live through years of abuse by white trash whores and know what their pervert husbands did. You don't feel those things by reading a book. Not to mention the school counselor undoubtedly had my records right in front of her on that computer. What was I thinking?

I sat in my car in the school parking lot for about ten minutes trying to decide what to do. I replayed the conversation we just had, and tried to remember what I had said to her before school got out last year. I asked her for Medicaid for a pregnant friend, of course she knew it was for me. Obviously she knows I'm pregnant now.

I had to tell Angel or someone, but who? Angel will shit a brick if I tell him. Who knows what will happen if anyone else finds out, I can't tell him. The counselor seemed nice enough, but a bit of a bitch too. She kind of overstepped her boundaries in my opinion. Who the fuck is she to ask if I'm pregnant?

I drove the car to the gate. Of course the Security Guard, Officer Dickhead, as he was known by students, came out to see why I was leaving early. I wasn't going to come to school at all today, but figured I was only going for three periods so I might as well. I agreed to go to the big hoopla with Angel. I didn't want to, but I thought I'd be nice. Plus he was right, people would get all bent out of shape if we didn't show.

"Jennings, I didn't know it was 2:25 already," he said. My only response was opening the window enough to show him the Early Dismissal Pass. He took the pass and looked at it for twenty seconds, nodding the entire time. He sure was a good dickhead acting like he wasn't sure if my pass was legit- a real pro. He did this every time a kid left early, even though he wouldn't have a clue if someone whipped one up on the computer and had it laminated at Wal-Mart. If I had to guess he was pissed that he was once a cop, but was now left sitting in a booth getting shit on everyday at 2:25 by about 800 teenagers. I know the 'Porky Pig,' calls from the buses had to hurt. Kids could be real mean, but so could cops. Sometimes I felt for the guy, just not when I had to talk to him.

"I gotta get going," I said.

"Whatcha in such a rush for?" he asked. I shook my head as I grabbed the pass back. He was so annoying. Get a life, I thought to myself. He smiled and took a step back from the car. I must have felt bad this time because I smiled back.

Chapter 14

Three days following the sun boiled display of Milton Hawkins' cranium the Mayor threw a party. It was more of a pat himself and his police chief on the back party, on the steps of Town Hall. It was announced in that morning's Special Edition Franklin County Journal. The announcement was boldly printed across the top of the newspaper, "A Day for the Children." The article praised the police and their master detective work. It failed to mention how Milton Hawkins never made an actual attempt to flee, even after his likeness was circulated all over town and on all three Network's Mid- Day news. It also failed to mention how Hannah was found by an intoxicated twenty year old girl, ten minutes after Milton dropped her off at a car wash two towns away.

Cammy had lived in Franklin County for eight months, and already did not care for Mayor Jacob Colvin. His answer to a faltering budget was to cut the police force. The education budget was slashed soon after that. Those cuts, did not carry the same bold headline or anything resembling- *For The Children.*

Bartholomew 'Boone' Cross sat between the Mayor and his daughter Hannah. He smiled at the camera, showing off his missing number ten upper incisor. The missing tooth, and Cajun roots left Boone with an accent/speech impediment that could only be understood by someone who knew him for some time. Cammy was curious if Boone had been trached at some point in his life. She listened to the father talk and her thoughts drifted to that of a young child learning to talk, and how only his parents knew what he was saying.

Boone's salt and pepper hair was long enough to curl around the brim of the backwards *Vietnam Veteran* ball cap. Boone looked like a war veteran, the type of vet who never quite acclimated back to society, the kind that never fully left the battleground. The lines across his forehead and under his eyes, added to the Al Capone like scar across his cheek, implied a history of violence. That type of violence that could not be hidden by his crooked smile, no matter how loud his laughter filled the small stage. He was trying to act like a teddy bear, but something told Cammy he was more of a silverback Gorilla. His smile seemed to be forced. He wanted to make sure everyone in the audience knew how happy he was, how happy Hannah was, and the entire Cross family. He continued to repeat it. The more excited he got about Milton's death the more it bothered Cammy.

"Just glad ol' Milton Hawkins gonna spend the rest of his days burn'n in hell, burn'n like the sombitch he be," Boone said. He referred to Hawkins as 'that sombitch,' as often as he let everyone know how happy they were to have Hannah back.

Given the rollercoaster of emotions over the past week, all appearances and comments deserved to be given the benefit of doubt. Boone never took his arm off of Hannah during the press conference, maybe he was just afraid she would be taken from him again. Cammy wanted to know if she would understand his reaction once she was a mother. She wanted to know the desire and love for a single person, and even the hate she could possess for anyone who threatened that love.

Cammy watched the great ape of a father with a curious eye. She turned to Pete Wellman, who was staring off at something to the side of the stage.

"What are you doing? Are you listening to this?" asked Cammy.

"No, I'm thinking," whispered Pete. He turned to the stage in an attempt to look like he was listening. Without delay his attention was lost. Pete turned to the phone in his lap to read the day's headlines.

"What's with the wife, Hannah's mom?"

"She's probably stoned. That's the usual story," he said without looking up. Pete was born and raised in Franklin County, but always considered himself an outsider. He went to college in Chicago and stayed there for a couple more years. His family's two hundred acres north of town added to big city rent on a second year teacher's salary brought him back. His future plans start with selling off his piece of the land the day after his father's funeral, but the old man is eighty- four and recently featured in the F. C. Journal for running a half marathon.

"She looks half his age, what is he, sixty?" asked Cammy. Principal Savard turned around from two rows in front of Pete to shush

Cammy. Cammy smiled at her, and today's lime green pantsuit.

"Don't drink the tap water, she's a poster child for that," he said about the Cross matriarch. "Celexa is causing fatal changes in heart rhythm, that's great, fatal." Pete read from his phone.

"So, what's that?"

"Celexa? It's a depression medicine, and now it's killing people."

"You take it?" asked Cammy.

"For almost two years now, this is," Pete said before sitting silent for a moment, "So depressing." The two listened to Boone Cross mumble something how he feared the police would not be able to find Hannah after a couple days passed.

"I didn't know you were depressed," Cammy whispered.

"Really? I live with my two kids and wife in a town where the restaurant that is lined with dead Deer heads is considered fine dining. Not to mention the only black leather is worn by men who just want to fight, smoke weed, do crank, ride Harley's, and eat dinner every night at a strip club," Pete smiled. "How would I not be depressed?"

"I don't want you to think I'm rude," said Cammy. "But that sounds a little drama, kind of like a high school girl." She smiled at Pete. He smiled back and shook his head.

"Not to mention, I'm kind of a hypochondriac, especially when it comes to my heart." Pete's biggest fear in life was that his health would be inherited from his mother, who died from a premature heart attack during his sophomore year of High School.

Pete looked up and to the right of the stage again. Cammy followed his gaze. There were eight men standing at the bottom of the stage. The men were The Vandals Motorcycle Club (MC); reputation dictated that much to Cammy.

"That's Elliott at the end, right?" Cammy asked. Pete looked away from the gang, and back to the stage, trying to hide the fact that they had been commanding the bulk of his attention during the press conference.

"Um, yeah that's him, talking to the cop," he nodded. Donovan Elliott was much bigger than Cammy expected, and younger looking in person. His jet black hair was slicked back, but not greasy. His clean shaven face and big smile reminded Cammy of a 1940's movie star. His blatant confidence was evident by the fact that he wore his M.C's patch while prancing around with the local Police Chief. That was the first time she had ever seen him in person. "How'd you know that was him?" asked Pete.

"I've lived in Franklin County for almost nine months. It's not hard to recognize Donovan Elliott- the most powerful man in Franklin County, right?"

"Probably," Pete knodded. The leader of the Club stood at the end of the line of bikers, furthest from the stage, laughing it up with a local police officer. Neither was listening to Boone Cross's inaudible ramblings. Instead, they were having a laugh like two college buds replaying the party the night before, in this case, most likely the strip club. If anyone in Franklin County frequented the Tattooed Lady as much as The Vandals, it was Franklin County's finest boys in blue. Cammy looked at Elliott and could only think of one word: untouchable.

Chapter 15

Laugh it up ass hole. I screamed the words over and over again, but of course, not out loud. It was sacrilege to speak like that to the great Donovan Elliott. He was Stalin disguised as freaking Robin Hood all through Franklin County. If you had a problem with Donovan Elliott and he found out- then you had a problem. This whole town lacked any integrity or conviction. He donated the majority of money for a new soccer facility, and a couple parks so he walked around like the King of the County. Where did people think that money came from? This town might be filled with stupid people, but they're not complete idiots. People here like to claim to be a God fearing bunch, always doing right. Guess God is good, but money is better, even when covered with the blood of their addicted youth. We all hate drugs, but they can buy us shit. That was the Franklin County way.

I tried to avoid looking at him during the Mayor's little pony ride of a celebration, human nature took over a few times when Elliott would be laughing loud enough to drown out the shit that was being gargled from the stage.

I would look away immediately. He caught me once. Gave me a wink and nod when he saw I was looking at him. I can't stand the guy.

"Can we go yet?" I asked Angel. He held his finger to his lips to shush me. "Don't fucking shush me," I whispered. I thought. The dirty looks I got from the people around me implied it was a little louder than a whisper. "I don't feel good," I definitely whispered. "Five minutes," he said. I barely heard him, but the five fingers he held up helped translate. I sat listening to the dad talk about his self some more. How he missed her, how worried he was. How happy he was the kidnapper was dead. I gave it three or four minutes and looked at Angel. He held up another five.

"Adios Fucker," I said as I got up. That wasn't whispered, nor appreciated by anyone sitting by us, which they let me know on my way out. A sixty year old lady with a hairdo from the 1970's shook her head at me, so I shook my middle finger in her face. Her old husband tried to jump up, but I was ten feet away before he managed to get to his feet. I hurried down our row of proud, sweaty citizens who were eating up every word that came from the stage, no matter what kind of shit- filled blabber was said. They had even given Chief Danville a standing ovation for finding her, and he had absolutely nothing to do with it. I was given a dirty look from each person as I pushed past their knees. I didn't care what any of them thought or mumbled. I'm sure none of them liked me anyway, for some reason or other.

Chapter 16

"Mrs. Cross, what were your first thoughts when the police told you a little girl was found?" asked a Channel 7 Reporter. The dark haired olive skinned mother smiled to the reporter, a nervous smile that relayed the message she wasn't asked to relay too many messages. The mother looked to Boone without saying anything. Cammy assumed the mother's opinion was a rare request.

"She didn't think too much, just seeing Hannah. Seeing her live and with us 'gain," Boone answered for her. Cammy was pretty sure that was what he said. She watched the silent wife. Esmeralda Cross hailed from Mexico, but Cammy was pretty sure she spoke English. So it wasn't the lack of a translator that kept her from speaking. Cammy heard Hannah speaking to her mother a couple times at the start of the ceremony, always in English. Boone also spoke to her in English, not to mention she seemed to understand everything that was being said. Which was more than most of the audience could say about her husband's newfound fifteen minutes of fame. "Ezzy don't like to say much," added Boone. Ezzy doesn't get to say much, thought Cammy.

Cammy didn't stay for punch or cookies after the mayor's disguised campaign tour. The Mayor hadn't yet turned back to his seat following his farewell, "Y'all drive safe," before the counselor jumped up to beat feet back to her car. It seemed everyone in town was there, so everyone would soon be on the narrow roads leaving as well.

Chapter 17

Cammy scurried between cars in St. Thomas Catholic Church's parking lot when a scream pulled her back. Cammy dodged and ducked her way between cars toward the scream. She spied on three up and coming Vandals high fiving each other as they walked away from the source of the parking lot scream. All three wore black leather vest with the M.C.'s rocker on the back, and "Vandals" across the top. If there were any witnesses they stayed out of sight, hiding between cars, no doubt.

Cammy watched the three make their way to the other end of the church parking lot, leaving their fresh crime scene behind them. She stood up from her concealed cubby hole between two Dodge Mini Vans and continued searching for the scream. Cammy walked through the parking lot, passing a handful of not so good Samaritans on her way, churchgoers who seemed to be stuck between cars as the three hoods beat, stole, pillaged or did whatever it was they did best. Cammy emerged from an aisle of parked cars only to come to a sudden halt when she saw her student in the middle of the parking lot. On the ground was the not- quite- ready- to- admit she's going to be a mother, Macie Jennings.

Macie was kneeling in the middle of the parking lot between Aisles 7 and 8. A red Ford Taurus swerved to its right to avoid her, the man driving looked straight ahead to avoid any kind of eye contact with the crying teen. The red and purple Mexican man underneath Macie was her freshly ass- kicked boyfriend, Angel Ortiz. Angel's long dark hair and his stomach alternated absorbing Macie's sobs. His arms moved to hug her, but just seemed to flail around unable to grab her seemingly slippery body. His eyes were closed, more from the immediate swelling than choice.

Cammy stood not more than twenty feet away, she wasn't sure how a student like Macie Jennings would feel about the school counselor stepping in on this part of her personal life so she slid back between two trucks. She wanted to say something or help, but was quickly discouraged when she saw the policeman appear from behind a black SUV.

The police officer Donovan Elliott chatted with earlier walked up to the couple. He looked around, Cammy ducked behind a Maroon Suburban. He had a slow, upright gait. That, combined with the thoroughly scanning eyes across the parking lot gave Cammy a strong inclination that staying hidden would be her smartest move. Cammy huddled under the truck, she watched past the bottom of the F-150 and right at the pair of recently shined black shoes. The officer's shined left shoe hovered over Angel until it hooked the flailing right arm. The shoe forced the hand to the blacktop, the solid rubber heel dug into the top of Angel's right paw. Angel winced before he let out the gasp of pain filled breath he had been trying to conceal from Macie.

Chapter 18

I could see the fucking cowards from the corner of my eye. They hid behind the cars of the god damned church parking lot, the hypocrisy. I laid there as our Police Chief dug his heel into Angel's hand. Angel let out a chilling yelp, but tried to mask his pain with a broken smile.

"You're a piece of shit Danville," I said. He raised the back of his hand as if he was going to slap me. I didn't even care at this point. To be honest, I was trying to get him to slap me. I knew there were fifteen people watching this, not that one of them would say a word about it at Sunday Mass. They'd sit there silent, only nodding when Father would say they needed to find who was responsible for this. He'd probably look right at Danville and ask him to make it a priority, and I'm sure Danville would nod to let everyone know- he was on it. I tried to bait him, but he wouldn't bite.

"Macie, you're smarter than this. Don't be stupid," he said. I gave him my best -rip your head off- look.

"You don't know shit dick head," I said. I tried to slap at his leg, but ended up with his boot in my shoulder, pinning me down.

"Listen, no stupido sista, eh? Don't listen to this spic piece of shit, he's going to get you in trouble. No more fucking games. He better learn his place and how these things work. Translate that for Rodriguez here when he's a little more with it," Danville said as he hovered over us. He stood straight up and tucked his shirt back into his pants. "Know your role dumb ass," he said to Angel. Then he looked at me one last time, "Don't fuck up the rest of your life girl?"

Chapter 19

The cop's ass chewing was animated enough to spray the girl's face with spit that seemed to be mixed with tobacco juice; from Cammy's point of view. She couldn't hear what the officer said, he was smart enough to keep his volume down, but body language and the physicality of the altercation told her enough. He threatened or warned them in some way or another. Was he working with the Vandals, on their payroll? Cammy felt no pity for Angel or Macie. The girl's boyfriend was getting something he deserved, she was sure of that. There was a reason The Vandals sought him out to teach him this lesson with this kind of force. They didn't mess with the public, that wasn't there M.O. This was done to get a message across. Angel was a bad person, getting punished by bad people.

Cammy never pitied the dead drug dealers or gang bangers she saw on the news. When she saw a meth lab blow up, she secretly wished the dealer or cooker blew up with it. If a blown up cook house was on the news Cammy watched to see if any children were inside, if not, she had no sympathy for the dead. If they wanted to kill each other or themselves all the better she felt, and this was what she was feeling at the moment. There was almost an excitement for Cammy. She found herself getting further under the pick- up truck, not to hide, but to hopefully hear what the officer was saying. What were Macie and Angel up to? Her breathing was loud, and fast. She couldn't remember what her initial thoughts were when she heard the initial scream. She may have wanted to help, but her objective quickly switched to enthralled spectator now, with little interest in getting close enough to hear what was being said.

Chapter 20

Cammy would find out the following day the cop was Sheriff Chad Danville. Danville was a homegrown hero of sorts. Fifteen years earlier he was quarterback of the only Franklin County team to ever bring home the District Championship. Danville was recruited to Mizzou, where he sat on the bench for a year. Two months before he was to start his first game for the Tigers his drunk ass climbed a car and fell off at two in the morning. His right kneecap was shattered from the fall. He was living his parent's basement in Franklin County before the season kicked off.

Danville was still considered a legend by local standards. Franklin County never had a football team or player worth watching before him, and they hadn't since. Danville grew up like any other lower middle class Franklin County boy, his family had enough to get by, but never enough to leave. The day he was named starting quarterback of the varsity football team as a sophomore was the last time he would be just another Franklin County boy. He was quickly known around town as the boy who would put Franklin football on the map. He was an instant celebrity in a town where the closest thing anyone got to celebrity was the rag papers in the supermarket check- out line. Everyone wanted a piece of Chad Danville before the end of that season. Recruiters showed up in helicopters to watch practice. Local businessmen wanted him to come to their stores, and would offer him whatever it was they offered. One of the QB's biggest fans was the town's biggest name, Donovan Elliott. Elliott always made sure Danville had money, girls, and anything else he desired while he was in school. When the prodigal son of Franklin County limped back from college he was still held in a high regard, so he had no shortage of options, or friends.

Danville bounced from job to job for a couple of years before landing on the police force, once he earned his Associates Degree. He was again looked at as the savior who would change the image of Franklin County. They would no longer be known as the county in Missouri ranked second in meth lab busts, and first in exploding cook houses, but once he became part of the law Danville showed that old acquaintances never die. Chad Danville's biggest fan when he was a football player was his biggest fan when he became the Authority. Danville wasn't out of the Academy for six months before the majority of his income was in cash, from Donovan Elliott.

Chapter 21

Cammy ignored the asphalt and pebbles that imprinted themselves in her knee to the point of just not piercing her skin. She watched as Chad Danville stood over Angel. The Cop looked around before he gave the young criminal one last kick, in case the Vandals missed the spot above Angel's left temple. Angel rolled over, unconscious.

"Learn your place, you mutt," Danville yelled as he kicked. It was the only time his voice was loud enough for Cammy to hear throughout the entire altercation.

Macie lunged at Danville, only to fall on Angel's bare stomach. His shirt was pulled up around his chest and ripped from the original beat down. Macie continued to call for help. Each time she called out Cammy's body locked and she held her breath for ten more seconds. Her beating heart the only sound she could hear over the crying girl. Macie had her face buried in Angel's chest when Cammy slowly slid out from her seclusion. She stayed low to the ground, crouching as she moved away from the couple. Macie continued to cry out. The town folk walked to their cars, they continued not to hear.

Chapter 22

The Franklin County Journal wasn't an award winning newspaper, Cammy needed no extensive research to learn this much. The paper was given away free to every house in the County, usually delivered sometime between Saturday night and Sunday morning. Cammy occasionally picked one up in the mailroom on Monday evening when she was getting her mail. There were typically about ten remaining in the lobby two days after delivery. The paper never did much for her, but she still read it religiously. The front page typically had a story about some type of car accident or trailer explosion and the subsequent arrest. The second story was the feel good story of the week, a thriving local business or future construction project. The second story always made her feel like the town had a chance, but as she would read she would remind herself the business would probably go belly up within a year and the construction project would never officially get funded by the bank. Still, she read it. The second section was more local info on High School sports, 4- H updates, and any other events going on around town. Nothing too informative, but now Cammy found herself on the website searching past editions of the FCJ.

She typed in *Chad Danville*. This was the only Missouri paper that contained his name in the last ten years. There was a little article in the Columbia News when he left Mizzou, but even that was no more than a paragraph saying the quarterback would miss the '94 season. Cammy knew this was actually the end of Danville's life outside of Franklin County thanks to her daily meetings with Pete Wellman. So she was left with the local paper.

The paper never wrote negative articles. The most recent article praised Danville in the finding of Hannah Cross, even though everyone within fifty miles knew he had absolutely nothing to do with her recovery. There were other articles praising the police chief for every drug bust, and every meth house that was busted. No article ever mentioned how Franklin County had grown into the Meth Capitol of the United States.

Cammy read every article that contained Chad Danville anywhere in the text. There were a total of fifteen. When she finished she realized one thing; Danville had accomplished absolutely nothing. The County had grown in population 11 percent, but violent crime had risen faster than any other County in Missouri. The paper commended Danville for a three percent increase in drug bust, but failed to mention the astronomical twenty- two percent increase in drug related deaths. One thing was clear to Cammy. Danville's tenure had been nothing more than an utter failure. How did he keep his job year after year? Obviously he had connections bigger than the tax paying public, and Cammy knew who that connection was.

Chapter 23

The first bell had rung fifteen minutes earlier, at 7:15 A.M. I sat on a curb in the Sinclair parking lot, underneath the statue of a concrete brontosaurus. The dinosaur had to be at least forty- years- old, it was one of the last of its kind at any Sinclair station. Chunks of faded green paint disappeared by the day, each patch of missing concrete brought the gas station dino closer its inevitable extinction.

I sat and watched the school's bus depot from the gas station. The lot slowly filled with the rusted buses, sitting on bald tires that were trusted to get all the little ass holes to school safely. The drivers slowly grouped in front of the large bay door numbered one. They usually stood around exchanging bad jokes, smokes, and gossip like high school girls. More often than not, they traded gossip about high school girls.

I lit my third cigarette from the pack I had just bought. It was already getting hot so I took off the long sleeve shirt and looked back at the gas station in need of a paint job. The thermometer read eighty-five freaking degrees. This humidity probably added another ten degrees for the heat index, so it had to have been at least ninety-five, not even eight in the morning. I didn't know what I was doing, I had been there just trying to hear what I could from these bus drivers. I started to get bored, thought about going to the small hole cut in the glass of the gas station. Did they ever card the High School students who asked for cigarettes there, would the hole in the glass card me if I ordered a six pack?

The drivers slowly gathered in the bus depot, but he wasn't back yet. I almost changed my mind when bus number 75 pulled into the lot. I stood up, and watched the bus until it came to a stop. A man in his late twenties got out smoking a cigarette as he stepped off the bus- Ray Lehane.

"Hey, hey Ray, really Ray? You can't wait two GD minutes?" I heard Sam Montero yell from across the street. Montero had run the depot for the last ten years. He had a knack for finding people willing to drive disrespectful teenagers around for minimum wage. This, combined with his ability to put up with even bigger ass hole drivers allowed him to keep the title of F. C. School District Transportation Manager.

I watched Sam yell and chase Ray down to give him an earful. I hoped he really gave it to him, but I knew the guy, I knew his story. He didn't give a shit what Sam said to him, and Sam knew it too. It didn't really matter what Sam said to him, he was only his boss on paper. I had met Ray twice, both times with Angel. Three weeks earlier he came over to buy some weed. A few days after that he came back for some crank, then sat inside the trailer and smoked it.

Ray unleashed a list of questions as soon as Angel was fucked up too. He wanted to know where Angel got his weed, where he got the crystal, did Angel cook it, where, with who? Ray implied to Angel that the two of them could work together.

He claimed he had a market that was endless. I had worked extra slow cleaning dishes in the kitchen to listen. Ray brought this idea of a partnership up three or four times to Angel. I knew what Ray was doing, Angel was kind of clueless, or just whacked out of his mind. The piece of shit was planning to use his bus as a roving street corner. He could sell before he dropped everyone off at night or for their lunch money in the morning. The bus driver was bad news, but I had known that.

I tried to end the little job interview, but typical Angel told me to get the fuck back in the kitchen. He would let me hang out when he was working (his name for it), but shit flew if I dared open my mouth. He was always an ass hole when he smoked.

Ray ignored Sam as he strutted his wiry ass to the smoke cloud in front of door number one. A couple of the older drivers looked at Ray and walked away, obviously not interested in his company. I didn't take my eyes off the scrawny object of my disgust as I walked across Highway 47, and walked right into lot. The closer I got to him the more I didn't care about anything, I hated him.

Ray thought he was something. The cocky attitude probably got him the shiner on the left eye, no doubt he mouthed off to someone he shouldn't have. He had on an orange shirt with ripped off sleeves even though his arms looked like they hadn't lifted anything heavier than a forty in five years. His hair was combed back, greasy and dirty enough to appear slicked. It was the same tan, brown color as the town's dead grass following the twenty days of heat advisories, and long enough to pass his neck to cover the collar of his sleeveless T.

"I would give a nut to be sixteen for a day I tell you, these little bitches love to suck dick," Ray proclaimed. He took a long drag off his Kool. The closer I got the more I hated him. He waited for someone to ask what he saw, what he was talking about. Someone finally did. So Ray obliged. "You know that little black haired girl Lyndsey Curry, I think, dresses in all black" he said. She didn't think I could tell she was in the back really going to town on this punk's meat, she knows what she's doing too." I was close enough to hear everything. The closer I got the more I wanted to hurt this low life.

Chapter 24

The life of Macie Jennings had been one few people would envy. Cammy thought about the girl, thought about what her upbringing must have been like. Pete told her all about the family's history in Franklin County. He wanted Cammy to understand what kind of family this was. So he started at the beginning, the story of Ma Jennings.

Pete pulled his piece of leftover cake from the other day closer to him. He picked up the plastic pink fork and took a bite. Cammy's first thought was the smile and nod came from his pleasure with the cake. They weren't, and she figured this from the look in his eyes. She just sat back, and refused to give him the satisfaction of delaying his story. Only a few minutes passed before Pete gave in. He gave Cammy an oral history of the Jennings's family beginnings, or at least the popular version.

Madeline (Maddie) Jennings was a woman who knew what the people wanted from an early age. She began hanging at the truck stop before she could drive, her first job (not the type where you paid taxes), was her first glimpse at breaking the law. On her sixteenth birthday she had earned enough money getting truckers off to buy a 1984 Ford, aptly named, Escort. She had also earned enough to leave home, and move into her very own used double- wide. That's when she moved to the ritzy Sun Valley Lake Trailer Park, that's where she met Donovan Elliott.

Elliott took her to his personal school of cooking crystal 101, and she aced the class. Soon if you were using in Franklin, it came from Maddie's trailer. They had more money than they could spend and all the drugs they could shoot, snort, or smoke. Elliott was quickly climbing the ranks of the Vandals Motorcycle Club, and believed his ceiling was much higher than a top earning drug dealer.

Donovan soon learned if you wear high ambitions on your sleeve, you're best keeping them covered. The leaders of the gang grew cautious of his growing popularity among other members, and local users. Rumors started, he overheard them: The kitchen would have to close.

Ty Harvick was President of the club at the time. Harvick was a user himself, and meth was the drug choice of the bikers, including the MC President. It allowed the bikers to stay up for days on end, whether it was a bi- state drug run or a weekend party when sleep was not an option. Harvick was no different than most the men, meth was his life, socially as well as financially. This did, however, carry the unfortunate side effect of being overly guarded, and extremely paranoid.

Donovan Elliott wouldn't be the first time Harvick ordered an up- and- coming biker's membership to be revoked. Through Harvick's leadership members had been taken out when it was necessary, but the club knew there had been a bounty of eliminations due to the paranoia of the M.C. president and many started to wonder who would be next. When plans moved forward to purge the club of Donovan Elliott word leaked, and this time Harvick's paranoia was dead on.

In those days club members hit up the Tattooed Lady when they were looking for some tail, and they were always looking. The Lady was a dance club that strictly sold beer, whiskey, and pussy. Smoke stayed thick in the Lady for two reasons: You didn't have to be picky on the pussy, and you never had witnesses in case things did go down- and things went down.

On June 19th, 1990 Donovan Elliott walked into the Tattooed Lady to announce his candidacy for Club President. When he walked into the bar seven club members were sitting at a table in the back corner, the table that only club members sat. It was the table behind the stage. Five of the men stood up and walked away from the secluded corner. They all nodded to Donovan as they walked out of the dance club to the parking lot. They got on their bikes, and drove off. A sure sign of each exiting member's approval for what they knew Donovan was there to do. The boys were telling Elliott what two members were planning to take him out or would have been taking him out.

Benny Jets and Sammy Snake Charms sat alone in the booth. Guns and Roses rocked the sound system. *Welcome to the Jungle* vibrated the speakers. Donovan smiled. He was the lion, and he was there to claim his throne- there was a new king of the jungle.

There were no witnesses to any of this, of course, but police believed Benny Jets tried to plead his case to Donovan. There was a bullet hole clean through his hand which resulted in the dead biker's mug getting painted in blood, even though the other five gunshot wounds were found in Benny's chest. The hand and arm of Benny Jets was also lit on fire, so they thought. Sammy was shot once, but his throat was slit, with an O.J. like rage that approached decapitation. Police later believed Benny was trying to make a deal with Donovan, a deal Donovan later learned was very time sensitive.

Ty Harvick was woken up twenty minutes after no one saw anything happen at the Tattooed Lady. Police reports claimed he was awake to read the close up of future Hall of Famer Andre Dawson's signature as it embossed his face. This was determined after no one in the Franklin County P. D. could name a big league ballplayer besides Dawson who would have a Louisville Slugger bat made that year with the initials A and D, so legend grew that it was an Andre Dawson bat. Those were the initials rumored to have been in the autopsy as being imprinted on Harvick's forehead. This was a rumor many believed, but never said aloud, to have been started by Donovan. It also led to the nickname A.D. for Donovan Elliott, although many would say the moniker was a result of taking over after the death of the long termed former president.

Chapter 25

Ray Fucking Lehane, I kept saying it over and over. He would ruin everything. I knew this wasn't the place, wasn't the time for this. Sometimes, none of that matters. The whole morning seemed like a blur, I really don't know what I had been thinking at the piece of shit green dinosaur gas station. Was I going to kill him? I thought about it. What would happen if I really did do it? What would it actually accomplish?

I wanted out of Franklin County. It's the only thing I've ever wanted ever since I could remember. I had nothing here, never did. The only people who ever gave a damn about me had been gone for years now. I wanted out, and Angel was my ticket out of this hole of a town. Angel had our plan. He had an escape route to get me far from this place. He had gotten in with Elliott and The Vandals, moving dope and meth here and there. It was fine and made extra money, but he had to get out on his own to start making any escape money. The plan was to stay under the radar and move enough at the Mexican Restaurant to start a future. Now it was gone. Elliott didn't trust him and made it clear in the church parking lot- he wouldn't hesitate to eliminate Angel if he strayed again. This was all because of Ray Fucking Lehane.

Broken Lullabies

Did I want to kill Ray? Sure, it crossed my mind, but I didn't think I could actually go through with it. I'd give it a hell of a try though.

Chapter 26

Pete Wellman would always stop when talking to Cammy to make sure she was listening. When he had told her the story of Ma Jennings and Donovan Elliott he stopped more than usual. Pete wanted to be sure Cammy gave him her full attention, she did.

"What next?" Cammy asked. "What about Maddie?"

"That's where the hand of Benny Jets comes into play. It wasn't lit on fire. It went up in flames when Elliott shot him. The lingering gasoline on his shirt sleeve made him into a human fireball. The gas from the bomb Benny jets and Sammy Snake Charms had just finished planting under Maddie's double- wide. Harvick figured Maddie's trailer would be the easiest place to get Donovan. He also knew the meth lab wouldn't need much of a kick start to go up, and it did go up." Pete looked wide eyed at Cammy. He loved having her full attention now. He finished telling Cammy the story of how Elliott became President of The Vandals Motorcycle Club. Maddie had survived the blast, but was badly burned. Her entire left arm and forty seven percent of her face and head were left scarred. If she ever left her house after that she wore an exceedingly large straw sun hat, with just as obnoxious large dark glasses. Most people never knew that because she rarely left after the fire.

Donovan Elliott was quickly named President of the Vandals. If anyone did object it fell on deaf ears. Maddie was in the ICU for forty days. She followed that with another month in a rehab facility. On August 24th that year Maddie left the rehab center. Two low ranking members of the club picked her up, and drove her to the three bedroom trailer she spent the rest of her life in. No one knew where the girls came from or when they were actually born, there never were official birth certificates given to the school district.

Chapter 27

Ray flicked his cigarette off to the side and smiled. He waited for someone to ask for more, but the circle froze. The entire group stared with dropped jaws. They wanted to tell him, but it was too late.

A fist ripped the air behind Ray's ear, it landed directly on his right temple. The cigarette that was held in the fist exploded on Ray's face. The fist opened up and grabbed the top of Ray's dirty mane, his head jerked up, then back. Ray fell to his knees. He was momentarily blinded by the sun, but could feel his attacker's left hand come around to put a four inch blade to his neck. Ray's eye's adjusted, he recognized the girl, the drug dealer's old lady. Macie looked Ray in the eyes. She didn't say anything until she was sure they were making eye contact.

"You told Donovan about Angel, you get what's deserved," she said in a rasping whisper. Her voice was steadier and calmer than her eyes. The blade pressed against Ray's neck, his head yanked back even further as she tugged his hair, his vision blinded by the sun. Macie leaned closer so he could feel her breath. Ray had nowhere to look but her piercing blue eyes as they turned black.

Chapter 28

Cammy stared at the stack of papers that would close the school's file on Macie Jennings. The counselor was the first signature needed to process the expulsion of a student, and Macie was getting expelled. No matter how low the life of Ray Lehane sat on the totem pole of society, he was an employee of the school. The fact that the school insurance had to cover the hospital bill for Ray's sliced arm left little for a parent to argue about. Not that Macie had anyone in the world who would defend her and help prove that Ray was a wannabe drug dealer, hired by a school that allowed two Class A misdemeanors and a felony go unnoticed, any digging around town would uncover that he had been involved in the drug underworld for the better part of that last two decades. These facts couldn't erase the attack of a school employee on school grounds so the fear of a lawsuit wasn't heavy on the minds of the school board.

First problem for Macie was no lawyer in town was foolish enough, or had the right sized balls, big, to go after a guaranteed loser. Second problem was the girl, Macie Jennings. For all Cammy knew no one cared enough about Macie Jennings to put up a fight for a hopeless case. How do you say guaranteed loser in Franklin County? Nine stitches and fifteen witnesses is a good place to start.

Macie flung open the door to Cammy's office. She obviously felt a knock was unnecessary since her fate was sealed. She was here for the formalities. Cammy could see the school Security Guard who escorted her to the office. He waited outside as Macie walked into the tiny office and froze. She stared at the counselor. Cammy gave the girl a crooked smile, letting her know she wasn't looking forward to this meeting anymore than Macie.

"You know, there's really no reason for me to be here. You're kicking me outta fucking school, that's not going to change," Macie said. She backpedaled back through the door she came in, and began to close it.

"Wait, Macie wait," Cammy pleaded. "We might be able to fix this."

"Bullshit," the girl said, but she was still there.

"Not go away, I won't say that," she did say.

"Then what?" asked the girl. "That fuck deserved what he got. You should see Angel's god damn face 'cause of him."

"Enough of the language," said Cammy. "My job isn't to sit and listen to some little girl with a smart mouth thinking she's someone anyone 'round here gives a dang about."

"What's that supposed to mean?" asked the sixteen year old.

"Means I'm the only one who's going to help you," Cammy said. She nodded to the chair across the desk from her. "So show some respect and act grateful." Macie didn't move. "Or you can leave, get hooked on whatever people around here get hooked on and raise your baby like one of the other crack head moms in the trailer park. It's your choice." Macie slowly walked to the chair, sat, and looked to Cammy. "Now tell me, what were you hoping to accomplish by slicing that bus driver's arm open?"

"I was hoping to accomplish killing the bastard."

"By slicing his arm?"

"By slicing his throat," said Macie without blinking. "I kind of froze up I guess. Chickened out."

Cammy nodded, "Well, I think wised up might be a better phrase. So what did this Ray Lehane do so bad to you that you need run in there full of piss and vinegar and go slicing him up anyway?"

"Got my reasons," said Macie. She looked around the office as she started to get tired of the conversation and questioning.

"Did you really think this was going to help or change anything?" Cammy asked. She wanted to know what this girl was mixed up in. Was this tied to the church parking lot?

"I don't know. Just really wanted to hurt or scare the shit out of him," she said. Macie wasn't in the mood to tell her soon to be former High School counselor much, she was more interested in fiddling with whatever she could reach on Cammy's desk. Macie reached across and pulled a pamphlet out of the basket on the corner of the desk. The pamphlet detailed the new law of pseudoephedrine, the main ingredient in meth, and how it can only be purchased with a doctor's prescription. "This don't matter anyhow, won't change a thing," Macie said to the pamphlet while Cammy talked.

Cammy was limited on her knowledge of Angel, Macie's man. She was obviously aware of his run- in with The Vandals, followed by the scolding from the local law enforcement, but had no intention of letting Macie know that. "Who's Angel?" Cammy asked as she watched Macie read about her boyfriend's new road block to becoming a successful businessman. That and the twenty- seven bikers who have threatened to kill him if he continued to sell.

Macie told Cammy about Angel. Everyday Cammy got to hear from one of her girls in school who was fortunate enough to connect with the one person in the universe she was meant to be with, her soul mate. Only to come in a week later in tears because that same soul mate found another soul to mate, or they were just lucky enough to have two soul mates in this world, both who lived in Franklin County.

Macie was one of these lucky girls, she found her Angel she told Cammy. She met him when she was fourteen, and he was fifteen. Macie said they hit it off and started dating that night. Love at first sight she said. Cammy eventually found out love at first sight was closer to love at first joint, as Angel got the Eighth grade Macie stoned for her first time. Angel had been her boyfriend since, she moved in with him eight months ago, right at the end of first semester freshmen year. Moved right into his cozy little trailer in the back of Sun Valley Lake, same park her mother moved to when she was sixteen. Cammy tried to smile throughout Macie's entire story. She caught herself rolling her eyes once. Lucky for Cammy, Macie was transfixed on the hole in her Nike, attempting to get a second finger through her sock to her toe.

Cammy explained the options available to Macie after she was officially kicked out school. She could appeal to the school board, who would shoot down her request for re-instatement. The girl had been alone since her older sister passed, and the fact that she OD'd left everyone believing Macie would eventually follow the same path. She was best off skipping the appeal all together. Truth be told, the school board was happier without her.

Macie could request a transfer to the Alternative High School in hopes they accept her, most likely they would not since she really had no one who would fight and make a case for her. Cammy could try, but she was new and had little influence on the small- minded small town folk. There was one other High School in the Franklin County District, but another long shot. This option usually worked for exceptional athletes. It would be easy to transfer to the local private school, but her last foster mother was a broke meth head who Macie had no relationship with. So Cammy skipped that option completely.

A public school outside of Franklin County would accept her. Her attendance was steady, and her overall GPA was respectable. Cammy could talk to the counselor at the other school and tell her the attack was a one- time incident. A story about why Ray deserved the attack probably wouldn't be hard to come up with either, if Cammy looked hard enough.

Macie had a final option too. Get her GED. If Macie ever wanted to write anything in the box that said Education, other than *some*

High School, a GED was her best option. The one she could actually complete. Macie continued to rip into her shoe, occasionally giving a nod.

"Are you going to respond at all, to anything?" Cammy asked.

Macie shrugged her shoulders as her eyes scanned the counselor's office. She finished her inspection and finally answered. "That's fine, I don't even care."

"I have some info on getting your GED, you want to bring those home to take a look at with Angel?" asked Cammy. Macie sat as if she didn't hear her.

"You ain't got any pictures. Have any family?" asked Macie, who finally looked at Cammy.

"I keep my personal life private Macie." Cammy paused for a moment, then leaned forward and put her elbows on her desk. She looked right at Macie. "Listen here little girl, you haven't given me your full attention since you walked into this office. Why would I answer anything you ask me that my job doesn't require me to answer? I'm here to help you. I'm trying to give you a life that doesn't lead to jail," Macie was taken aback by the snap, almost at a loss for words.

"I'm not going to end up in jail."

"You'd be there right now if the knucklehead you cut up wasn't a fucked up tweaker hiding from his past. It also doesn't hurt that there are ten bus drivers who seemed to blink long enough not to see anything when you sliced up that man's arm. You do know that if one of those drivers would testify your little ass would be in jail right now?"

"Miss Hart, the language please," Macie raised her eyebrows and smiled at Cammy. The cursing provided a connection for Macie. At the moment, she liked the counselor.

Macie smiled big, a pretty smile. Cammy had seen her as another trailer park trashed sixteen year old waiting around to get knocked up or addicted to something, most likely something hard. The girl's translucent pale skin looked like it had seen sunshine in recent days; it suddenly had a glow to it.

"By the way," Cammy looked at Macie. "Don't talk like you're white trash. I'm reading your grades right now, when you first started school you did well." Cammy tapped her computer screen. She made small talk with the girl as she read. She might be interested in helping Macie after all. She didn't want to read the mandatory script typically fed to students in these situations. She read through the file, Macie was a high B student in Junior High. Her first semester freshmen year she had five A's, and a B. The B was in Phys Ed.

"You had pretty good grades last year," Cammy said. She tried to look like she was staring at the computer as she said this, but really wanted to see Macie's reaction.

"I guess," she said as she pushed the ring in her upper lip with her tongue.

"What happened?" asked Cammy. She was pretty sure it was Angel, and partying in the trailer park. She continued to read the file as they talked. "Out of nowhere your grades dropped."

"Curriculum got more difficult, second semester of High School, ya know?" Macie looked away. Cammy knew it was a bullshit answer. The curriculum didn't get harder, much of it was review for her. She stopped doing the work, she stopped caring.

"You don't go from A's to D's in three weeks Macie, first to second semester is a continuation it doesn't get harder, you don't get dumb. You get lazy." Macie huffed and shook her head in defense. She didn't have an answer for Cammy.

If Cammy was the counselor when Macie first registered for school she would have skipped Spanish 1 all together. She was a smart girl, very smart. Cammy read and tried to keep up a conversation as she imagined what the young girl's life might be like if given a chance. Macie answered most the questions answered with one- word answers. Cammy tried changing the subject from grades a few times, tried talking about Macie's home life. A topic the girl had no desire to discuss. Cammy had driven by the trailer park a few times. It seemed there were always groups ranging from sixteen to forty- five years old walking around, all fucked up on something. It was a constant trailer park bash that always went nowhere.

Cammy read through the file, learning just how intelligent the girl was with every line she read. In the sixth grade Macie scored in the top five percent of students in the state, which made her the smartest girl in her class at Franklin.

The red flag Cammy was looking for would have been apparent to anyone looking, if anyone would have looked. Cammy had been hired to start the second semester the prior year, Macie's grades had already taken a nose dive. Teachers would have seen the grades drop in one class only. They wouldn't have known the large scale decline in the student's overall GPA. They wouldn't have known the potential held by the petite girl who preferred to wear too small tank tops designed with last night's dinner. No one would have cared to notice it all started last December 11th. Ten days before the end of first semester.

Cammy wanted to ask Macie if she thought the paper thin long sleeved shirts hid the food stains or the baby bump. She wanted to tell her it hid neither. Instead, Cammy stayed professional.

"Macie, why did you miss the final ten days at the end of first semester last year?" Cammy asked. She didn't expect to hear the truth, but she was interested in what kind of story the girl would come up with. Macie sat back, pulled her hands away from Cammy's desk, then shrunk into the petite child she was.

"Oh, um, I had a cyst. I had to have surgery to remove it."

Bombshell.

Cammy sat back and thought of the meeting with Wellman the morning Hannah Cross was found. Wellman had told Cammy that Macie's sister J.C. used to tell people she had a cyst. She never admitted to being pregnant, then she was found dead in the river. Now Macie had a cyst, so the story goes.

"What'd the doctor say about that, how do you get those?"

"The GED, I'll do the GED," Macie said. She tilted her head at Cammy, hoping she'd end her interrogation. They were silent. Cammy waited for an answer. Macie refused to give in. She couldn't get into it with the counselor. She told Cammy it was a cyst, and that was all she would say about the topic. Cammy discussed the GED for a couple minutes before she pressed the once confident girl again.

"Have these cysts been a problem for you?" asked Cammy. Macie grabbed the arm rest on her chair. If she heard the question, she didn't acknowledge it. She crouched down in the chair with a knuckle whitening grip on the arm. Cammy half expected the girl to make a run for the office door. "Do you have-" Cammy stopped. "Have you experienced more than that one cyst?"

"I just want to disappear."

"Disappear from where?" Cammy asked.

"Everywhere, this piece of shit school, town. This place sucks, you'll learn."

"I guess. I don't mind it so far. So these cysts, how many have you had?"

Macie glanced backward at the office door as she shrugged her shoulders. Her left hand pressed her stomach, hoping to push the baby bump back in. "Who knows? It was one, just that one. They're hereditary I think."

Cammy thought the same.

Chapter 29

Pete Wellman jumped when the door flung open to his kitchen classroom. Cammy looked around, it took her back to that small kitchen from her childhood home. She felt as if she stepped into a time machine to 1985. She was six years old again in Cedar Rapids, Iowa. The yellow and brown striped wallpaper in the classroom was cracked and peeling between the seams. The linoleum tile looked like it was once a tan color, but was closer to the rusty Franklin County clay people tried every spring to grow a lawn in.

Cammy nodded and smiled to Pete, then leaned against the door jam. "She's pregnant."

"I knew it."

"Again," Cammy proclaimed, almost victoriously.

"Again?" Pete's head stretched from his body, lead by his ear to be sure he heard correctly, "You sure? How do you know?" He tried to wait for Cammy to answer, but she didn't flinch. "Did she tell you that? Did you ask her?"

"Hell no," Cammy looked at Pete like he just asked for a quickie on the kitchen counter. "What makes you think I'm going to ask a fifteen year old girl if she's pregnant, for the second time?"

"Then what, how do you know?"

"She told me," Cammy smiled. Pete raised an eyebrow, was he hearing things?

Cammy just smiled, knowing he was on the edge of his seat.

"What, what'd she tell you? You just said she didn't tell you."

"Last year she missed the last ten days of the semester," Cammy waited. Pete nodded, then held his palms up with shrugged shoulders, and waited for them to be filled with the secret Cammy held. Cammy gave him a boastful smile and almost announced, "Because she had a cyst."

"Shut the front door!"

"Nope, isn't that what tweak the sister used to say?"

"That was her story," he said and jumped up on the counter, then stared at his dangling feet. "Why don't they want anyone knowing they're pregnant? For half these girls it's like a right of passage." Pete said this with an excitement of a detective discovering the first piece of evidence in a new case thrown on his desk. The question was: evidence to what?

"Well, I called her bluff," Cammy smiled. "I set up a doctor's appointment for her. She didn't want me to, obviously, so now we just have to wait. See if Macie shows up. It's for next Tuesday."

Pete took a deep breath. He looked at Cammy. Something was bothering him, didn't make sense. Pete shook his head. "No, something smells funny," he sat up. "What's the big deal? I mean, why they hiding it, the pregnancy? These girls get knocked up, it's what they do. They're trailer trash for Christ's sake."

Cammy looked at Pete, her head tilted as she listened to Pete. "She's different, she's not what you think, she wants everyone to believe she's like the rest of 'em. She's not." Cammy opened her leather binder and pulled out a file. She leaned across the stove and handed Pete the manila envelope.

Pete reached into the envelope and pulled out a folder. Not too thick, but thicker than most sophomore students, in the neighborhood of seventy pages.

"Her file, since fifth grade. You won't believe the grades she used to get. If you ask me, she's one of the smartest kids in this school. They had her taking foreign languages in the fifth grade," Cammy watched as Pete thumbed through the file. She told him how not only did she take Spanish AND French, she excelled at both.

Cammy looked over Pete's shoulder and out into the hallway. She nodded to his brief case, then tilted her head toward the file. Pete half turned toward the door, and quickly turned back to Cammy.

"You can lose your job," Pete looked at her. A phys- ed class was filling the hallway outside the kitchen. The sneakers of the students whistled as the majority of the insecure non-athletes dragged their feet toward the gymnasium. Cammy nodded to the file again and mouthed, "Read it. You should see what this girl's been through."

Pete made one more over the shoulder glance before he knocked the file on the floor, a line formed a trail of papers to the door as they sprang from the folder. He shrugged to Cammy and laughed at his clumsiness.

"A visitor, huh Mr. Wellman?" asked a red headed fifteen year- old girl standing in the doorway at the end of the paper trail. The girl's smirk reminded Cammy of the whispers of her passionate affair with the in-the-closet choir teacher. "Heard something fall on my way to gym, thought I'd see if you needed some help?" The girl was an undeveloped six foot tall red head who was still learning to control her new lanky arms and legs. Outside of basketball week, finding a way to get out of gym class was a twice a week occupation for 'Big Red,' the nickname her creatively challenged classmates had given her. That or Micky D, after Ronald McDonald, the name used behind her back by the much crueler faculty.

Pete held a finger up to Cammy as he leaned over to pick up the spilled file. Micky D was already down picking up the file before Pete or Cammy could stop her. "Hey, ain't this that girl who stabbed that bus driver?"

"What, no, no I don't think so," said Cammy.

"You're the counselor, yes it is. Whatcha got it out for, she expelled?"

"I, um I have to go over some stuff with Mr. Wellman about the student," Cammy weakly attempted to recover.

"Sure ya are," the red headed Micky D winked. "She's getting expelled isn't she? She shouldn't. That guy had it coming. I don't even know why he was allowed to work here. Just cuz he's friend's with Donovan Elliott n'all."

"What's that?" Cammy grabbed Micky D's hand that was holding a stack of Macie's file.   She looked in her eyes. "What about Donovan Elliott?"

"That bus driver, he's one of his guys, isn't he?"

"I don't know, is he?" Cammy looked at Pete. He shrugged his shoulders.

"Beats me," said Pete. "Why do you say that Michelle?" Micky D's given name was Michelle Donahue, Irish. "Why do you think Ray is one of Donovan Elliott's men?"

Micky D shrugged her shoulders, "Just one of those things people know around here." She looked away from the teacher and counselor to avoid eye contact, and save them the embarrassment she was sure she caused for being so out of the loop. She excused herself from the outdated kitchen classroom.

Cammy looked at Pete, "Are you kidding me, a member of the town's biker gang is driving a god damn school bus?"

Pete stacked the papers in a pile. He bounced the stack off of the counter until it was relatively neat. He reached for Cammy's binder.

"Did you see how she looked at us? Like we were god damn idiots! She knows what she's talking about. Does anyone else know this, does everyone?" Cammy was talking loud now, she almost approached yelling. Pete's silence wasn't helping his case either, he was born and raised in Franklin County, he knew how these things worked. "Did you know?"

"I didn't," he paused, "and she said a friend of, not member." Pete was putting Macie's file back into Cammy's binder instead of his briefcase.

"What are you doing?" Cammy asked. She grabbed Pete's hand and looked him in the eyes. "Why are you putting that back in my binder?"

Pete pulled his hand back from Cammy. He shook his head. "You don't get it, you're not from here, hun." Pete told Cammy what Donovan Elliott wanted in Franklin County, Donovan Elliott got. He wanted Ray to be working as a bus driver. Those plans were fucked up by Macie, which in Franklin County made her a DNR. Do Not Resuscitate, as in school, or any other kind of help someone may need- like career. Cammy and Pete would both be better off staying away from her, far away.

"How many guys does he have selling to kids on busses?"

"I have no idea, that was probably it," Pete said. All the while he avoided any eye contact with Cammy.

Cammy shook her head at his lack of subtlety. "I'm guessing you were more of a song and dance man, huh?"

"Excuse me?"

"Acting wasn't your thing?" she stared at the Theater, Home Ec, and Choir teacher.

"What does that mean?"

"Bullshit, that's what it means. I'm going to go down to that depot and ask that dipshit who runs it just how many of these guys are Elliott's men." Cammy headed for the door, Pete ran behind her and grabbed her shoulder.

"Cameron, listen to me. I don't know what goes on down there, but I'm pretty sure it's best left the way it is."

Cammy yanked away from Pete. "This town is fucked." The door was halfway shut as Cammy approached it, she flung it with a brute force and it slammed against the wall, open. She walked out. Pete watched her leave, he took a deep breath as he leaned against the warped brown cabinet.

Cammy took a few steps and stopped. She knew Pete had nothing to do with what went on in this town. He didn't like it any more than her, but he wasn't the type to stick out his neck. Pete was a gay man with a wife and two children. The last thing he was going to do was mess around with the food chain of Franklin County.

Cammy stuck her head back in, "Sorry, this town isn't fucked, not all of it." She smiled, Pete nodded back to her as he pointed in the direction of the bus depot.

"Listen, Donovan Elliott, if he's involved in this you might just want to push it aside. Forget about it, you got enough on your plate," he said as he nodded to her stomach. Cammy nodded and smiled to Pete, who knew her mind had already been made up. She gave him a half wave as she backed back out of her childhood styled kitchen.

Chapter 30

Angel's truck wasn't in the drive when I pulled up. He finally left the trailer after three days. He only works at the restaurant three to four shifts a week, and had all his shifts covered since the beating. I guess he decided to go back to work. That or he had a pick-up, but I was pretty sure the Vandals got to him in the parking lot, enough to keep him hidden in the trailer for a few days anyway. Maybe he had finally worked up the courage to work his tax paying job. I really didn't give a shit to be honest. I wasn't pissed at Ray for messing up Angel's little drug ring, I was pissed that he was messing up my plans. My plans to get the hell out of dodge. Not to mention, I was getting sick of seeing Angel's fat ass on the couch, and really needed some time alone. I needed to start thinking about a Plan B.

I tossed my purse on the table when I walked in. I looked around real quick, something that didn't really require any movement besides my head in our gigantic home.

"Angel, hey you taking a shit?" I yelled. I waited a second to be sure he wasn't there. Relief, he really was gone. I rushed to the bedroom and my side of the bed. I reached under the mattress and pulled out the notebook- it was still there. A rush of adrenaline raced through my body. I could finally read it. Finally talk and hear from him after all this time.

Chapter 31

The bus depot was originally built in 1926, for the United States Army. It was officially listed as Army barracks in Franklin County history books. The depot was a row of four completely identical buildings. The half mooned buildings had two large windows, one at each end of the 120 foot tube. One hundred and sixty soldiers bunked in each building back in the day, awaiting their deployment to save the world. That was the Army's official stance on the barracks. Local legend had it that the barracks were an entranceway to an underground lab, the lab where the nuclear bomb was tested and created.

Cammy walked into the depot at 2:55 P.M. She knew the drivers would be bringing students to their homes, she wanted to be sure to have Supervisor Montero's full attention.

Cammy knocked on the open bay door, but the place was empty. She called out, no one answered so she walked in. The floorboards were worn down to the point that there was no mistaking it to be an eighty-year-old floor, a third of the wood had been worn away. If anyone was there and didn't hear her yell, they were sure to hear the creak of the floor call out with each step Cammy took.

"I'm not hiring, if that's what you want," Montero yelled out from behind Cammy. He was standing in the bay door Cammy had just walked through, she must have walked right by him as he stood there lighting a cigarette.

"Oh, I didn't see you there, I mean, um sorry," Cammy stuttered. Montero was maybe five foot tall, when he wore cowboy boots. He was the type of guy who could be described as wide as he was tall. Cammy couldn't tell if his head was abnormally large, or if the missing neck just made his head look that much bigger. That, and the goatee that ended somewhere around his sternum gave Sam the look of some kind of Hobbit warrior. Sam had spent most of his adult life trying to compensate for his never-ending battle with the earth's gravitational pull. His free time was spent in the gym, and extra cash on the newest and greatest bodybuilding supplement. The two full sleeves of tattoos also gave Sam the looked he desired, but lacked in elevation. "I mean I saw you, see you."

"I watched you from across the street, I wasn't here. What do you want, who are you?" asked Montero. He held the cig in his right hand while his left quickly rat- a- tatted on a stack of aluminum siding that sat inside the garage. His fingers banged loud on the siding as if he was the underdog in a dueling piano bar.

"What's the siding for? Are you remodeling?" Cammy tried to ease the setting, but to no avail.

"What are you the freaking school accountant? I'm storing it for someone. Listen lady, I'm a busy guy, can I help you with something?"

"School counselor," Cammy responded. Montero's look told her he didn't get the comment. "You asked if I was the accountant, I'm the Counselor."

"Oh," he said. He paused with embarrassment but quickly and calmly collected himself. "What can I do for you?" he asked. He didn't know much about the office politics up the hill in the main school, but he knew the Counselor worked close with the Principals. She could have been sent by one of them, so it was in his best interest to accommodate the woman. "Sorry about that, we had some reporters and people snooping around asking questions," he said.

"I'm here to ask you some questions too, about the incident last week with Macie Jennings."

"Figured. Yep, that was a first, student stabbing a bus driver. Even in this crazy town," he said.

"I'll bet," Cammy smiled.

"Yeah, I figured they were screwing or something like that, ya know? He swears they weren't, and Ray ain't the type to deny something like that."

"I'm pretty sure it wasn't that," said Cammy. She then apologized for not introducing herself or giving her name right away. Sam smiled and apologized to her, and the mood was given a much needed sedative.

Sam told Cammy how he didn't see the actual incident, but was there shortly after.

"You can tell she just wanted to scare him, maybe hurt him a little. Did you see the wound? It wasn't deep or anything. She kicked out?" he asked.

Cammy nodded, "Yes, but I'm interested in this Raymond Carter Lehane. You know, the victim." Cammy's sarcasm was heavy on the way she said victim. She was now only a couple feet away from Ray, and six inches higher. Cammy looked down at Ray, "Did you know Mr. Lehane had a police record? A rather active police record at that," she said. Cammy took another step forward, "Are you in charge of hiring all the drivers?"

"You for real?" Sam Montero stood up on his tip toes. Cammy realized she had struck a nerve. "Who do you think you are?" He shook his head as he walked around Cammy and headed for his office in the back of the barracks. Sam had spent much of his early life getting bullied by boys and girls alike. Those days were over, he liked to tell himself. He wasn't going to put up with some High School Counselor pushing him around. He had to kiss enough asses and take enough from the higher ups in the school that he would be damned to put up with her shit. "Beat it, lady. You don't have a clue."

Cammy followed, creaking boards right behind him. "Mr. Montero I'm asking you very valid questions. Do you know what will happen if word gets out that a guy like this is driving a school bus? I promise you, Statutory Sodomy driving a school bus is the lead in the evening news, on all three networks."

Sam stopped, he didn't turn around. "Statutory what?"

"Sodomy."

"You saying Ray's a pedophile?" he asked. Sam turned around, his eyes looked up at Cammy but his head laid low.

"Not necessarily, um, she was sixteen years old," Cammy told him. Sam turned away and headed for his office, he moved much quicker than before.

"When? How old was he?"

"Twenty- four."

"That's god damn bullshit, they told me nothing was sexual, and nothing with kids. Now I got to deal with this shit, and that son of a bitch last week. Could you imagine if he ended up working here, or if the press got a hold of that? I'd be the freaking fall guy, and no one in this town would hire me, and I'm a good guy. A good fucking guy!" Sam spun toward his office and punched the door as he walked through it, "Fuck!" He walked in the office and fell into his desk chair, still mumbling to himself as if Cammy was gone.

"They, who's they? What'd they tell you, what guy last week? Who's they?" she repeated. Cammy quickly looked over Sam's office. The desk was metal made to look like fake wood, with a computer that was bigger than any computer produced in the last ten years. Two file cabinets were along the back corner behind the desk. On the right side of the back wall was his tiny college boy fridge, in front of that was a coffee- stained card table with two chairs.

Sam sat at his desk and picked up his phone, he started to dial a number when he remembered Cammy in the doorway. Cammy was staring at the card table, and the newspapers spread out all over it. The table had all the newspapers from the last seven days; *The Post-Dispatch, The Franklin County Journal,* and two more she had never heard of. She slowly walked toward the table to scan each paper.

The newspapers were mainly just the front pages, and the continuation of the articles that Sam had cut out. They were all the same topic, same story. They were Franklin County's story of the year- *Milton Hawkins and Hannah Cross*.

"Please, Miss, Miss," Sam snapped his fingers at Cammy, unable to remember her name.

"Cameron," said Cammy, "Cameron Hart."

"Cameron, right, Miss, uh, Cameron I need to make a call. Maybe you can come back some other time," he put both hands on his desk.

"Who were you talking about out in the garage?" she asked without turning from the table.

"Please, I don't have time for this right now," Sam walked over to his door. He gave a wave of his hands from Cammy to the door, hoping she would get the hint and leave. Cammy picked through the newspapers. She held one that was headlined, *"Hawkins History of Violence."* She read the headlines out loud.

"Why are you so interested in Milton Hawkins?"

"Who?"

Cammy smirked as she nodded toward the newspaper filled folding table, and held up the article in her hand. "The Milton Hawkins you seem to have an obsession with. Was it him, is that who you were talking about out there?" Montero looked at the door to avoid Cammy's stare.

"I don't, please, I think you should leave," he pleaded. Montero gave Cammy one last look before he walked out of his office. Cammy followed him with the article in her hand, and asked again what his interest in Hawkins was. Did he give him a job? Montero ignored her the entire way to his car. He opened the door and was getting in when Cammy finally forced him to answer her.

"You leave and I'm going straight to the *Post Dispatch*," she threatened. Sam got out of his car, he stood in front of Cammy, and pointed right in her face.

"You don't know what you are talking about lady. You want to go to the paper, be my guest. They won't print shit, and you know what, you won't make it back to your fucking shithole apartment," Sam was fired up now. The beads of sweat converted to drips, his giant face was crimson red. "That sick freak was going to work here, never made it, and I didn't hire him. Just like I didn't hire god damn Ray the jerk off. If I could have I would have let that dick go six months ago. I can't. I want a job. I know you're new, but even you've probably figured out the job listings aren't exactly overflowing around here. I do what I have to do to keep this job."

"What do you mean you do what you're told, what were you told to do? By who?" she asked. He looked around to make sure they were the only two around, he then wiped his face and opened the door. "Mr. Montero, who tells you who to hire? Who is doing the hiring?"

"Quiet, will you just shut up? What's wrong with you Lady?" Sam pleaded. He held up his hands while he gave one last coast- is-clear head swivels. "Not everyone. Every six to ten months I'm sent a guy here and there. Like Ray, and you know?" He knew he had told her too much already. Cammy asked again who was 'you know,' and who was telling him to hire the men. Sam told her he had no choice, even though the record might be a little tained. He told her he was stuck with ass holes like Ray who would smoke on the buses, even leaving cigarette butts on the steps.

"Why, who is telling you to do this?" she asked as a bus pulled into the depot parking lot. The first bus of the afternoon was no one to be worried about though. The driver was Ashley Renaud, a single mom who had another job just to pay for a small two bedroom apartment. The last thing she wanted was to be involved in any type of altercation, no matter how mild it might have been.

Sam got in his car and leaned over the fast food wrappers. He grabbed one of the empty cigarette boxes, ripped it open, and wrote something on the inside of it. He folded the box back to its original state, and handed the empty smokes to Cammy. "Not here, not smart. Call me tomorrow night. I'll be home alone." Sam started the car and drove off.

Cammy watched him turn out of the parking lot, and drive off. She saw the lone bus drive around the back of the depot. Cammy heard a bird whistle. She looked around to see the bird was far off on a broken down bus, no one else was in sight.

Chapter 32

My Dearest Macie,

Where do I start? How? An apology? There are no words to express my sorrow, sadness, and feelings of guilt when it comes to what has happened to you. I am responsible for the situation you find yourself in. I know that. I don't know if I can make up for any of this, but I hope by the end of this letter you will find forgiveness is possible somewhere in your heart.

I am clean, I want you to know that, have been this entire time. Not one slip. I have spent my time trying to make myself into a better man. I have devoted everything to improving my intellectual health, as well as my physical being. This has included opening myself up to God, I feel I have only touched on my spirituality. It is a relationship that I will push to grow until I stand before my ultimate judge, and ask for his forgiveness for everything I have done wrong in this world.

Everything you have been told since I last saw you is a lie. I know this because the only people who would tell you the truth are now dead. This is the reason I had no choice but to write you. I understand you may not want to hear from me, but you must read what I am going to tell you. I have wanted to talk to you this whole time, but couldn't. So I have spent my time learning to read and write so I could write this one message to you. Trust no one. Don't trust the people in town who say they want to help. Don't trust the people at your school. I have feared that you have already learned this fact about Franklin County. If you don't know the truth about these people, you must. Something else you must know, don't trust the police. Danville is a piece of the puzzle whose authority is not handed down from the law of the Government, but the law of our County. He's just another arm of the corruption that has run Franklin County since Donovan Elliott came on the scene. These are people who have one God- Money. There is no value on human life, only how much they can make off it. Danville has been on the take since he started. I can't say he's in what I'm going to tell you or condones it, but I believe he's been turning a blind eye for years. As long as he gets his monthly stipend from Elliott he's not to be trusted...

Chapter 33

The lumber industry once thrived in Franklin County. This lead to a large hotel and restaurant industry since the county never could man the jobs with its population alone. Franklin County resembled a small touristy town back then. If there was an internet remotely similar to todays, Main Street would have made one of those *Best Streets in Small Town America* lists- back in the day. The street was lined with European style cafes, antique shops, fudge and candy parlors, hotels, bed and breakfast, taverns, and a giant ice cream parlor, Lizzie's, but that was all gone now.

Cammy drove cautiously down the cracked brick road that was now Main Street. If she went any faster her Toyota would bottom out in one of the dips or potholes. Most the businesses were now boarded up with plywood, some just had a broken window that allowed the homeless a place to take shelter. She had looked through the town's 125th Anniversary book from 1983, the history book of promise that made the town's current state difficult to digest. Cammy pulled over at a small 8 by 10 foot log cabin that sat alone on a quarter acre yard at the heart of the main drag. An oak sign that was now a warped gray stood in front of the cabin, the sign had a wood burned title: *Kinsey Log Cabin, Franklin County's First Resident.* The cabin was over 150 years old, and in better shape than half the buildings on the street. Cammy got out of her car. She walked toward the cabin to a bench outside the town's original residence. Franklin County's first bench she wondered, she sat on the bench and worried it might have been 150 years old too. A police car parked behind hers. The officer got out of the car, and walked her way.

The black boots methodically tapped the pavement, silence, then two steps as he crossed the sidewalk. Cammy didn't have to turn around to recognize the slow walk of Chief Chad Danville. Her mind raced back to the parking lot after the Hannah Cross press conference. Danville would never lose his job for his actions against Angel, but even Cammy knew there was something more than what she saw; he was something more than a simple officer of the law.

Chapter 34

There were probably a thousand reasons I wanted to leave Franklin County. If I wrote a list of pros and cons, the pro list for staying would be pretty short. Really I couldn't think of one good reason to stay. I had no friends, or family. Now I didn't have a school to go to.

Angel knew I wanted to leave and liked to tell me he had a plan. He wouldn't tell me what it was, but I was pretty confident it no longer involved dealing drugs. I think he was done with getting his ass handed to him for awhile. He said he was working on something, that's all he would tell me. That's what scared me.

I sat under my Willow tree telling my sister all of this. It wasn't really mine, it wasn't even close to my house or any of the houses I had been put in over the past six years. It was a giant Willow in River Road Park. There was an island in the middle of the river and the only thing on this little island was the Willow. It was the place my sister was found when they murdered her. It was now the place I went whenever I got depressed, lonely, or just lost. I'm not a psychiatrist or anything- but I was pretty sure I was all three at this point. So I needed someone to talk to, and my sister was the only person I ever had.

"Hey sis, I can use some help right now," I said. Whenever I did this I talked pretty quiet, it was really just a low mumble if even out loud. I figured if she could hear me at all she could probably read my mind. I don't know. I really wasn't sure if I believed in any of that afterlife or God stuff anyway. The thing was, it made me feel closer to her, and usually helped cheer me up. I knew I wouldn't get an answer, but sometimes I felt like she gave me a sign. That's what I was looking for this time. I asked her for this, then decided maybe I should just skip her and go right to the main guy. I figured it couldn't hurt. So for the first time in a long time I said a prayer to God. "I mean not to question you or anything Lord, but maybe this time, ya know, you can give me a little help. I don't want to sound ungrateful or you to think I'm some kind of a bitch but I don't know. I think ya owe me one, just this time. Thanks, um, see you later. Amen."

Chapter 35

Cammy sat her bag down on the bench, shuffled through it, and pulled out a paperback. The book wasn't even opened when her peace was interrupted.

"This is an excellent place to come read. A real nice place to do some thinking, ya know?" Danville asked, but more just said. He wasn't sure if Cammy heard him till she dropped her book into her lap.

"It's typically quiet," she said.

"I don't mean to be a bother," Danville said quickly just to say it so he could be a bother. Maybe he didn't catch her subtle hint. "Just wanted to introduce myself, Police Chief Chad Danville," he held out his hand as he said this. Cammy looked at him, but didn't move her head. Sensing that he had successfully annoyed her he extended the hand a little further, then flashed the quarterback smile.

"Cameron Hart," she forced a smile when she finally looked up at him to return the handshake.

"New counselor at the Frank, huh," he said. He stared right into her eyes. She smiled to mask the cringe from his attempt to sound hip by calling Franklin High, 'The Frank.' Cammy had heard a few of the football players and Coaches call the school by that name, it had been just as annoying when all of them had used it. She tried not to look nervous when he held on to her hand a little too long.

Cammy's hand quickly flew back to her breast when he did let go. He smiled, as if realizing he got to her.

Danville paused for a moment before he said, "I apologize if I frightened you." He gave her the smile, but it was different, only his mouth moved as his eyes held a strong gaze. "When I snuck up on you," he said as he started to back up. "I'll see you around."

Cammy said goodbye and opened up her book. She felt Danville watching her for an extra second before he finally turned around to leave. Cammy looked up to watch him go when he stopped and turned back, his eyes stared into Cammy's. He had turned too quick for her avert her gaze, they stared in silence for a moment that felt forever.

"Oh and before I do forget Ms. Hart there was something I meant to talk to you about. That Macie Jennings thing that happened is now a police matter, just so you know," he said. Cammy nodded, the realization that he had been following her was now without doubt. "She was expelled I've been told, so she's no longer a school issue. We got it from here."

The temperature of Cammy's blood rose a few degrees throughout her body. Cammy showed her best poker face, but she was never good at poker. Her face felt like it was bright red and one hundred ten degrees. She was unsure if the comment embarrassed her as if she did something wrong, or if it angered her like he was telling her she did.

Danville just smiled. He walked backward away from Cammy for a couple of steps. He then pointed both his hands like fake guns with his fingers and thumbs. "And that boyfriend thing you thought you saw, well, ya didn't," he winked and pulled the fake triggers. Cammy didn't move as he turned to his car. He yelled while turning that he hoped the best for her with her new job in 'his town.'

Cammy watched for a moment, then down at her book. She wanted to look like she was reading, but if someone was looking close enough it was quite obvious that the shaking book would be very difficult to read. Cammy looked up without moving her head. She watched as Danville's squad car numbered 3 started and drove off. He never looked back as he sped away. Cammy looked around, if there had been anyone else at the little park, they were gone.

Danville did not show up by accident, he had followed Cammy, or was told where she was. Sam would not have given her his number to call later if he was the one feeding Danville her location. Someone else, did Macie tell him about the appointment that Cammy had set up? The other thing that frightened Cammy, terrified her actually, was how long had he been following her? How much did he know?

Chapter 36

The next day Cammy called into work sick. She did the same the day after that. When she did finally show up that Friday Pete Wellman was already sitting in her office. He told her that Macie had been calling the school for two days, and even called his house the night before. Cammy threw her bag on her desk and fell into her chair. She looked at Wellman without saying anything. He started to talk, she began to work on her computer.

"She brought up the doctor's appointment you set up for her, to tell you she didn't need it," Pete said. Cammy stared at the computer as she stopped typing, she finally looked up at him.

"I know, well, I figure she wouldn't go," she stated.

"Did Macie actually admit to being pregnant?" he asked. Cammy shook her head no. She had set up an appointment for Macie with a doctor who would be able to take care of the cyst, and possibly prevent another reoccurrence. The appointment wasn't really for Macie, it was the proof Cammy needed that Macie was pregnant for the second time.

"Listen," Pete looked around to make sure no one was outside the office. "I'm not into talking bad about students, but this one," he leaned in. "I'm telling you again, get away and stay away. Bad, bad news," he whispered. The concern was not unwarranted. Pete didn't know how much Cammy knew about Macie's sister J.C. He had told Cam about the family's past, but he gave the Lifetime network version. The real story was more Cammy's style, True Crime TV. Then there was the issue of the drug dealing boyfriend who was on the wrong side of the playground when it came to neighborhood bullies. Any ties to Donovan Elliott were not good, and if you were on his hit list it made things even worse.

Her sister and mother were both rumored to have dabbled in prostitution. Neither was ever arrested for it, but it was a rumor that was out there. Rumors like that eventually become fact by most townfolk. There was also the rumor of J.C. and Macie's real father. He was murdered, chopped up, and buried somewhere in the field behind Ma Jenning's trailer- all at the hand of Ma Jennings herself. Pete was pretty sure that was just old town folklore, but none the less. The story was out there. The history of the Jennings family wasn't what really scared Pete, whether these rumors were true or not he wasn't even sure. It was the secrets that always scared Pete. The way Pete saw it every family had something that would embarrass them, from a DUI or someone had an abortion to more extreme stuff like the second cousin who was arrested for child porn in Kentucky or murder. Those were the secrets that scared Pete, that was the scary stuff. Pete felt like those were the types of secrets of the Jennings Clan. Now Macie was the only one left, she was bitter. She had been dumped on her entire life. Pete feared what she could be capable of, or involved in. He looked Cammy in the eye and whispered one last time, "Bad news."

Cammy smiled and nodded. She pointed to the computer to say she had to take care of something. Pete smiled and left. Cammy leaned back when he was gone. She looked at her stomach as she ran her hands along both sides, then slightly pushed in with both hands.

Chapter 37

The road was winding through a very heavily wooded area, most the trees were one to two hundred feet high. Maple, Evergreens, and Oak trees dominated Cammy's view. The road dipped and veered and turned enough that twenty five was her max speed, until finally, an entrance.

The entrance was a gravel road, but even the gravel had seen better days. It was more of a dirt road with loose rocks that randomly shot up to bounce somewhere under Cammy's Toyota. The first trailer on her right had been abandoned long ago. The back end had collapsed due to a rotted out base. The wood had finally given up on itself and the rest of the trailer looked like it would soon be doing the same. Cammy thought of a giant gray filled ashtray as she drove past it.

The car continued down the graveled dirt road, every few hundred feet a trailer could be seen back in the trees. The further from the main road, the more hidden the homes got. Cammy slowed the car as she approached Lot 54, she pulled into a bare space amongst the overgrown grass that seemed to be the parking spot. Cammy turned off the car and surveyed the area, she looked at her notebook one more time to be sure she had the right address. She did, but it could have been wrong, wouldn't be the first time. She was here, so she was going to try. Cammy stepped out of the car and walked to the front door. She had to step over a faded dull pink big wheel, she guessed the original color was red. The rest of the yard was empty with tall grass, not obnoxiously tall, but well overdue for a mowing. Cammy guessed the yard to be a little over an acre. Outside of the assumed property there was tall wheat grass for a couple hundred feet until it reached the woods, then that was all she could see, trees.

Cammy shuffled hesitantly to the front door. The entire time she was trying to watch where she was stepping while keeping one eye glued to the front door. Turning around flashed through her head with each step, as she neared she realized only the storm door was between her and the inside of the trailer, surely if anyone was home they would have heard the car, and they did.

The hammer on the gun was as identifiable in person as it had always been when Cammy heard it on TV or in a movie. The initial body numbness and the lost control of her legs was a completely new feeling.

"Turn the fuck around or you will be shot in the face bitch. I might'em take a chunk out a back'em of your gad damn head for the principle of coming here. Don't ya fuck'n read?" the voice from the other side of the screen said. Cammy stood at the bottom of the short rusty stairway looking into the dark trailer through the door. She couldn't see the person; she only knew it was a woman by the voice.

"I, um," Cammy stammered. She wasn't sure if her heart stopped when the tip of the shotgun came into view against the screen.

Cammy could also make out a figure, at least a tiny woman's figure.

"Nuff said, you fuck'n dead."

"NO, NO, please Macie told me to come here, I'm here for Macie," she pleaded. The figure sat silent for a moment before telling Cammy that Macie hadn't lived there for almost a year. Cammy said she knew that, she was from the school.

"She's been trying to contact me, I was gone for a few days."

"Why you not there for then? It's yo job," the petite figure said as she lowered her shotgun. Cammy ignored the question thinking she wasn't about to get lectured about doing her job from a lady in broken down trailer home that may or may not have working electric.

"I already went to Angel's apartment, I had heard she stayed there often. No one answered," Cammy said as the woman nodded.

"We don't talk."

Cammy told her she did all she could to get Macie's expulsion reduced to a suspension, but the school board would not allow it.

"Personally, I don't know why they were so adamant about expelling her, he ended up fine, and probably did deserve," Cammy trailed off for a couple seconds. She shrugged her shoulders as she peered into the dark room. "This is my first full year. Seemed like a harsh punishment though," Cammy watched inside the trailer as she said this, trying to see if she reacted at all. "No kid left behind, huh," Cammy chuckled. She received no reaction from the other side of the screen. There was silence for a long moment. Cammy began to step backward.

"What that dumb bitch gonna do with an education," she finally said from inside the trailer. "Wouldn't use it."

Cammy watched inside the screen door. How were people like this paid to take care of children? Did the state really investigate these people at all?

"I'm sorry to bother you Ma'am, but I do have one last question," Cammy said.

"What is it? Can't wait."

"Did you know she's pregnant?"

"No she ain't. Why you saying that?" the woman asked. She moved closer to the door, then pulled it open. She stepped into to light to get a better view of the counselor, and Cammy got her first view of the last meth head responsible for Macie's well being.

"I've seen her stomach," Cammy told her. She waited for an answer, there was none. "To be honest, I think she was pregnant when she was here last fall, winter I guess."

The silence answered the question that Cammy didn't ask. The woman raised the gun again, she pointed it right at Cammy's head. This time no screen hid the barrel. "Macie and I don't talk, and I don't really give a damn about that girl. Haven't seen her since she left last year. I do sense you may be threat'n me about tell'n the state she left. That ain't a good idea'r, now I think we're done here Miss Hart."

"So you do know who I am?"

"I do know you've worn out your welcome. Goodbye ma'am."

Cammy took a step back, and froze. The woman could tell that Cammy was ready to give one more last shot. She thought about asking her again about the previous year, and she thought about asking what happened with the baby, until the question was answered for her.

"She was pregnant last year, the girl ain't smart, didn't take it serious. Poor child, she lost it, end of story. Now leave."

Cammy nodded. "I understand, I'm sorry about the loss. Which hospital did she go to when. . ."

"You can leave," she said. She gave Cammy a look to break ice, but eased as her eyes dropped. She looked at Cammy's bumped out stomach in the middle of her opened button up shirt. "Miss Hart, if you are as smart as that Master's Degree says you are, you will let Macie be. That'd be best for you both." The woman was still looking at Cammy's stomach. For the first time since pulling into the trailer park she felt her palms heat up, she wiped both hands on her hips, and hoped to herself that they were not wet enough to leave a streak of shaky fingers.

"My husband is in the war," Cammy said, unsure if she was being judged.

"Lady, I don't give a fuck if you're on Maury because it could be ten dads, leave me alone."

Cammy felt the nervousness turn to anger. She was here to help a student who could be in trouble, not get insulted.

Cammy tried to see the woman behind the screen, then just gave her a sympathetic smile. There was nothing else here. The only connection she had to Macie was getting her monthly check. Cammy gave her a slight nod with a sad, slight smile.

"I'm sorry for bothering you ma'am," said Cammy. She slowly backed up as she gave one last apology. Cammy pulled out her card and set it on the bottom, rotted out step. She asked her to call her if there was anything she could do to help Macie. She walked back to her car wondering if her business card would make it off the step before it became a part of the broken down trailer. A twisted backwoods version of "Cat's in the Cradle," spun on a record through her mind. The only thing was how did she know about Cammy? Did Macie have a connection to the woman? Who all was watching every move Cammy made?

Chapter 38

I laid next to Angel, he was already asleep. He was always asleep right after I gave it up. It was gross, he was gross. It wasn't always this way, I might have loved him at one point. That was a long time ago. The more I thought about it I think I just loved the idea of someone. Someone to take me away from everywhere I had been. I listened as Angel slept, it was all I would hear. Every thought was interrupted by his snoring. How did I get here? How was I going to get out?

I laid there trying to think, his breathing interrupted every thought. I watched my bare stomach rise and fall. There was a baby in there, there was no doubt if anyone looked at me. I'm sure everyone knew I was pregnant. Maybe they all thought I was just getting fat. I don't know what's worse? I rolled on my side and rubbed my freshly shaven legs. My arms wrapped around my stomach, everyone was probably thinking I was gaining weight, getting fat. Was it obvious I was pregnant? I hardly ate, I couldn't. When I ate in the morning I puked, same happened when I used to eat lunch at school. For dinner I'd have maybe a potato or half a jar of peanut butter, the only food that seemed to stay down. Anything else was rejected by my body.

I listened to Angel sleep, his sleep blocked every racing thought. I tried to go over the plan he had laid out earlier in the night. It wasn't a good plan. It wasn't bad, but I couldn't do it. I told him no, but he was persistent. He said it would work, and I couldn't disagree. That wasn't my problem with it. I just didn't know if I could actually go through with it. I wanted to get out, I wanted my baby more than anything. I wanted to do it my way though. I had to think of a way out because like usual, no one else was going to do it for me. I closed my eyes and curled into a fetal position, or as close as my stomach would allow me to. I think that's how I fell asleep that night, like the night before, and the one before that.

Chapter 39

The doctor watched Cammy leave the office, neither said anything as the door shut. She moved like she had nowhere to be because she didn't.

Cammy left the two hundred foot metal shed turned into an office building, it was like every other business in Franklin County with a generic name, initials were popular like CT Grocers, H and H Hardware, etc. The other similarity new businesses in the county had was they were all housed in aluminum sheds. Cammy still couldn't bring herself to catch a flick in a giant shed called The OFC Movie house, hardly the place she would watch a first run movie. She bared the forty minute drive to the next closest theater for the one movie she saw since living in Franklin County. She'd accepted the fact that she was now a renter- strictly Red Box, at least till Russell wanted to take her to the movies again.

She needed Russell to come back soon. He'd see everything would be different once they started their family. In the near future they would be hitting the town again, like they used to. They would have to find a babysitter. Would she use Craigslist, or maybe the school had a program where she could get a student to babysit. There were a few girls in the Honor Society Cammy would trust with her child, but plenty she wouldn't. She would be sure to give the student a lengthy interview before she allowed any babysitting. She thought how Russell used to dance with her till the bars closed, often they were the only two people dancing in the bar. She held those moments, the times when they didn't have a care in the world. It was young love.

The rain pounded the street hard on Cammy's drive home. The little bit she could see out of her windshield told her the short run from the apartment building's carport to the covered awning around her building would be far enough to soak her clothes. Her mind drifted as she watched the rain explode into the puddles in front of her. The giant craters dissolved as quickly as they were created, only for a giant drop to start the process over. When she walked into the aluminum office building the sun was shining, and there was no doubt in her mind it would be shining again before the day ended. Cammy took the long way home to pick up a coffee, and delay her arrival. There was an old saying in Missouri, "If you don't like the weather, wait ten minutes."

The sun was making its way through broken clouds when Cammy pulled the car into the apartment parking lot. The surprise wasn't the piece mealed pink sky she glanced at as she parked in front of the apartment, but the broken girl who sat outside Cammy's door. It was Macie, and from the look on her face- she had nowhere else to go.

Chapter 40

Now Macie sat outside the apartment door, she had been waiting for her. Cammy put the car in park, the girl looked through the windshield right at the counselor, trying to see if it was indeed Cammy. Cammy put her hand on the ignition and froze. Macie had been expelled; there was no obligation to help her anymore. If the girl really was bad news this was the time to get her out of her life for good. This was her out, her last chance. Macie took two steps toward the car and stopped. She watched Cammy, waited to see what her former counselor's decision would be. Cammy looked at the sixteen year- old girl. She turned the ignition to kill the engine.

"Hello," Macie called out. "Miss Hart?" Macie asked to see if it was Cammy, but she was really asking if Cammy was going to help her. With what? Was Macie ready to come clean with the truth? Cammy wasn't sure. She knew this was what she had signed up for, to help students get to, and succeed as adults.

Cammy got out of her car. She walked toward the apartment. As she neared the girl she could see her eyes were red, her cheeks streaked with black mascara. "You don't call your students back, what the hell's with that?" Macie barked as Cammy approached.

"You're no longer a student Macie," Cammy said. Then followed it with a comment she immediately regretted, "You got kicked out."

Macie covered her eyes with her sleeve as she tried not to cry. Under the oversized sweatshirt that covered her face Cammy could hear the little girl apologize for yelling, then apologize for everything else she had ever done wrong.

"I'm so sorry, I'm sorry, I don't know what to do," Macie cried as she fell into a ball in front of Cammy's apartment. Cammy's eyes darted all over the apartment complex in hopes that no one was seeing the teenager bawling at her feet.

"Get up, come on, get up and get a hold of yourself," Cammy pleaded. She helped Macie to her feet, Cammy looked around again, then at Macie. Her eyes were sunk back in her skinny face, her hair and shirt looked like a crusty rag that had been sitting in the sink for about three days too long. Cammy held Macie's face with both hands and looked the little girl in the eye. "Jesus girl, when did you eat last? Or shower? Come on, let's go get some food, we can talk there," Cammy said. She half- heartedly waved toward her car. "Come with me."

Chapter 41

Twenty two miles north of Franklin County was nothing. The last ten minutes of their drive didn't even have any farmhouses visible from the highway. There was an old time diner six miles off the highway at exit 87, Cammy knew this because when she moved to Franklin County she misread Exit 67 on her directions in a caffeine haze. She ended up driving north to 87 and got off, she followed her MapQuest printout until she knew she was lost so she pulled over at this diner where the waitress was kind enough to tell her she was at Exit 87, rather than 67.

The diner was similar to the new style retro diners where everything is stainless steel, including the booths and walls and tables. The only difference was this one was real- *Established in 1947,* according to the sign. The restaurant had 12 seats along the counter, then one long row of twelve booths. Over each booth was a faded photograph of a local farmhouse, all circa 1947. Cammy led Macie to the last booth, they both sat down.

The diner was much more crowded than the first time Cammy wandered in, but it was seven thirty at night now as opposed to two in the morning the first time. Cammy sat across from Macie who just looked up and down the counter at the customers. There was an older couple with empty plates at the counter near

Cammy and Macie. They were about eighty years old each, and neither spoke. They had finished their meals and were now taking sips of coffee between cigarette puffs. The rest of the crowd was dispersed in the first six booths and chairs at the counter, Macie didn't seem to notice them.

They sat silent for a few minutes, a continuation of the car ride. Cammy had already spent the half hour drive in silence, the girl obviously had something to get off her chest, and Cammy wanted to make this as quick as possible. Cammy was about to speak when Macie threw down her menu and looked right at Cammy.

"Is this still Franklin County?" the girl asked. Cammy looked around and shrugged. She didn't really know, and she told the girl she hadn't seen any signs to tell her otherwise on the ride up. They were far from town though. That and the surveyed crowd seemed to be good enough for Macie. "I'm sorry for coming to you, but I need someone, someone-" Macie said and stopped. She leaned across the table and whispered, "not from around here."

Not from around here, the thought danced around Cammy's head. "Why does that matter, Macie?" Cammy asked.

Macie blinked a couple times, her eyes filled up with tears, and the fourth or fifth blink knocked a tear from her left eye and then her right. She took a napkin out of the tin holder and wiped her face. Then she looked at Cammy.

"Did you know I had a sister?" the young girl asked. Cammy nodded, then held out her hands.

"I did, do I guess. I don't know much about her though," Cammy lied. Macie watched Cammy's eyes for a moment, trying to get a read on the counselor. What did she know?

"The thing is," Macie started to say and stopped. She then took out a pack of cigarettes. Cammy looked around and realized she was the only adult not smoking in the diner. She made a quick comment half under her breath about finding it hard to believe you could still smoke in restaurants here, the comment fell on deaf ears as Macie tapped her cig on the table.

"I don't want to involve you in what goes on here, or my situation. I need someone who might understand my plight though," the little girl said. Cammy didn't say anything as she calculated what Macie had just said. She remembered how this wasn't a typical girl from the trailers, this was a girl whose intelligence would rival anyone in the county, age not being a factor. Then the opening of the sentence came back to Cammy. "Someone not from around here," and how she had just said, "What goes on here." Cammy asked her what she was getting at, Macie was silent for a moment. Was Cammy more of an outsider than she suspected?

"I was happy when I didn't see any pictures in your office," Macie told her. "It told me you were a single woman.In the same, well, you know, situation." Cammy had already told Macie she wasn't single, then she asked her how she knew where she lived. Macie told her she figured it out due to the lack of family photos combined with the fact that Cammy was a new counselor meant she had no family, and most likely lived in the complex where much of the younger, single faculty members lived. Macie had gone to the main building and searched the mailroom for the name Hart, then sat outside Cammy's door for two and a half hours waiting.

"What situation is that Macie? I told you I'm not a single woman, just a victim of war," Cammy said as she rubbed her stomach. "I actually got word that Russell will be returning next month." Macie leaned closer to Cammy in a state of shock. She quickly became more agitated than Cammy had ever seen her.

"Returning? Why don't you have any pictures in your office then?" she asked. The news seemed to be a setback to Macie, something she didn't want to hear. Cammy told her how their belongings were in storage in her mother's basement, the little they had. Cammy didn't know how long she would be in Franklin County when she moved here. It all depended on Russell. There was a momentary silence.

"Shit, sorry, I'm sorry Miss Hart," Macie said. Again they sat in silence until Macie lit her smoke. "We don't have to order, we can go."

"You're pregnant?" Cammy asked. Macie nodded. "Should you be doing that?" Cammy said as she nodded to Macie's cigarette. Macie gave her a look to tell the counselor that it was none of her business. Cammy shook her head. "If you want me to help you, with whatever this problem is I'm not going to allow you to hurt the baby," she said. Then she leaned across the table, "And I'm not going to help you unless you start being honest with me. Half you girls are knocked up in this town, and not to offend you, but I know you were pregnant last winter. So we either start talking straight or I'm bringing you home and won't see you again till I read you got arrested or see your Obit in the paper. Right damn now," Cammy said. Macie's eyes got wide at the counselor's abrupt change of attitude. "Put the cigarette out."

"Fuck, fine," Macie said as she stabbed the cig into the ashtray. "Jesus Christ."

"Not Jesus Christ," Cammy said. Then pointed right in the girl's face, "I got my own shit sissy, I'm not going to listen to your little sob story unless you tell me what is up, and I'm certainly not going to sit with you while you smoke and hurt this baby."

Macie sat silent. The waitress finally came over to the table. Macie ordered a Mexican Skillet, Cammy just ordered coffee. The waitress left and they sat in silence for what felt like a few minutes to Cammy. Finally, Macie came clean.

"I was pregnant last year Miss Hart. I was," Macie started to cry. Cammy sat silent, and watched as Macie tried to come clean. "I have, I had a sister," she said. Macie wiped her eyes as she looked at Cammy.

"She passed away, right?" Cammy asked. Macie shook her head no.

"Murdered," she whispered.

"Murdered?" the counselor asked. Macie quickly scanned the diner, then shook her head at Cammy.

"Shh, please. People around here don't believe that, or won't. They know what happened though, it's just these aren't the type of people to admit that kind of thing. I know, and they know what happened. Things are different here, the truth isn't always important when it comes to people like me and my sister."

Cammy let the girl go on about how she had no one who cared for her, even Angel. If she said anything he didn't like or didn't check in at the right time he would threaten to throw her and their unborn baby on the street, or get physical.

"Have you ever asked yourself which is worse: being a violent person or just sitting in the back of the theater to watch that violence?" Macie asked and stopped. She looked around the diner again. "No one helps, ever." Macie stared off toward the door. Her face lost all expression as Cammy answered her.

"I'm here trying to help you Macie."

Macie smiled as she softly asked, "Are you?" She paused and looked at the counselor. "People don't go out of their way to help, not unless there is something in it for them."

Cammy sat silent for a moment, then answered the girl, "Eventually you'll let your guard down, you'll see people can be good."

"See that guy in the front, that wannabe who just walked in?" the girl asked. A young man walked in the diner and sat in the first seat at the counter. Cammy nodded. Macie just looked at the guy sitting in the first seat at the counter. Cammy heared the man order a coffee and ask for a menu in broken English. She wasn't for sure, but thought he had a Bosnian accent when he ordered. Cammy knew there was a pretty large Bosnian population closer to the city, she was pretty sure that was his first language. "This isn't good," she stopped again, and looked at Cammy. Macie watched the counselor and wondered if she was going to help the girl.

"What's that? What's not good?" Cammy asked. Macie's face was pale as the napkin she held. Cammy could tell her mind was racing. She was looking all over the restaurant as if it was closing in on her. Cammy looked back at the man and saw that he was watching them. He was wearing black hat with a gold St. Louis Cardinals emblem, he smiled, and revealed that he was missing his two front teeth. He wore an oversized black hoodie, and oversized jeans. Cammy thought about her theory that most young men in town either dressed like they were country music stars, camouflaged hunters, or gangster rappers. The foreign looking guy at the end of the counter chose the latter for his wardrobe.

"I want to leave."

"Who is that man?" Cammy asked as Macie gathered her purse.

"Please Miss Hart," Macie stopped and started to gag. Her body convulsed as she dry heaved, then she threw up on the black and white checkered floor right in front of the booth. Cammy winced as vomit splattered off the tile onto her slacks. Macie grabbed a napkin and wiped her mouth. A pimpled boy about Macie's age wheeled a mop bucket over to the table. He mumbled something to himself. Macie stared at the man in black, almost oblivious to the mess she just made.

"Let's go, come on," Cammy said as she grabbed Macie by the elbow. She led her down the narrow diner along the row of booths and past the fixated eyes on Macie. The Hip Hop Foreigner didn't move, he watched Cammy the whole time as he seemed to draw a mental picture of her face. She did the same.

Chapter 42

The drive home was silent. I didn't care I'd just puked all over the diner. The thing was I didn't know if I could go through with Angel's plan, but I didn't want to stay either. There was nothing more important to me than this baby, but now everything seemed different. Maybe Miss Hart did want to help me.

I didn't recognize the man who came into the diner, the one she thought made me sick. What I recognized was the type he was. The guy was up to something, I could see it in his movements. He tried to act like he was minding his own business, but I caught him looking at me three times. He tried to be sneaky using the mirror behind the counter, he tried to hide his shifty eyes to see what we were up to. I don't know who he was, but he was sent by someone. That much I was sure of.

I felt bad not saying anything for the ride home, but too much ran through my head. What was I going to do? How was I going to get out of here? When I saw that guy I knew my plan needed some fix'n. They were watching me. Someone knew I was thinking of a way out.

Miss Hart pulled up to the trailer and stopped the car. I looked over and saw she wasted no time before she shifted the car to reverse.

"Sorry, 'bout all this," I said.

"It's fine Macie," she said. I tried to smile, but could feel my stomach tighten at the weak attempt. I could have burst out in tears if I said anything else. I wanted someone to tell me what to do, she wasn't the person though. There wasn't someone. Just me. Miss Hart nodded to the trailer. "You're being summoned."

I looked to the trailer where the screen door was propped open by a bare foot. Angel stayed inside, out of sight. He just held the door open and waited. I turned back to Miss Hart, but didn't say anything. I didn't do anything, just held her gaze for a moment, then got out.

Chapter 43

Thursday and Friday came and went without any kind of contact from, or mention of Macie Jennings. The most exciting incident at school was when a Special-Ed student found out she was getting a detention. The girl emptied her book bag and began to throw each book around the counselor's office until security finally showed up after two and a half minutes. A lime green flower pot was the sole casualty of the situation.

That Friday started as lonely as most. Cammy ate alone at Applebee's. That was followed by a solo trip to CJ's Ice Shack, an orange pop- up camper parked at the top of Main Street that sold Sno- Cones. Cammy had a friend who craved Sno- Cones during the last trimester of her pregnancy, even though the baby was born in March.

The head lights behind Cammy were no different than any other cars, but they started to give her the impression they were following her. Cammy wasn't one to be paranoid, so she drove a couple blocks and made two turns off the beaten path. The same headlights with a bluish tint were still behind her. Cammy drove down Western, she turned right without using her signal on Washington Street. The blue lights did the same. She was being followed. Cammy sped up, so did the car behind her. She was driving quick, and after a few turns to shake the car found herself in a new subdivision. There were only eight houses in the neighborhood. No other cars, except the one following her. Cammy slammed on the gas and raced the car back through the dark road past the eight new houses. The road turned left, then another left, the car was still behind her and closing in. She realized she was heading back toward the entrance to the neighborhood and accelerated with conviction. Cammy took the right on the residential road at fifty and hooked a quick left back to the road she came in on. She ended up on Highway 47, which had a few restaurants. She drove to the first one she saw, McDonalds- of course. The car stayed behind her.

Cammy saw a police car at the gas station across the street from the McDonald's. Her car flew over the highway just ahead of an oncoming pick up. She pulled into the station, and watched the car that had been following her. It didn't cross the road, just sat at the entrance, then turned and drove away. Cammy stood outside her door as she watched the car drive off. He was gone, but not before Cammy saw who had been following here, again. It was The Bosnian, from the diner.

Chapter 44

The next morning a police car sat outside the front doors of the school, directly in front of the fire hydrant. A *No Parking* sign was within a foot of the front bumper, impossible to miss, but apparently easy to ignore when your name was Chad Danville.

The Navy Blue Squad Car had been there for almost a half hour, at least that's was when Cammy first noticed it, and she'd been watching it from her office window ever since. She was expecting an officer and Principal Savard to come marching in her office any moment. Cammy was always next in line to be notified when a student was arrested.

The blinds to her office were closed, she liked to keep them closed until tenish, it helped to keep from being bothered. The door finally opened, without a knock. Roberta, the office Secretary stuck her head through the opening that was just big enough to stick her head through. She was quickly pushed aside and replaced by a frail woman in her late thirties.

"I tried to tell her she needed an appointment," Roberta yelled from behind the woman. Cammy nodded to Roberta. The morning's intruder smiled a tooth rotted victory smile in Roberta's direction, then to Cammy. Cammy forced a return smile. The one thing she couldn't stand was the parents who barged into her office with no appointment or warning.

139

Cammy had sent out countless e- mails and letters (since many families in the District still lacked a computer) informing parents that meeting with her would be much more beneficial if she had time to prepare. Most the parents ignored this request.

"I wanna see my boy," the woman slurred. The woman was on something, maybe a few something's. She looked like she could have been anywhere from early thirties to mid- forties. A person who didn't know the toll Meth took on a body might even mistake the woman to be about fifty. At any rate, she looked like hell. Cammy guessed the woman weighed in the neighborhood of eighty- five pounds, mainly skin and bones. Her brown hair was dirty and thin, Cammy thought of a stray wet dog. When the woman scratched her arms Cammy saw they had been scratched to the point of bleeding. "Get my boy down here, right the fuck now."

"OK, easy," Cammy told her, "Have a seat." She pointed to one of the chairs in front of her desk. She told Roberta it was fine, and asked her to close the door on her way out. Cammy pulled the chair out for the woman. She then opened her blinds and looked at Roberta to let her know she should keep an eye on the situation. She walked back around to sit at her computer. "Now ma'am, what's your son's name?" she asked calmly and slowly hoping it would ease the woman's attitude.

"I don't know, don't know, let me see him," she said as she put both palms on the desk. Cammy leaned back as the woman leaned toward her. "I know his face."

"The chair," Cammy said. She eyed the chair until the lady sat back in it. The counselor sat back in her chair, another parent fried out of their minds. She didn't need to know the kids name because she already knew the mother was going to be banned from seeing him, hence the visit. A number of parents who were court ordered to stay away from their children would come to the school to try to bully the faculty with threats of lawsuits if they couldn't see their children. Cammy always wondered if these parents knew that Cammy had all records concerning the students. All court orders were listed, and even highlighted, on each kid's school page.

"I can't look him up without a name."

"I said I don't know it," the woman said. "How would I? Please I want to see him, I just don't know his fuck'n name God Damnit."

Cammy peeked out the window through the blinds; the police car was still in front. Cammy made eye contact with Roberta to let her know this one was really off her rocker. If this woman did do anything Cammy wanted to be sure Roberta saw everything.

"How about we try something a little easier, what's your name?" asked Cammy. She hoped the woman didn't think she was being too sarcastic, but then again, how would it not sound that way. The strung out wannabe mom responded with some inaudible mumblings.

"They took him, see him, I want to see HIM," stumbled out of her mouth. Cammy wondered what the woman was on. She seemed to be somewhere between a dreamlike trance and a drunken stupor. Cammy thought of a child talking in his sleep, that's what the woman was, walking and talking in her sleepy dreamlike trance, another self- induced blackout.

"I can't help you without names. Now what is your name or your son's name," Cammy said. The woman's head swiveled around the room once, and ended up almost in her lap. She covered the back of her head, and moaned as she pulled her head down to her knees. Cammy looked outside at the squad car, it was still there. She nodded at Roberta who picked up the phone to the school's security officer.

The woman continued to talk, never telling Cammy her name. Cammy turned around to her usual binder of local counselor's and rehab facilities. "Do you have insurance miss?" asked Cammy, she waited but got no answer. She took the lack of a response as negative. She started to explain to the woman how these facilities could help her. "Once you get better we can work on getting you more time with your son."

The woman jumped up as she screamed to the ceiling. She swiftly swatted the pamphlets out of Cammy's hand.

"I don't need help, I need my boy!" she yelled. Roberta finally heard the commotion and looked at Cammy. Cammy shook her fist toward her ear to let Roberta know it was getting urgent. "They did this to me, I'm not crazy, they fucked me, they fucked me up like this. You have to listen," she yelled. "Please help," she barely whispered. She fell to the ground and curled up in the fetal position. The door flew open.

The thirty pound overweight man in blue was the school's security officer, Officer Nate.

He looked at the woman on the floor, then to Cammy. "What's with her?" he asked.

"Well Nate, I'm pretty sure someone took a little of this, and a lot of that," Cammy said. He pulled out his handcuffs. Cammy's eyes widened as she held her hands up. Officer Nate looked at her with a tilted head until he realized she was looking right past him.

The office door bounced off the wall as it flung open. Cammy stared at Chad Danville standing in the doorway.

"What's this woman doing here?" he said as he stood over the weeping mess of a mother.

Cammy watched the officer. Something about him seemed much more vulnerable as opposed to the day in the park, maybe it was because he was now on her turf. It could have been the way he stormed in and everyone else in the office just looked at him like he was some kind of lunatic. At any rate, she didn't fear him like she did just a few days earlier.

"Oh look everyone, it's super cop," Cammy said. The words exhilarated her as they left her mouth. Danville shot her a look to keep quiet as he whipped out his cuffs. He grabbed the woman's wrist and pulled them high up behind her back.

"What do you think you're doing?" Cammy shouted as she jumped up.

"Sit down and shut up Counselor," he yelled back. Officer Nate jumped up between the two as Cammy lunged toward the town's most famous police officer.

"This is my office Officer," Cammy said loud enough to make Nate take a step back.

Danville and Cammy stared eye to eye, she wasn't about to back down to him, even if she did think the woman was crazy.

"This here is Katherine Siebert. There are currently three warrants out for this woman's arrest. She is a known meth head, and dealer, not to mention sexual assault of a fifteen year old boy. She's a piece of garbage. Let me guess, she was here to find her son or some bullshit like that."

Cammy didn't say anything as Danville lifted the woman up and threw her over his shoulder like a straw filled scarecrow. He turned around and started for the door. He stopped and turned his head to Cammy.

"By the way, your former student Macie Jennings has been brought in for questioning for the murder of Ray Lehane," he said. "Thought you'd like to know." Danville walked out with the woman over his shoulder, her seemingly lifeless arms hung down his back. He took the woman and left without saying another word. No one did.

Chapter 45

The slippers slid in red death as the Mother Lehane tried to run, not really toward or away but a shuffle because she didn't know if she should wake her son or go for the phone. She ignored the splash off the dirt from the dog's urinal mist as it hit her ankles, and son's face. She told herself Ray had passed out in the backyard, again. She leaned down to wake him. Her hand touched his head, but instantly retracted. The mother silently cried out as she held the crushed skull of her recently deceased son. The silent cry turned into a chilling squeal that told the neighbors someone better call the police.

The police arrived just before sun-up, the media sometime before the orange burn on the horizon and after the wet misty blue of dawn. Donovan Elliott and a couple of his guys showed up in between. Elliott walked around without talking to anyone. No one talked to him. He was even able to walk up to the body, he watched closely as officers gathered evidence. A bloody baseball bat sat in the lawn next to Ray's dead body. Donovan stood over the bat and stared at it for a long moment. He turned to his three henchmen, nodded to the bikes, and they all got on and left. Regular conversation returned to the crime scene once the bikes were out of sight. The local gawkers all discussed Elliott's reaction to the bat, each opinion varied, of course.

Chapter 46

The television in the faculty lounge was around well before the wave of flat screen and plasma televisions appeared. The TV was probably around before DVD's ran Laser Disc out of business since the TV came with a built-in VCR. The color was bad, the picture was wavy, but Cammy heard everything she needed to hear. Someone was about to take the fall for this murder. Someone innocent.

The phone rang in Cammy's purse, she took it out and looked at a local number she didn't know. Cammy answered the phone and listened. She nodded even though the person on the other line could not see her. Finally she said OK, and hung up. The reporter on the TV was asking Chad Danville about Macie Jennings. "Is it true the juvenile had been arrested the week before for an attack on Mr. Lehane?" asked the Reporter.

"No Comment," commented Danville. He gave the same answer for all questions. The reporter then asked why Donovan Elliott was at the murder scene.

"Is Elliott a suspect?" she asked. This was the only question that Danville gave a definite response to, a flat out No. "Why was he there this morning?" the Reporter asked Danville.

"He's a concerned citizen, there was a brutal murder in our town. A lot of our local community was milling around the crime scene this morning. Some concerned, most just nosy."

Cammy watched the Police Chief, she had seen enough. She got out of her chair and headed for the door. Pete Wellman walked in the lounge. He stopped in front of Cammy and put his hands on her shoulders as he looked in her eyes.

"Did you hear about Macie?" he asked.

"She didn't do it."

"Where are you going Cammy?" Pete looked at her, then shook his head. He urged her to stay away from Macie, she was in trouble, the worst kind of trouble too. "I'm not talking the law Cammy, Elliott was there, he's pissed."

"She didn't do it."

"I know, and so does Donovan. It was the boyfriend, her boyfriend. They're going to kill him, and anyone he's with. Jail is the safest place for her right now. That's might even be why Danville had her brought in, her own protection."

Cammy nodded, then looked down. She thought to herself for a moment, shook her head. "Pete, she's sixteen- years old, and has no one. I have to help her, that's what we do, right?" She looked at Pete, he gave her a crooked smile, but didn't say anything. Cammy walked by Pete and out of the lounge.

Chapter 47

The Franklin County Police Department was nothing like the police stations Cammy had seen on TV. The building was a typical white aluminum shed, of course. Cammy saw it fitting that the only way to identify the station from the outside were the initials FCPD. Inside of the front doors was a small room that was about six by eight foot. A glass window was to the right when she walked it. The window had a small hole eye level, and an opening like the ones Cammy had seen at gas stations when the owner knew better not to let customers in after dark. There was a small silver bell next to the opening. Cammy rang it.

The station was silent, she wondered if anyone was there. She rang the bell a couple more times.

Chad Danville appeared on the other side of the glass. The former quarterback stood tall in front of Cammy, he wore oversized Top Gun style mirrored sunglasses. Cammy felt him staring at her- silent.

"Gum, Officer?" asked Cammy. It was more to break the silence than a legitimate offer as she held out a green pack of spearmint Trident. Danville acted as if he didn't hear the counselor's generosity as he slowly lifted his glasses to the top of his head.

"I think you're stepping out of your job description Ms. Hart."

"It's Mrs. Hart, MISTER Danville. Is she being charged?" she asked. Cammy stared right back to let him know she was un-intimidated by the former small town hero.

"Macie?" Danville asked, playing dumb. "No, not yet."

"Then why is she still in there?"

"She's free to go, for now," he said. He leaned closer to Cammy and slid his business card through the slot in the counter, "If you think it's a good idea." Danville stood back up straight and tall, "Here's my number," he said. She thought he was making an attempt to be a real police officer, "If you ever need someone to talk to." Cammy couldn't tell if he was being sincere, "Or if you just want to get a hold of me," he said.

Cammy smiled and tossed a piece of the Trident into the metal pan below the slot, "Take the gum." Cammy gave Danville one last look to let him know she wasn't interested, or intimidated. She walked to the closed hallway door that led to the jail's holding cell. She stood in front of the door until Danville finally buzzed her in.

The hallway was long and narrow. It was painted a typical off white- yellow that most the offices in Franklin County were painted. Cammy wondered if there was deal on the paint years ago, or if the local pastime of smoking had just turned all white paint to this new shade of yellow. She also wondered what Danville's angle was, why give her his card, and follow it with a blatant sinister flirtation? Cammy could see the room at the end of the hall on the right side, the holding cell. There were no bars, but a giant thick Plexiglas wall. The door was the same Plexiglas. Cammy was about ten feet from the cell when the door opened and Macie walked out. She looked at Cammy and smiled.

"Thanks Ms. Hart," Macie whispered. "Can you take me home?"

Cammy nodded as Macie walked past her. They walked down the hall, the door buzzed as they approached. Macie shoved the door open and continued to walk through the lobby. Her eyes were focused on the front door the entire time, her head never turned. Cammy followed the girl out of the building. They walked to her Toyota. Macie got in the passenger seat, Cammy sat in the driver's seat. The keys jangled in her purse before she pulled them out. Cammy put the car key into the ignition, and started the car. She looked at Macie before shifting to reverse.

"Have you heard from Angel? I couldn't get a hold of him," Macie said. Cammy shook her head. She reached out and rubbed Macie's shoulder for the second Macie allowed before she slowly pushed Cammy's hand away. "I have to go to the trailer, I need to find him."

"Hun, I don't know if that's a good idea. People will be watching it," Cammy informed her. Macie already knew that.

"I didn't hurt that guy, not yesterday at least, I certainly didn't kill him."

"I know that," Cammy said and smiled to Macie. Macie didn't see though because she was looking at her knee under her jeans. "They know that too, that's why you're out here. There are people though," Cammy stopped. Macie was staring off out the window now, somewhere in thought. "Macie, some people don't care about innocence, they see you as a connection, a weakness-"

"Angel didn't either, he ain't a killer," she said to cut Cammy off. Cammy didn't respond. Macie looked out the window as she thought out loud where Angel could be.

"Does he have a temper?"

"Who Angel? Heck no. He's as sweet as a teddy," said Macie. Cammy shrugged her shoulders, Macie turned away back to the window.

"Well, there aren't many teddy bears selling meth to teens sweetie," Cammy told the girl with instant regret.

Macie whipped her head around, and tried to yell, but stumbled over her words. Cammy nodded and said, "I'm just saying, I mean, what's the deal with Ray? Why did you guys get into it last week?"

"What are you talking about? I told you he was spreading shit about Angel."

"So you attack and slash him? I'm not going to lie, this kind of story doesn't end well for you."

"He turned Elliott against Angel. That ain't good Miss Hart. I ain't sad Ray's dead, he was a piece of shit, but I didn't kill him."

"How about Angel, how upset was he with the whole thing about you and Ray? What kind of temper does Angel have, has he ever hit-" Cammy asked but quickly got cut off.

"Fuck no, I told you Angel is a giant teddy bear," Macie repeated.

"Maybe, I don't know, maybe he saw him out alone and thought he could get away with it? I mean is there more to the Bus Depot?"

asked Cammy. She waited while Macie ignored her, staring out the window.

"It's for me, he's doing it all for me and I just treat him like shit."

"Doing what for you?" asked Cammy.

"What do you think? The dealing, selling is all for me. He's trying to get some money so we can get out of this town. You know what though?" asked Macie. She didn't wait for a response from Cammy. "My plan from the beginning of this stupid idea is to ditch him as soon as I have enough cash to make it on my own. He's risking everything for me, and I just shit on him over, and over again. I'm not a good person Ms. Hart."

"That's not true Macie."

Finally she turned to Cammy. Macie wiped her tears away with her sleeve. "Miss Hart, I think if they find him," Macie said and stopped. She looked down at her knees again and wiped her eyes with her shirtsleeve. "They're going to kill him."

"Who Macie?" Cammy asked. Silence. "Is it The Vandals? Are they going to kill Angel? Is it another dealer?"

"Who knows?" Macie said as she looked right at Cammy, "Is there a fucking difference?"

Chapter 48

School got out at 2:15, the last bus usually returned around a quarter after 4. Cammy waited till almost 5 P.M. before she made her move. Forty five minutes should be long enough for Sam to finish all paperwork, and unless there was a problem with a bus, all drivers and mechanics would be gone too. She circled the bus depot twice, the only cars in the parking lot were two clunkers that had been there since summer. Cammy pulled her Toyota into the lot. She drove around to the back of the depot and parked. She turned off the car and got out.

The newspapers from the Milton Hawkins case were gone from Sam's coffee table. Just about everything was now gone, it no longer resembled the cluttered mess it was just a week earlier. The computer and telephone remained. Everything else had been cleaned off. The paper from Ray Lehane's murder, when he learned what it felt like to be a baseball was by itself at the end of the coffee table. Cammy skimmed through the three paragraphed article. The headline read *Body Found in Franklin County,* no details or names were given in the article, despite the fact that Ray was found dead by his mother- in his own backyard.

Cammy looked through the newspaper. She thought there were more Ads than normal for a Tuesday. She flipped through and realized they weren't Advertisements. Sam had all the articles about Milton and Hannah hidden in the newspaper. Why was he so interested in this story? Was Milton Hawkins tied to Elliott too?

Cammy moved to the office door and peaked out, still alone. She scurried behind the desk and knelt down to the file cabinet. She sifted through the drawers and files in each drawer. Apparently Sam hadn't had enough time to get around to cleaning out his files yet. She started to look for something, anything that caught her eye. She couldn't find Ray's file, she couldn't find any employee files in the cabinet. He got rid of the necessities. A small cabinet was tucked behind the college boy fridge in the corner. Cammy slid along the floor to the cabinet. She grabbed the handle- locked. The handle would not budge no matter how hard she shook it.

She stood up and quickly scanned the office, no keys hanging anywhere. She opened the desk drawer to find a few pens and paperclips. Cammy gave the office a final once over, then to the clock. It was almost six o'clock, she had to get out before the school's custodian locked the parking lot gate.

Cammy grabbed the day's paper. The clippings of Milton and Hannah flew out from the inside. Cammy glanced at them, but her eyes made a swift jump back to where she had grabbed paper from. A binder had been underneath. Cammy opened the binder, Macie's picture was photocopied along with some scribbling next to it. Cammy didn't even read past Macie Jennings. She grabbed the binder, and practically fell over herself as she fled the office. It was 6 P.M.

The Toyota reversed along the side of the depot until Cammy could spin the car to face the gate. She raced the car to the gate, slamming on the brakes when she realized she had nowhere to go. The car slid along the gravel for about fifteen feet, coming to a complete stop in front of the closed gate. She looked down at the clock on her dash, it read 6:02. The beat in her chest jumped to third gear.

The driver's side window was slapped so hard Cammy covered her face expecting glass to shatter. The scream she howled would have been heard if anyone else was in the lot, no one was, except Sam Montero. Cammy stared at him through the window. His face showed no expression, just a blank stare directed at the counselor. Cammy tried to control her shaking hands as her finger shook over the window button. She rolled the window down. Sam's mouth moved to resemble a smile. He scratched his head, never looking away from her.

Chapter 49

When you are told by all you know that this is how life works, well, one day you wake up and just believe it. That is, till someone finally shows you the truth. I had waited most my life for the answers to my sister's death, to this town and how it works. Finally I had the answers I had been looking for, and it was worse than I had ever dreamed. I laid in my bed trying to control my sobbing. Angel would be home at any moment, I couldn't let him see me like this. I finally sat up in my bed when I heard the barking. I slid the notebook under my mattress and listened.

The neighbor dogs barked wildly. The frenzy they were in momentarily soothed my pain as it re-directed my attention. I got out of bed and saw Cooper Lawson in the street trying to calm them down. His focus wasn't entirely on the dogs though. His eyes jumped from the dogs to my front door, the focal point of the barking Dobermans. The storm door shook when someone knocked like he was trying to put a hole in it. I leaned against the bedroom window so I could see who it was. Shit! The Bosnian.

My heart kick started against my chest. Why was he here? Where was Angel? I didn't know if The Bosnian was after me or Angel, and I wasn't up to finding out. I sunk down from the window to stay out of his view. The door rattled as if it was about to be my former storm door. I reached under the bed for the shotgun, and crept back into the corner of the room. I loaded two shells and held the gun toward the door. If he got in the trailer with any intended malice one thing was certain, his head wasn't leaving.

"Hey, hey what the fuck man, you're going to break the door," Cooper yelled. Shut up Cooper, you don't know who this guy is. "They obviously ain't there, not like it's Graceland, or something."

The Bosnian ignored him and knocked again, louder and harder than before. Cooper said something, but couldn't make it out over the dogs that were now in a rabid state. The foreigner wouldn't make it five feet if Cooper let go of them. That fact finally broke through the Bosnian's language barrier. Through the curtains I saw The Bosnian walk down the steps. He held out his hands to make it clear he came in peace.

Chapter 50

"Sorry about that," Sam Montero said to Cammy. His eyes remained focused on hers. He pointed to the ring on his finger. "District Championship," he said with no change of expression.

"Excuse me?" asked Cammy.

"I said sorry Ms. Hart. I think my ring may have frightened you."

"I wasn't frightened," she forced herself to say. She knew he didn't buy it. Cammy pointed to the gate and told him it was closed.

"I know. Was there something you needed?" he asked. Cammy shook her head no. Sam leaned down, his massive head only inches from hers. "Shame about Ray, huh?"

"Um, yeah, it was." They were both silent until Cammy nodded toward the gate. "Think you can help me out and get that gate?"

Sam nodded in slow motion as both his elbows rested on the half- opened window, his hands were folded together just inside her car. "Sure can," he said. He pointed to Cammy's bag on the passenger seat, "Soon as you give me back what you took from my office." Cammy felt the rush of blood to her face, her stomach quivered. "I'm not an idiot lady. Give me the bag."

Cammy felt Sam's elbow smash against her temple as he lunged for the bag. She instinctively threw her body at the bag, knocking it to the floorboard. At the moment her first priority was to protect the sacred contents Sam needed so bad. His thick bratwurst fingers grappled at her nose and eyes. She leaned further from him, but felt him manage to get a hand around the end of her long hair. He had enough to pull her so he could re- grip to get a giant handful of hair along her head. He yanked her back to him. He pulled hard, the side of her face smashed against the half- opened window, she was sure he would have pulled her out of the car if the window had been down all the way. She felt the spray across her face as the red faced behemoth barked his demands.

"Now give me back my fucking bag," he tried to turn her around through the window to face her. Cammy's head felt like it would be crushed along the car door. He pulled so tight she couldn't nod without her hair ripping out of her head. She barely managed a moan. "You don't get it Counselor, I'm your friend. I need that binder."

The grip loosened enough for Cammy to nod. He kept the handful of hair as she slowly leaned toward the bag. "You better grow longer fucking arms or let go of my hair ass hole." Fear was suddenly absent.

"Not a chance."

"Bag is on the floor, I can't reach it," Cammy short armed her reach toward the floor. Sam looked at her hand, seeing the ten or twelve inches she was from grabbing the bag.

"Don't be funny, or I bust this window," he threatened. Cammy nodded and held up both hands. She felt his hand open, his arm backed off. She waited a moment, in the corner of her eye she saw his open palms pull back away from her.

The bag was only inches away from Cammy's hand. The elation that flowed through her body was hard to contain. Her head made a half turn toward Sam, and he saw it. He saw the glint in her emerald eyes that told him one thing, he just fucked up. Sam tried to dive at Cammy, but his forehead slammed the top of the door. The same door that a moment earlier he had Cammy pinned against. What he saw sent a tremble through his body. In one move Cammy had flipped open the glove box with one hand and caught the falling 38 Special in the other. Sam didn't have time to comprehend what happened before the counselor had the gun pointed directly between his eyes. Cammy winked. Then laughed.

Chapter 51

"No trouble, buddy," The Bosnian said. Why is it foreigners always call Americans 'buddy?' Do Hollywood Westerns do that? I remember hearing that foreigners would watch a lot of old westerns and old gangster movies, do they still? Do American men do it to them? I didn't know many foreigners really, just met a few working at gas stations. They always called Angel, or whoever I was with buddy. It kind of annoyed me really.

I watched The Bosnian attempt to communicate with Cooper. Cooper may have understood the broken English, but he had no interest in negotiating with the much larger man. "Buddy? Who you calling buddy?" Cooper said. Maybe it was the two ferocious Dobermans at his side that gave Cooper the balls to stand up to the big man.

"I'm friend, friend to you, to girl."

"I ain't no friend with no Muslim, n' you sure ain't my buddy." Maybe it was just that Cooper was a racist redneck who thought anyone with an accent must be Muslim.

"Just shut up and let him get out of here Cooper," I whispered to myself. I saw both of them perfectly in the opening of the drapes. Well, the old bed sheet that earned a second life as window drapes. The Bosnian said something about trying again to see if I was in the trailer. I could hear Cooper screaming to get the hell out of there when the dogs leapt hard enough to loosen Cooper's grip. The little moment of ease was all the dogs needed on the leash, they both broke free and made a bee-line for The Bosnian. The now frightened man jumped back, but his body was big and clumsy and he landed flat on his ass. He held his hands in front of his face in case the dogs attacked. Cooper regained control of the leash as their teeth chomped down inches away from the foreign face of their disdain.

"Please, please no, I beg. . ."

"Shut the fuck up," Cooper said. He laughed as the big man pleaded to leave. The Bosnian scooted backwards away from the dogs, Cooper and the snarling beasts followed.

"Please, please I'm to help," he said. I think. The dogs were in such a state that I could see The Bosnian wipe the spit and snarl from his face. I couldn't hear what Cooper said, I couldn't hear either of them now, only the dogs. I watched Cooper. His expression was of nothing. He had no feeling for The Bosnian, Cooper looked like he didn't care about anyone at that moment, I knew he was going to let the dogs loose. In a matter of minutes I was going to have a dead man on my front lawn- never a good follow-up to a murder interrogation.

"Don't!" I jumped up and slammed the window. Cooper and The Bosnian both spun their heads toward me. They both watched as I pressed myself against the bedroom window and begged for Cooper to spare the life of some foreigner I never met. The dogs didn't look. They were zoned in on The Bosnian, and attacked. Each Doberman latched on to a forearm of the momentarily distracted man. I could hear his screams over the dogs, their growls muffled by his ripping flesh.

"Get off, heel, heel I say," Cooper yelled as he yanked back on the leashes. It took him a couple seconds, but he got the smaller dog off. The bigger one got a chunk of Bosnian scalp as Cooper pulled his counterpart from the Bosnian arm. The Bosnian curled in the fetal position; his bloody forearms covered his just as bloody head. "Awe damnit, shit," Cooper said to the dogs. He pulled them back away from The Bosnian.

I watched as he removed the dogs from their fleshy snack. I looked back at the bloody man on my front lawn. Cooper bent down to the dogs and said something. They both stopped barking immediately. Cooper led them across the street, all three as calm as a foggy morning.

The Bosnian uncovered his head and watched them cross the street. He slowly got up and walked toward the street. He walked with his arms folded, wrapped around each other. His car was parked in front of the next trailer. I watched the whole way, not knowing what I should do. Should I help, was he a friend? He stopped at his car door and looked at me. I didn't move. I couldn't. We both stared at each other as if we knew a secret. A secret shared by only us. He may have nodded, telling me he knew. Then he got in his car and drove off. After that I would never view The Bosnian as a threat. Was he a friend? If he was telling the truth, was he the only friend I had?

Chapter 52

"That was disobedient, wasn't it?" Cammy asked Sam. "Because this is all kinds of funny," she smiled.

Sam stared for a moment, "You're not going to do it, you'd never get away with it. Someone will hear you, or see." Cammy pulled the hammer back on the gun, she had a determined look in her eyes he hadn't seen before. A stare that made the neck- less meathead question if she would try to get away with murder. Would she be able to get away with it, after all, she was an innocent High School Counselor and he was a rough, tough weightlifter who had a stable of ex- cons in his employment.

"Open the gate," she demanded. She motioned the gun and her head simultaneously to the gate. Sam looked at the gate and back to her. "Yes, I will do it. I know what you are thinking and yes, I would get away with it. Now open the gate."

Sam walked to the gate and lifted the rusted- over lock. He pushed the gate away from the lot, and it swung open. Sam walked in front of the car. Cammy steadied the gun toward his chest.

"What's so important in this? Why do you need it back?" she asked. She waived the folder as she leaned toward the window.

"I don't."

"You're willing to get shot over this," she said. She watched as he stepped closer to her and shook his head no.

"I'm not trying to get it for me."

"Then what?"

"I'm trying to keep it from you," he said. Sam held out his palms as he approached her window at a snail's pace. "To protect you. You don't want this, this ain't your fight."

He held out his hand one last time, one last chance for Cammy to give it back. She told him he wasn't getting it. His head tilted to the left, his eyes looked into hers. "This ain't the real world, this ain't your world. You should give me that, then leave here, this whole place."

The folder was now on the passenger seat, the bag still on the floor. She leaned toward the passenger side. Sam told her she was making a wise decision just before she picked up the bag and covered the folder with it. He shook his head.

She smiled to Sam. "Have a good day Mr. Montero," she said as her foot pressed the gas.

He stuck his head close to her window, "I'm not just saying this, you have to leave." Cammy wasn't listening so Sam dove in front of the car, she slammed on the brakes.

The car door flung open as Cammy jumped out, her gun leading the way. "What the hell's wrong with you? I could've run right over you!"

"You want to know what's in there? It's the shit I'm starting to see around me. It's what's been going on here way before you got here, before I got here. Listen, I'm on your side, but

165

I'm in this. You can get out, this ain't your fight."

"Something tells me I'm going to read this and bring it straight to the law."

"Forget the law!" Sam slapped the hood of her car so hard she was surprised he didn't leave a dent. "Are you listening to me? This ain't the real world! There's no law, forget everything you know is real, it don't exist here. You're about to have a baby, go focus on that. That's what you should be worrying about. Just leave," he paused. He turned from her and started to walk toward his office door in the bus shed. "Before you can't." Cammy sat a moment, she watched Sam through the rearview mirror. Sam sat on a broken down bench outside his office door.

The Toyota pulled out of the lot and turned left. Sam sat alone in the parking lot. He watched her car drive off till it disappeared around the bend.

He watched long after she was gone.

Chapter 53

When Angel wasn't at Chihuahua's Mexican Cantina, his only legitimate job, I knew where he was. I had decided I was done with Franklin County. I had made this decision a few days earlier, but after the dogs and near scare with The Bosnian I decided it was time to get the out of Dodge. I was pretty sure The Bosnian was no longer a threat, but that's not what was freaking me out. It was the next 'Bosnian' or the one after that. Eventually someone would show up who wasn't there to help me, if that's what he was trying to do. Christ knows Angel won't be there, and who's to say my nut job neighbor and his two dogs would save the day again. There was no doubt if I stayed I would end up dead, or worse. The only thing worse I'd been through already and I couldn't go through it again. I had to get out, soon.

Earlier that afternoon I had watched The Bosnian drive off. Once he was gone I packed what I needed. I filled my backpack with a couple shirts, some underwear, and a couple pairs of jeans. I threw the notebook in my bag on top of it. The last thing I did before leaving my trailer was climb up on the kitchen counter to get Angel's handgun in the cabinet above the fridge. It was loaded, safety on. Angel had taught me how to use it a few months back, probably a stupid decision considering the only time I've ever considered firing the thing was in his direction. Not to kill him of course, just to scare the jalapeno shit out of him when he was a dick, not all the time. There are things about our relationship only we know; I guess that's true of all relationships. That's why I think those relationship columns are usually bullshit, I don't want advice from someone who doesn't know what happens when we're alone. I don't want to know what would work in your relationship, because I know that won't work in mine.

I didn't find him at work so I headed south on 61 to Route C. I got off at C, went left back over the highway and turned into the first parking lot. The Tattooed Lady.

Chapter 54

The row of mail boxes was a good bet to be occupied by two or three stay at home meth head moms, no matter the time of day. The evening hours were worse, so I always tried to get my mail early. I hated walking through the stench of cheap beer and weed. None of these people cared about these kids walking around, and what the kids saw. If the temperature was over 45 degrees kids would be out till they decided to go in on their own. Some of the parents passed out well before that, others would still be going strong when their little kids woke up the next morning at the crack of dawn. I hated going to the mailbox.

The moms were out, as expected, when I walked down to the mailboxes. A twenty year old mom sat on the bench. I knew her once, but I was pretty sure she didn't remember much of her life before she it got iced over. One look at her dazed eyes and I knew she was high as hell. She had two little boys with her, they were probably about three and five. The girl's face was covered by her dirty hair as she stared at the gravel under her bare feet. I had to do a double take to be sure she was even breathing. When I passed I noticed her cigarette ash seemed to be in a fight against gravity. The ash lost.

I walked to our box trying to hide the fact I was looking at the deadbeat mom, trying to hide how disgusted I was by her. The two boys were poking a pile of dog shit with a long stick, I hoped they didn't notice me either. I opened the box, a phone bill and late notice from the Franklin County Water and Trash. Something else was tucked in the back of the box, it was an envelope with my name on it. The envelope had no return address or even my address. The only thing written on the envelope was my name written really big in the middle. I stuck the envelope between the two other pieces of mail. The two boys stared, the three- year old waved. Who put this in here, and what was it? I smiled at the boys and raced back to the trailer.

I ripped open the envelope with a key as I made my way up the trailer steps. I opened the door and dropped the rest of the mail when I saw what someone sent me. I threw everything on the table. Ten or twelve pictures fell from the envelope. I just stared at the table. I picked up the stack of pictures. My hands were shaking so most squirted from the stack, the rest I dropped the on the table. I looked close at the top picture, held it with both hands to steady myself. Then I fell to the floor. I tried to throw the pictures I could get to, but they didn't go far. Why would Angel have done this to me? Why would he cheat on me right before our baby? I yelled this a couple times till the answer hit me square in the forehead. Why wouldn't he? I guess even he knew when he was being used. I shouldn't blame him or be pissed-but screw that and screw him.

Chapter 55

The red wine rippled as the vibrating phone shook the table. Cammy leaned forward to see who was calling. She silenced her phone to stop the small quake that was Macie Jennings. She turned her phone off so she could delve into the research Sam was so adamant about keeping from her, and so she could enjoy her wine.

The newspaper article she read first was from the day after Ray's murder. The article lacked all details, it actually lacked any details. Cammy read it twice, double- checking to see if even the slightest facts were written, like the address were the body was found. Ray Lehane was found beaten to death with a baseball bat at his home. He was found and identified by his own mother. He was referred to as John Doe in the article, 'who was found at an unknown residence.' All this nothing was found in Cammy's first piece of local reading material saved by Sam, the article *Body Found in Franklin County.*

The newspapers from the two days since Ray's murder were still in Cammy's car. She was in tight cut off sweatpants and a thin, white tank top. Clothes she would never dream of wearing out in public, but loved to lounge around in when she was alone. The last thing she wanted to do was run down through the apartment complex parking lot to her car, but she needed those papers. She set the paper on the couch next to her, and took a long sip of her wine.

The Missouri evening was sticky hot, more like early August than late September. Cammy didn't bother putting on shoes, breaking a childhood rule of not going outside in your stocking feet. She was careful not to step on any glass or rocks as she tiptoed between cars. She could feel the beads of sweat forming on her forehead as she ran to the car. Cammy got home late after the ordeal with Sam. The late return forced her to take a parking spot in the back of the lot, away from the streetlights.

A drip of sweat ran between her breasts as she arrived at her car. Cammy opened the door and reached for the passenger seat. "What the?" she mumbled to herself as a pain shot up from each finger through her arm. She looked in to see shattered glass where she had left the newspapers. All that remained from the passenger window was the bottom half of spider webbed glass that was ready to dive into the seat with the slightest nudge. Her black bag, sunglasses, and a case of CD's were still there. It appeared that everything was there, but someone was definitely looking for something. The black bag was opened and dumped out. Loose change and a few pens were all the thief had found. Cammy made sure to bring the binder that was originally in the bag earlier. She was waiting to read that last. Or should she read it at all? Cammy heard Sam's warning again- he didn't want it for himself, but trying to keep it from her. What if he was right and she was better off not getting any deeper into this? It was a decision she wouldn't have to worry about as she walked back to her apartment. It sat thirty feet from her. She was now in this.

The fog lights lit up Cammy as she started to make her way back. She adjusted her eyes and could make out a silhouette of a truck behind the high beams. The Pick- up truck had been sitting there the entire time she was at the car. The truck slammed on the gas, tires squealed as it took aim at the stocking footed counselor. Cammy's instincts overcame all thoughts of who it could be as she took off across the lot. The truck jerked toward her, more to scare than crush. That was the first thought that went through her head as she landed from an airborne head first dive in between cars. The truck squealed as it swerved through the lot, and another elongated screech as it made a hard left out of the parking lot.

Cammy was on her feet in time to see the attacker drove a red GMC truck, she knew that much. A GMC made the odds better that it was one of the locals trying to scare her. That's what most the men drove in town because up until two years ago many worked at the GMC truck plant ten miles south. That's when the plant shut down for a sweeter deal somewhere in Mexico. For some reason unbeknownst to Cammy, the locals insisted on still taking their business to South American made GMC. A few cartons of eggs on her Toyota announced this loyalty to GMC, or hatred for Toyota, during her first couple of months in Franklin County. Her first weekend in town was spent peeling fifteen *Buy American* bumper stickers off her car. Her second week in school she had posted a sign on her car in the parking lot that read, *Made in Indiana.* This only infuriated the Buy American police even more and pushed them to re- sticker her car. She had a teacher's salary so there was nothing she could do about what she drove, she figured that the most loyal Americans in town finally figured this out. Unfortunately, what it all boiled down to was absolutely nothing for Cammy. A GMC meant it could have pretty much been anyone in town.

Cammy winced as she grabbed the throbbing wet patch of missing skin on her knee. She was covered in a cold sweat now, she reached down to feel the sweat mix with the blood and rock in her knee. Cammy yanked her hand away as she started to hobble back to the apartment. She could see the crimson streaks across her shirt where she wiped her hand, the scraped up palm being the original home of that blood. Whoever it was wanted that folder, and wasn't afraid of the law to get it back. He would be back, but when. The attacker could have killed her, but didn't.

Chapter 56

The Wild Turkey sat half empty in the center of the table. I was hunched over the table, my chin rested on my hands. I watched the empty rocks glass that I was pretty sure I had out only to guard the whiskey bottle. The photographs were in a neat stack face down on the other side of the bottle. I just stared at the pictures through the muddy whiskey. I hated whiskey, and I hated those pictures more. My stomach turned at the thought of both.

The mind of the depressed can wander I had heard somewhere, not sure where. I was off somewhere far from this place, far from my Franklin County trailer. I watched the whiskey, and imagined what it would be like to float down the Mississippi. In the whiskey I could see myself on a wooden raft just floating down the river lit by a full moon. There was a little girl with me on the raft. We floated till we reached the summit, the Gulf of Mexico. It was a beautiful sight with nothing but the open water. Where would we go from there? Anywhere we wanted.

The thunderous smack of the storm door slammed so hard I almost shit myself. I jumped out of the trance and was spun around before I was on my feet. I had the Sig- Sauer pointed at Chad Danville's heart before I was fully home from the Mississippi. Danville stood inside the trailer. He had his hands out to tell me he came in friendly, I suppose. Danville was in his usual LCPD blues, shoes shined like a championship bowler's ball. You had to admire the dedication to appearance, even if he was crooked as a Chicago politician.

We looked at each other in silence for what felt like an eternity; eventually my heart started beating again.

"Yer lucky to be standing right now," I said.

"You, my friend, are lucky I'm standing right now. Put that thing down," he said. I took a deep breath but held the gun steady. He was in my house.

"Whatcha doing here?"

"Come to check on you," said Danville. He nodded to the gun again. "Please."

He seemed to be sincere enough. I dropped it from his chest, but made sure it was close. I laid the gun right in front of me next to the whiskey bottle. Then I sat back in the chair.

The second I looked away from him his hand shot across the table, he was a lot faster than I expected. I didn't have time to react so I just closed my eyes. I sat for a second and nothing happened. I thought for sure I was about to get the crap smacked out of me. I opened my eyes, part of me half expected to be looking down the barrel of a gun. He just stood across from me, he watched me, but didn't say anything. I figured then he wasn't there to arrest me.

"What the fuck is this?" he asked. I looked to the table and the gun sat right where I left it.

"You don't know? That's my baby monitor."

"Huh?"

"You heard me, a baby monitor. The next time one of you dick heads puts my baby and pregnancy at risk it's going to monitor your fucking ass," I said, then smiled. I thought it sounded good, for just coming up with it at the moment. Truth was, I didn't care what he did to me. I didn't care what anyone did anymore. I was going to leave this town and start a family, as fucked up as that was. Or I would end up dead in Franklin County.

"A fucking drink?" he asked. I realized Danville wasn't talking about the gun at all. He went for the empty glass, surely thinking the pregnant girl had been getting bombed on some Turkey.

"Oh that," I smiled again. "That's an empty glass officer." I felt like being a bitch to him, he was just another man in my life who had let me down over and over again.

Danville flung the glass across the room and into the stove. Pebbles ricocheted throughout the trailer. What a dickhead, I thought. I just sat there, he wouldn't scare me this time. I didn't care about anything he did. He could have burned down the whole trailer for all I cared. I knew my days were numbered there anyway. He stared at me like he was still trying to make up his mind if he should smack me or not. I watched for a moment, but just got more pissed at his silence.

"There's not a fucking thing you can do to me. You know that, right?" I asked. He wandered over to the broken glass at the stove then back to the table. Still silent. Danville picked up the bottle of Wild Turkey, he smelled it before he took a long swig. Finally, he looked back to me.

"I don't know that, but I have a feeling you're fix'n to tell me," he said.

"That's right, 'cause I don't give a damn anymore. 'Bout any of this, this town, these people," I said. I stopped for a second, I could tell my eyes had started to well up for a second. I took a deep breath and looked at him. I calmly told him, "I don't care anymore. I just don't."

A tear rolled down my cheek. I thought I had it under control, but the way he stared at me, the way he sat and judged me just pissed me off more. I couldn't help myself and charged with both fist in the air. He caught both my wrists before I had a chance to hit him. His thumbs jabbed my pressure points and I fell to my knees.

I dropped to the floor and started to cry. I don't know why, I guess it was a bit of everything from getting kicked out of school, the shit with Angel, to having no one to help with this baby, and then there was this baby. I was sixteen; this was shit I shouldn't have been dealing with. Danville stood over me silent. I knew he didn't want to say anything to upset me more. That's one thing I've learned about men, many hate a crying girl. There are those that would just give it to ya worse of course, but somewhere in Danville there was a man who once wanted to be a cop. He may have been a dirty cop, but there was still some police officer in him. I felt his hand on my back and heard him say something to try to calm me down. There was some good.

Chapter 57

The front door flew open when Cammy pushed, it flew a little easier than she liked. Given her recent trade- in of a lonely life filled with books like *What to Expect When Expecting* for the new action packed life filled with being an attempted murder victim, who would blame her. She leaned into the apartment, keeping her feet outside the door on the sidewalk as if it were some kind of safe zone. She looked down and noticed the bright red ring at the top of her sock, a la 1980's style striped tube socks. She quickly surveyed what she could see in the apartment.

"I'm armed ass hole, I have a gun," she said as she retraced her last fifteen minutes. Did she shut the door all the way when she left, she brought her keys so why wouldn't she have locked up? Cammy thought back, she was going to run to the car and run back in less than three minutes. She wouldn't have locked up. Her right foot stepped from the safety of the sidewalk, her bloodied left followed. She was all right. "I know how to use it too," she insisted to anyone who might be lurking in the apartment waiting to pounce her. She did have a gun and was actually a very good shot. Unfortunately for Cammy the gun was in her purse on the couch.

The black folder sat underneath the loaded purse, everything she needed was fifteen feet away. Cammy quickly tapped her foot like she was taking off for the couch. A little something to throw off the attacker in hopes that he dove out of his hiding spot. If anyone was hiding, they didn't bite. The apartment was complete silence.

Chapter 58

Danville could see Macie was alone due to the lack of places to hide, especially for a giant like Angel. Although he could have been hiding as one of the giant piles of dirty clothes, Danville thought to himself. He finished surveying the trailer and bent down to pick up the weeping teen.

"Come on, get up," he said as he grabbed her elbow. She didn't move so he bent down and picked her up by both arms, he placed her back in her chair. Danville picked up the bottle of whiskey and nodded toward it before looking back at Macie. "Think this is the answer?" he asked. He got no response, like he expected. He expected the same answer, or lack of one when he asked of Angel's whereabouts.

"I'll tell you what Danville, if you do find him tell me where he is because I'm fix'n to cut off his balls and make the fat fuck eat'em." Danville admired the girl's crass mouth, a direct product of the local Trailer University or Trailer U.

Trailer U was an unofficial name the local police referred to as the kids who grew up and ran with other kids from the trailer parks. It was a group of kids who were children of meth users, dealers, and the majority of the County's cookers. Eventually, they learned the tools of the trade and followed in Mom and Dad's footsteps. Macie was like the Reverend's daughter in

Footloose and a bunch of other stereotypical rebellious teen flics. The only difference was instead of up on a pedestal parents/bad kid, it was meth cooking and dealing mom/ Good Daughter.

The photographs were still face down in the middle of the table, Macie's eyes turned to them. Danville leaned down and picked up the source of her current misery. He started to shuffle through the pictures. He shook his head in what seemed like slow motion. A couple of the pictures even got a whistle from the cop. He made his way through the dozen, then asked where they came from. Macie shook her head and pointed toward the envelope. He gave it a quick enough glance to see that her name was the only thing written on it. "Who's the girl?"

"If I knew I wouldn't be sitt'n here," she said. She slowly looked up at him and added, "Would I?"

"Well, come on, you knew this day would come, didn't you?" he asked. Macie now had both arms sprawled on the table, her face down between them. Without saying a word she turned her right hand toward Danville, and extended her 'Fuck You,' finger. At least that's what it was referred by the kids who were part of Trailer U.

"Did he do Ray Lehane?" Danville asked, trying to change the subject. He also knew this was his one chance to get the truth from the girl. Macie raised her wet, black streaked face and shook her head no.

"Haven't seem him since, but I don't see why he'd hurt Ray," she said. Danville's face seemed to squish up on its left side as his head tilted to his right. He looked Macie in the eyes and believed she was telling the truth, the truth about not seeing Angel at least.

"We both know why, same reason you took a blade to his forearm."

"He's no killer, trust me. He almost shit a brick when he found out what I done to Ray. Angel might be a piece of shit, but not a killer," she said. Her chin went back to its earlier resting spot on the table. "A real piece of shit," she repeated as she stared off in some random spot on the trailer wall. Danville continued to talk about Angel and the murder. He even asked Macie if she killed Ray, something he had never actually asked at the station earlier. Danville had assumed all along it was Angel, but at the moment he believed the girl was telling the truth. When he finally asked if she did do it he got the answer he expected to get. She said no without saying a word, just the return of the Trailer U finger.

Chapter 59

The black binder was still sitting under her purse, so if Cammy's attacker did have a partner in crime he wouldn't have been in the apartment for long being that the folder was in plain sight. Cammy thought how he wouldn't be able to miss it. What was her mindset when she left for the newspaper in the car? She wouldn't lock the door, she was going to be gone three or four minutes. No one was there, she told herself this enough that it had to be true. The apartment had to be empty.

Cammy gave a final surveillance of what she could see in the apartment. She took a deep breath. She quietly recited self defense techniques she had learned from a kickboxing class. Arms up, elbows in, "Gut, balls, GO!" she yelled. She took off. Cammy sprinted for the couch in three steps, with the third step she went airborne, leaping over the coffee table and landing on the couch next to her purse and folder. Her fists were up ready for whatever was coming at her. Silence. She was alone. She grabbed the purse and folder. Time to go.

Chapter 60

"Listen, a lot of people are looking for Angel, certain people," Danville said. She knew he meant Elliott and his Vandals, so she didn't bother looking up from her fixed spot on the table. "I'm trying to help you, so you might want to listen up sugar pie. They want Angel, so they're going to get him. If you're not careful you'll be with him." Macie shook her head then gave the officer a smirk that told him she knew more than him. "No one's going to touch me, you of all people should know that," she said.

Danville figured she had heard the rumor that Elliott had gotten in his face after the parking lot incident. The message was clear: Do whatever to Angel, but no one touches Macie. He all but admitted the rumor to be true when he turned from her, she would never believe him if he tried to deny that the MC called all shots. Something Macie knew since she was six years old.

"Plus, I got something in the works then I'm out of this shithole, forever." Macie got up and walked to the stove. She stared at the shattered glass with her back to Danville.

Danville watched her. He picked up the bottle of whiskey and motioned it toward the girl's back. "I'm taking the Turkey," he said. She didn't move. "For your own good." Danville gave Macie one last look and left the trailer. He made good on his promise to take the Wild

Turkey, the storm door crashed shut on his way out.

Chapter 61

Cammy wondered if she had landed on a piece of glass when she dove from the truck. She needed stiches, but for now a dirty kitchen towel would have to do. Cammy didn't know who was trying to give her a headlight imprinted t- shirt earlier, but she figured he would be back. Luckily she was on the ball enough to grab a towel off the counter on her way out. It would have to do for a half- hearted attempt to clean up the wound.

The drive was twenty minutes north. She was heading to the diner again. It seemed to be far enough out of town to be safe, yet close enough to get back and start figuring out where her current situation turned into an episode of *Breaking Bad*. She knew she had to sit down and find out what was so critical in this black folder before she was being featured on the season premiere of *Forensic Files*.

Cammy could feel the blood swish between her toes with each push of the gas or brake pedal. Her shoe felt wet as she accelerated up the exit ramp, and made the left toward the diner. She pulled in, only three other cars. She should be safe.

Chapter 62

The whiskey burned his throat on its way down. Danville sat in his squad car. Something didn't feel right to the twelve- year veteran of the LCPD. He took a second drink. Something was on his mind; he couldn't stop thinking about the last thing Macie said. The way she said, "something in the works."

Danville went back into the trailer. Macie hadn't moved from the stove, she slowly turned to him. "Looking to break something else, it'd be a big help if you broke it in this general direction. You know, since I'm already over here cleaning up your first mess."

"I'm sorry, why don't you sit down, I'll clean the glass," he said. Danville almost jumped through the door when Macie raised the nine inch bread knife to him.

"Don't you touch a damn thang!" she said without raising her voice.

"Whoa, easy, I'm leaving. I, I just want to ask you a quick thing."

Macie watched him, she lowered the knife so it wasn't blocking their view of each other. "Go ahead."

"Where's Angel?" he asked. The knife came back up, even closer to Danville than before.

"What the- what did I just tell you? Trust me, if I knew you wouldn't be seeing this knife 'cause I'm gonna be using it to make sure that

188

ass hole don't whip his dick out for no more of these slut bitches."

"What did you mean by in the works? What are you planning to do?"

"Aren't you the detective?" she said as she rolled her eyes. "You figure it out. Ain't that your job?" She went back to picking up the glass without giving him a chance to answer her. He watched her; she seemed to be void of all emotion but anger.

"You know where he is, he can't have many places to go." he said. His voice had a little quiver to it. He wanted to try one more time to see if she really didn't know where Angel was, but he was nervous asking. Nervous that she might know where he actually was, and that they might be up to something, something no good. So he had to ask one more time, to see if he truly believed her.

"You saw the pictures Danville. I'm here bawlin' my eyes out. Why'd I be doing that if I knew where he was? Please, just leave me alone."

Oral sex would be grounds for many women to leave, and she wouldn't be the first woman to snap from her man getting some on the side. Receiving photographs of your boyfriend in that situation would make the situation that much worse, throw in the roller coaster of emotions of a pregnant teenager and Angel's life might actually be at risk. He thought about it all, maybe she was telling him the truth.

Danville just didn't buy Macie as the killing type. He viewed her more as someone who would threaten and obviously attack, but not kill. She wouldn't do anything without thinking it through. She sat in the gas station for two hours before she walked over to the bus depot to slice Ray Lehane's arm. Is that what she was doing? Thinking about which body part she would maim on the big Mexican.

"Listen, I hope you're not, um," he stopped to search for the right words not to set her off. "I know you've been seeing a lot of that new counselor," he said. "She seems like a good woman, maybe you should talk with her."

"What should I talk to her about?"

"I don't know, um, what you're feeling, I guess."

"Don't you have to take any kind of intelligence test to be a cop in this damn town? Danville, I'm asking nice like, please get the hell out of my trailer," she said as she turned back to the stove. He watched her for a moment as he started to open the storm door. If she knew where Angel was, she was doing her damnedest to convince Danville otherwise.

"I'll be keeping a watch on you, just so you know. Let's not forget, I am the law," he nodded to her, but it was more to reassure himself what his job was. Danville watched the back of her head, then left.

Chapter 63

Cammy flipped through the black binder. It was made to look like a book with a female student's school page on the left side of each page. The right side was just one name and a number. Cammy wasn't sure what it was till she reached Macie's page. It had her picture at the top, then all her school stats. Her address was listed, along with her year in school, any sports which she had played at her time at Franklin High, her missed days, and even her class schedule. The page opposite Macie was the same as each girl's. There was a male name and a number.

Ray Lehane was the name on the page across from Macie's picture. The number was his bus number, the bus Macie rode.

"Ma'am, how you doing tonight?" a voice boomed above Cammy. She had been locked in on the folder, she wasn't sure how long the large Mexican man had been standing over her, watching her. She gave a half smile, and even less of a nod. "Mind if I take a seat, always nicer to eat with someone to chat with," he tried to convince her. Cammy looked at the waitress behind the bar, and the one old man drinking coffee at the opposite end of the counter. They were oblivious to Cammy and the man. She nodded to the seat across the booth.

Angel sat down in front of Cammy.

Chapter 64

The River Road State Park had become a dumping ground for overdosed meth heads. If you drove through the campground on a summer night the majority of the license plates were out of state. The only locals who would stay at the park were kids in their late teens or early twenties, usually there to get ripped on their drug of choice.

The families that stayed one night in the park usually did just that, stayed one night. When morning arrived after a long sleepless night they would see the strung out addicts on the picnic tables and the camp sight littered with garbage. They would quickly round up their kiddos and gear and get the hell out of dodge shortly after sunrise. The first body that most locals remember turning up dead at the park was J.C. Jennings. Authorities never did release details of her death other than the fact that she overdosed. Off the record, it was considered the start of Franklin's Meth Era.

Macie was ten years old when her sister was found dead. She never did learn about the details of the death, until recently. The emotions that swirled through her head when she learned the official version of J.C's death were a mixture of disgust and a fear that bordered sheer terror. There was a regret that she was so naïve with everything she had learned since that day, somehow she always knew her sister would not have died from a simple overdose. The details of her death were the push Macie needed to make a change in her life. She had to, and would, do anything she could to leave Franklin County.

Chapter 65

Sam had taken up the hobby of playing amateur detective, and he seemed to be on to something. Cammy knew this by the time she turned to page three, not to mention the earlier scare someone tried to give her earlier that night. The black folder was worth killing a High School Counselor who seemed to have no real family or friends. If it was Sam who was keeping these notes, he wasn't discreet about what he wrote. It wasn't hard to figure out what was in the folder, especially for the High School Counselor. Sam, or whoever the writer was, believed he would be its sole reader. Now that would change.

Jaclyn Christine was murdered. That was what Macie had told Cammy. She had said no one else believed her, or would say it out loud, apparently Macie never talked with Sam Montero. It was the first thing written in a column he had marked: Facts. She now drove south on the highway back towards Franklin County. She couldn't go home; the red truck could be there, whoever it was. Cammy heard Macie's voice again, assuring her that her sister was murdered. Who was the driver of the red truck? How many people were involved in her murder?

A pair of high- beam headlights had been behind Cammy since the Diner. Were the headlights behind Cammy the red truck? At any rate, those were the only other pair of lights besides Cammy's on the road. She pulled off the highway an exit early, the headlights followed. The lights were less than twenty feet behind her.

Cammy made a hard right into the Tropicana Apartment complex without using a turn signal. The truck didn't have time to turn, but slammed on its brakes about fifteen feet after the entrance. Cammy stopped her Toyota and looked at the truck. It wasn't the same red truck, she was sure of that. It was black, navy, or maybe even a dark green. Cammy didn't move. The truck sat idle for what felt like an eternity. Her chest felt as if it would rip through her shirt. Her breaths were short. She could feel the driver watching her. Finally, the truck moved. It drove slow, but continued straight down the road. Cammy waited until the truck followed the bend to the left, disappearing from her sight. She took a deep breath and pulled a u- turn. She went left out of Tropicana, the opposite direction of the truck.

Chapter 66

The first page had two columns, facts and suspects. Cammy cleared her mind of the possible stalker and tried to get back to what she discovered in the folder. The next two pages in were bus schedules. Page Two contained the bus schedule, and the driver of each bus. Nothing any employee didn't have full access to.

The sounds of the High School in the middle of the night were a stark contrast to the days when school was in session. The school was dark and silent when she came in. Cammy was leary about going home after the parking lot incident, the second truck on her way home from the diner convinced her, but she was pretty sure it was the same guy.

She had parked around back to hide her Toyota. The rear entrance to the cafeteria was the most secluded at Franklin High so she used the moonlit backdoor to get in the school.

Cammy had never noticed the roar of the boiler room that must have been somewhere near her office, or right under it. Was that the water heater, or air conditioner that seemed to kick on every twenty minutes? She jumped the first couple of times, a possible side effect of having her first ever stalker. After two hours the sounds went without notice like it was 1 in the afternoon. She continued to research the girls written on the third page of schedules, even though she knew all of them.

The third page had grabbed Cammy's attention while she was at the diner. The moment she could shake Angel she knew she had to get to her school computer. Cammy had to double check what she already knew. She read down the sheet. Bus numbers 12, 103, and 25 were the attention grabbers for Cammy.

Janice Tompkins was written next to bus 12. Sienna Adriano and Michelle Sale were written next to bus 103. All three girls had spent numerous hours in Cammy's office. In a school with 1,200 kids that meant something. Cammy had been at the school less than a full year. She could recognize four or five hundred names, tops. Cammy knew all four female students on the list. The last name was the trigger that told her what this list was. She knew the first three for the same reason, the same reason she knew the girl next to Bus 25, Macie Jennings. They were the four pregnant girls who had met with Cammy in the past year. They were four pregnant girls who never became mothers.

Chapter 67

The full length wicker shade was all that stood between whoever entered my trailer and the Sig Sauer hand gun I had aimed to blow clear through it. A high- pitched squeak came from my stomach when I first called out, or tried to. The rustle of covers was the only sound in the trailer. I listened without breathing, if that was possible. I sat for another minute- silent. With a little effort I started to breath.

"Leave me alone, I ain't doing nothing against the rules. Who are you?" I yelled. No one answered, but I was sure as shit I'd heard the door shut. That's what had woken me up. I listened, I could hear heavy breathing. I was pretty sure I wasn't losing my mind completely. I heard someone breathing. "I can guarantee you this. I will not miss from this distance with the heat I got point'n at this door. I promise you that," I was calmer than expected now that I got my wits back. "I know you're out there, I hear your breathing."

"Mace?" Angel whispered. "It's me Mace." That son of a bitch had some nerve showing his face back here.

"Even more reason to start shooting. Give me one reason I shouldn't blow your cheatin' cock right off your illegal ass!"

Angel was silent. He mumbled something that sounded like sorry. I really didn't give a damn what he was saying though. I ignored it, I'd at least make him sweat another minute or so.

"I don't want to see you yet. You can stay out there," I told him. I wasn't exactly sure how I felt. Company would be nice, but so would putting a bullet in his leg. I ain't gonna lie, I'm still pissed. Real pissed. Why wouldn't I be, what girl wouldn't be. Even if I treated him like shit I was carrying his baby, less than a month from having it. "Sleep out there. If you try to come in her I will shoot you," I finally told him. I could hear him drag his sorry ass from right outside the room to the couch. A few minutes later he asked where the blankets were. I told him to find something from the pile of dirty clothes. He messed around the trailer a little more until he finally settled in on the couch.

I laid the gun in the spot usually occupied by Angel. My head hit the pillow, but I didn't close my eyes. What was the point, I knew I wouldn't be falling asleep anytime soon. I wasn't sure how long I stared at the ceiling. I went through about fifteen things I was going to say to the cheating ass in the morning. I was pretty sure he wouldn't like any of them, but wouldn't argue either. I held my stomach. What was I supposed to do? He was the baby's father, it kept going through my head, over and over again. He was also the only person who gave one shit about me. After the pictures I started to wonder how much he actually did though. I would need him, at least for now.

Chapter 68

The recently deceased Ray Lehane was scribbled down on page 2, next to Bus 25. Cammy flipped the pages back and forth three times to be certain she was reading what she thought she was reading. Macie Jennings rode Bus 25, the same bus driven by dead Ray.

Third trimester pregnancies are illegal to terminate in the United States unless they are necessary to preserve the woman's life. Some states like Missouri will allow a third trimester abortion if needed to preserve the physical and/ or the mental health of the mother. Mothers having a miscarriage after 24 weeks, which are considered a stillbirth, are drastically decreased when the mother is less than 35 years old.

These four cases of girls late in their pregnancies not giving birth were enough for Cammy to raise an eyebrow. She read over the records of the girls. There were no doctor's notes to get out of gym class, or any other kind of evidence that they were pregnant. The only reason she knew the three girls were pregnant was because they were all scared teenagers who needed someone to talk to. They came to Cammy because they had no emotional tie to the school counselor. They all gave her the same impression that they were going to have the baby. Abortion was never discussed as an option by any of them, and Cammy was pretty sure she was the only adult any of them had told.

The fourth girl was Macie, who denied she was ever pregnant until left with no choice but to tell her this was her second pregnancy.

Cammy had a friend in college who lost her baby 42 days before her due date. Anything was possible, but something in the counselor's gut was telling her this wasn't right. It was time to find out everything Sam knew about these four never pregnant teens? Was he getting suspicious of the forced hires? Would Elliott really risk drug deals on a bus? Maybe Sam started to wonder the same thing and started his own game of playing detective.

Chapter 69

"Freeze, don't even breath 'cause if I see your chest move I'm puttin' a hole in it!" Cammy froze as she stood over the dead body of what she would soon find out was once Sam Montero. She had come down to the bus depot to surprise Montero when he arrived for the day. Cammy got the surprise as she realized she was staring down a Glock 19, not to mention the dead body at her feet.

Cammy wanted to know what Sam Montero knew about each girl. More importantly, what did these men driving his buses have to do with each girl? She suspected he had the answers for her, but someone else had those suspicions first.

Angel had knocked up Macie, she was pretty sure of that. There would be no real reason to be with such an ass hole otherwise. Cammy knew Macie was blowing off the whole X- Rated photograph incident, and that would have been a deal breaker had he not been the father. The other three girls all told Cammy who the baby's daddy's' were. All three were just careless over- anxious high school kids who didn't know what the hell they were doing. So who were the men? Cammy was hoping an early morning surprise, aided by her 38 Special, could persuade Sam into giving Cammy some info. Now the only thing the 38 was going to do was go into the evidence box toward Cammy getting three square and a cot for the rest of her life.

"Listen, I, I just got here. I didn't do this," she yelled back into the darkness. The only thing she could make out was the glare of a streetlight through the window bouncing off the Glock pointed at her. "Please I'm the school counselor, Cameron Hart." Cammy could hear deep breaths from across the depot. She made out the figure holding the gun as his shoes began to thud on the wooden floor. The floor cracked and squeaked with each step.

"Hope you have a good reason to be here at this hour, dressed like that." he said. Cammy realized with the next step who it was, Police Chief Chad Danville came out of the darkness to reveal himself. He kept the gun on Cammy. "I think you got some explaining to do Counselor." He smiled at her, "This time, in my office."

Chapter 70

The crackle of gravel was the only sound as the red GMC truck slowly drove through Sun Valley Lake Trailer Park. The headlights were off the entire way, the truck pulled over, and the engine was killed. The passenger door slowly opened. A black boot stepped onto the gravel, froze, and was followed by the other. A large, formidable image of a man materialized in the shadows of the trailers. He looked at a trailer four doors down, then stepped out from the truck. Donovan Elliott took two steps, turned back to the truck and nodded.

"What's up boss?" a scrawny thunderhead asked the MC's President. Elliott stood under the street lamp; he didn't turn to the kid.

Vampire Eddy shot the kid a shut the fuck up look. "That's it, 1127."

"Looks like, that's his piece of shit truck. Go get 'em," commanded Elliott.

Vampire Eddy led the young Thunderhead and another Prospect toward the trailer. Elliott turned back to the truck and pulled out his pack of smokes. He got back in the passenger seat, lit a cigarette, and watched his men off to follow his orders. "Eddy," he yelled in a whisper.

Eddy turned back to his boss. "No one touches the girl, remind those two," Elliott said. Eddy nodded and could be heard by Donovan as he relayed the orders. Donovan took a long drag. He watched as the invisible smoke announced its existence when it hit the beam of light from the street lamps. He took another drag, and waited.

Elliott took out his phone, he touched the game *Cut the Rope*. He tossed his cigarette and started to play the game. The goal was to try to get a piece of candy into a frog's mouth after collecting three coins. The candy was moved by a series of swinging ropes, or bubbles that you had to pop. He was never into video games till a couple of club members started to play all the games on their phones. Elliott by his competitive nature went out and got a smart phone so he could play the games too, but mainly so he could beat his brothers. The plan hadn't gone as planned, and he found himself spending more and more time trying to improve his scores. It was supposed to be used as a way of escaping the world he was in, but worked in a way that had made everything worse. His low scores and losing ways only lead to more stress and lost time playing the game. After he finally passed the level he realized they had been gone almost twenty minutes. This plan was fucked in one way or another too.

Inside the trailer the men were looking in kitchen drawers, at post- its on the fridge, and anywhere else they might find some kind of clue. Elliott let the storm door slam shut; all three looked at him and froze.

"They've split," said Vampire Eddy in almost a whisper. He waited for Elliott's reaction while he stared at the floor.

Donovan nodded and slowly paced the kitchen. The men jumped out of the way as he walked toward them in the claustrophobic kitchen, knowing he was not going to stop for them. He circled twice, never looking at any of them. "How long?" he asked, when he looked at Vampire Eddy. "Were you going to let me sit in that God Damn truck and freeze my fucking fingers off trying to feed candy to a damn frog before you came to tell me this?" he said. It was more of a yell by the time he finished. No one said a word, or moved. "Did you forget I was out there?"

Eddy stammered, "No, no man. We were just, you know, trying to figure it out is all."

"Figure what out? If there's a three hundred pound Mexican hiding in the fucking drawers?" he yelled now, there was no doubt about that.

Chapter 71

Ten minutes earlier Angel dropped the driver's seat straight back as Vampire Eddy turned his truck into the park. Macie was ducking when she saw an old man looking out a window from the trailer. The man looked at Macie, then watched the truck with no headlights drive by. He looked back at Macie who was holding her finger up to her lips. The old timer had been around enough to know if she was hiding behind his trailer as the Vandals stormed the park his best bet was to back away from the window and go back to his TV, so he did.

The car shook with each deep breath from Angel. It had only been about four and a half minutes when Macie received a text from a number she didn't know that read; *Sam M dead- Elliott coming 4 U- RUN.* The text got the point across. It took half a second for her to contemplate leaving Angel. She couldn't though. Macie jumped up with the Sig Sauer, which now sat comfortably across her chest, yelled for him to move if he wanted to be breathing in ten minutes, and they fled. Macie was smart enough to remind Angel they knew his truck. If they did make it out of the trailer and ended up passing whoever was coming they were as dead out there as they were in here.

They ran two doors down to an old retired couple's trailer. In the ten months of living there Macie had never seen either one of them get any further than the back deck. The navy blue Ford Escort had only been driven when a mooching neighbor needed to borrow some wheels. They seemed to always allow this so she figured they wouldn't mind. If they were really lucky the elderly couple wouldn't even notice it was gone for a day or two. Macie hopped in the passenger seat as Angel did his thing with the steering column, and forty five seconds later they were on their way toward the back of the trailer park.

They were approaching the exit when the trees across the street went black. "Get over, over, behind that trailer," Macie ordered. Her guess was right that the killed lights were Elliott and his men. The red truck had turned moments after the Escort came to a stop behind the old man's trailer. Now it had been five minutes, she knew they were about to discover Macie and Angel were in the process of skipping town.

"Get the fuck up, let's get out of here," she said somewhat calmly.

"I think we're better off here, that old man ain't saying shit," Angel said. Macie gave Angel a look he had known since shortly after they first started dating. "Ok, ok, we'll go." He started the car, but kept the lights off. The car crept back around the trailer and toward the entrance.

"Get to the highway, hurry," Macie instructed. Angel drove without saying a word. He was almost a mile out of the park before he felt safe enough to turn the lights back on. The sign to their right pointed straight ahead for Highway 61, so that's where they drove.

Chapter 72

The three almost fell over each other as they ran out of the trailer. Elliott watched his three subordinates as they stumbled down the steps. He thought to himself how each guy was more clueless than the one he followed. He shook his head as he took out his phone. He dialed a number and followed the three men out the trailer. The other line picked up. "They're gone," he said. He listened to the other line, and nodded. "Keep the bitch there, time we had a face to face." He hung up.

Elliott turned to his men; they each strained to look at him. "Let's get. Danville might have something, it has to be more than this shit hole will have," he said. He instructed his first Lieutenant, Vampire Eddy, to get some men and start hitting some of Angel's hangouts. He took the Kid with him.

Chapter 73

The interrogation room in the FCPD was everything Cammy had expected. The room contained one table, two chairs, a small video camera in the upper corner across from her seat, the walls were an off white, and a large dark window was next to the solid wooden door. She sat alone in the room. She noticed her eyes had found a routine in which they moved from the camera, to the window, and ended with a quick glance over her left shoulder at the door. The walls were thick, or outside there was silence. She sat for at least a half hour before the silence was broken. The doorknob turned.

At first glance he reminded her of a fallen rock star. The dirty black leather jacket, and ripped jeans reminded her of someone she would have seen on *Behind the Music*. When he spoke she focused on his face, this is when her interpretation of Donovan Elliott changed. He fell somewhere between the good looking politician and the slacker grunge type who had the looks to get away with bad behavior in society. Cammy always felt many men got away with sexual harassment and other wrongful deeds when they were good looking. She blamed it on the women, but none the less, those men seemed to get away with murder, in her mind. Donovan Elliott was one of these men who got away with murder, and then some. He stood in the doorway of the interrogation room. Now it was just the two of them. His wide shoulders seemed to expand the entire door.

"Would it offend you if I said you are even better looking up close?" he asked. Cammy didn't respond, but seemed to shake her head no. Elliott walked into the room and sat in the chair across from Cammy. "I thought it was time we met," he held out his hand. She didn't move.

"Very much so," Cammy said. He looked inquisitively at the counselor. She finally made eye contact with the most feared man in the county. "It does offend me."

Elliott smiled, "I'd apologize, but ain't my style. Momma used to say I didn't know how. Drove her ape shit." He stared at her, a look of intimidation that probably got him what he wanted most of the time. Cammy didn't give a shit, she stared right back. "Here's the thing Miss Hart, I don't think you murdered Sam. I don't think you could, to be honest. He was a paranoid man, kept a gun in the desk. Not to mention, the man was as strong as a fucking ox," he said. He watched her to see if the language would offend her. Elliott went on to explain how strong Sam was, being the only man whoever beat him in a drunken arm wrestling match. Elliott almost shot him over it, as a matter of fact. His eyes never wavered from hers during the conversation, a common tactic he used to intimidate people he dealt with on a regular basis. What he couldn't believe was how the much smaller pregnant woman held his gaze, and could look pretty intimidating herself.

Cammy leaned toward Donovan and used her finger to draw him closer. He leaned toward her, she gave him a smirk. "Mr. Elliott, I don't give a rat's behind what you think," she said to his amazement. Cammy continued on about how Sam was a piece of shit and she knows they were up to something. "I am interested in what kind of Police Chief would allow a known felon into his station. Not to mention into the interrogation room alone with a suspect?" she said as she turned to the black window. She stared through the glass to be sure Chad Danville could feel her burning glare.

"I don't think you're a suspect," Elliott told her.

"Then I want to leave," Cammy said without turning from the glass.

"And I ain't no felon," he said with a smile.

"Where's Danville?"

"You can leave whenever you want," Elliott said. Cammy started to stand when he grabbed her by the wrist, squeezing till she sat back down. They were eye to eye once again. "As soon as you answer a couple questions for me, that's all. I have an issue you might be able to help me with."

Cammy looked into Elliott's eyes, then toward the glass. "Macie?" she asked.

"Boyfriend."

"Never met him," she said. Elliott stared at her. She kept his gaze, which only added to his current state of anger. "Heard he's pretty much like the rest of the men in this town, ya know, a real piece." Donovan took a deep breath. He watched her as she took his intimidation head on.

"Listen lady, I don't know who the fuck you are, or what your angle is here but this is Franklin County. Do you know what that

212

means?" Elliott stood up and leaned toward Cammy, resting both hands in the middle of the table so he could get closer to her. Cammy looked up at Elliott. She tried to keep it cool, but she did know what he meant. She knew who he was and what he was capable of. Still, she managed to shake her head no.

"It means you are looking at the HMIC. Head Mother Fucker in Charge," he said with a smile. Elliott now hovered further over the table, she could feel his breath as he spoke. "Now I'm only going to ask this one time, you got me Counselor?"

Cammy nodded. She found herself looking over his shoulder toward the door, wondering if Danville or any other officer might show up.

"Where is the black book you stole from that dumb cocksucker Sam?"

Cammy waited, then shrugged her shoulders and shook her head simultaneously. They both waited for the other to speak, neither did. "I don't know what you're talking about."

Elliott almost chuckled as he bit his lip. "I told you," he paused to be sure she was looking right at him. "I am only asking you one time."

She sat in the seat wondering what his next move was going to be. Clearly Sam was on to something, he was at least in the ballpark if not dead on. Somehow Elliott knew this, and he knew it would be the end of his biggest money maker, if not him.

"So Sam was on to you?"

"What'd you say?" asked Elliott. He squinted and leaned his right ear closer to her.

He wasn't used to being questioned, or having to work for what he wanted. Especially from a woman. He seemed to wait to see if she would dare repeat her questioning of HIM.

"I said," Cammy braced herself for his explosion once she finished. "Sam figured it all out, didn't he?"

"These little teenage whores," he said. Elliott was losing his cool, he started to show his cards. "None of them would have a place to sleep if it ain't for me, understand, I put that roof over their heads." Cammy didn't flinch. She didn't disagree with him, not at all. "Where's the black book?"

"By pimping them out to white trash bikers and meth heads?"

Elliott's hands both slammed on the table, his face was red and his breathing was that of a locomotive. "Where's the fucking book!"

Cammy took a deep breath. Donovan Elliott might control every move in Franklin County, including the local police. He might even frighten her, right now he did, but he wasn't going to intimidate her. "We both know," she said as she took a long, slow breath. She looked Donovan right in the eyes, making sure he was looking back. "I have a lot of black books."

His intimidation tactic had failed, backfired. The woman had no fear. He lost his cool.

The back of his hand flew up from the table and smacked Cammy across the face. He stood up over her and began to scream, "What the fuck is wrong with you, you god damn cunt. I have two dead men and I know you talk to the

214

little bitch that's starting all the trouble. Now where are they!"

The door to the interrogation room slammed open so hard it bounced off the door stop only to be held by Chad Danville. Danville took one step and launched himself over Cammy and the table taking out Elliott. It was a tackle that would be outlawed by today's NFL standards. Danville pinned Elliott on the ground with his knees and went face to face with the diminished motorcycle God.

"Are you nuts? What's wrong with you she's a pregnant woman!"

"Get the fuck off me now," Elliott growled. Danville could feel his heart racing, spit lingered on his chin from screaming. They both stared at each other for what felt like an eternity to Cammy.

"I'm fine," she said. She wiped the drop of blood from under her nose with her shirtsleeve. Cammy stood up next to the chair, she straightened her clothes to compose herself. "If I'm not getting arrested can I leave?" she asked as she pointed to the open door. Neither man said a word, so she turned to the door.

"Miss Hart," Danville called out. "What were you doing in the bus depot at four in the morning?"

Cammy stopped in the doorway and turned back to the men. "Your job."

"That girl and her boyfriend are bad news. He's been running a fuck'n muck since he was twelve when his mom broke his nose when she was all cooked up on meth," Elliott yelled. "Get the fuck off me Danville."

"She's pregnant, but you knew that." Cammy said. She looked at both of them one last time and shook her head. Cammy headed for the door.

Elliott stared at her for a moment with a tilted head. He smiled, "She's a whore, they all are." Cammy stopped and looked at him. "Ask her, ask who the father is, if she can narrow it down to a fucking handful or two." He laughed as he said this, but quickly transformed back to pissed as hell when Danville pushed harder on his shoulders.

Cammy watched Elliott, looked to see if he was telling the truth. "She's turned her last tSam for you."

The men watched her leave. Danville looked down at Elliott, "What the fuck is going on?"

"Get off me now or you won't see another sunrise," he said. Danville slowly got off, then took two quick steps back. He eyed Elliott to be sure he wasn't going to come after him. "I made you Sheriff, I can ruin you just as fast and you know it. You ever pull that shit again and you're done."

"I'm still the law. I can't have you beating women in my jail."

Elliott gave Danville the same look he had used on Cammy as he flung an errant elbow toward the officer on his way out of the interrogation room. "You ain't the god damn law," Elliott mumbled as he walked to the door. Elliott stopped at the door and turned back to Danville, "You're looking at the law." Elliott walked out of the interrogation room. Danville grabbed his hand to get it to stop shaking. He took a deep breath as he stared up at the ceiling fan. Elliott yelled back from down the hall. "I'm the fucking law!"

Chapter 74

"What the fuck is happening!" Angel screamed as he drove us north out of Franklin. "We're fucking dead, what the fuck did you do?"

"Are you kidding me?" I asked. Was he seriously asking if I killed Sam? "You aren't being serious right now?"

"Who sent you the text then?"

"I have no clue," I told him. It was the truth too. I didn't know who sent the text. Whoever it was though saved our asses. For now.

Angel was right about being dead, for once in his life. If Donovan Elliott isn't behind their murders then we are his obvious guess. I did attack Ray after all. We didn't really know what we were going to do. I wanted to get away and regroup. I had to get back to Franklin for some unfinished business, and how I was going to do that I didn't have a clue. Angel knew of a small family run campground ninety minutes north near the Iowa border so that was where we headed to figure out some sort of plan.

We drove in silence for the next twenty minutes, we were about an hour out of town now. No one had followed us. Two semis had passed us since we left town, there hadn't been another car on the road otherwise.

"Did you whack those two clowns," he dared to ask me again.

"You think I'm lying, or fucking stupid?" I asked but didn't give him a chance to answer me. "NO," I said for the final time. He knew I didn't, I couldn't figure out why he kept asking. Did he know who did if I didn't? "I'm starting to wonder if you did it."

"I'm no pedazo de mierda," he said. I couldn't stand when he spoke Spanish to me. Angel grew up in Franklin County trading foster families more often than I had. He knew curse words and stuff he learned in restaurants. I think he thought he sounded hard when he used his limited fast food Spanish. "I know how this all works, these hijos de putas." To be honest I didn't even know if he knew what he was saying half the time. I was pretty sure he said bitches or fuckers. I really had no clue, and that pissed me off even more.

"By the way you fat fuck, why am I getting pictures of some whore sucking your Mexican dick?"

He was silent, just shook his head like he was disgusted with me asking him. "You said it yourself, we ain't nothing here, nada," he said. He looked out the driver's side window to avoid me all together. I wanted to punch him in the throat, but couldn't. He was driving me seventy-five on the highway for one, and he was right. "Just business, your words," he said.

"I get it," I said. I looked out my window so he wouldn't see my face. He got it and shut up. I wasn't going to cry or anything, but I was hurt. I don't know why, he had been talking shit lately about a future together. I always blew him off, but maybe somewhere I did want it, wanted someone. "Let's just figure out what we're going to do."

We drove the rest of the way in silence.

Chapter 75

The excitement of the Ray Lehane death the week before was short lived. Danville and the powers that be in Franklin County wasted no time in wrapping the case up as a drug dealer's revenge.

The story was that Lehane was a recovered meth head, but hadn't been in trouble since he was a kid. That was how the school overlooked his past addiction from his days as a minor. He fell off the wagon hard, and fell behind with the dealer. When he couldn't come up with the dough the dealer had to make an example out of him, played a little Home Run Derby on Ray's brain. While many assumed that meant Ray had a falling out with the County Kingpin, D. Elliott, the man wanted for murder was someone most of them had never heard of, one Angel Ortiz.

Franklin County's newest dead body was going to a bit tougher for Danville to cover up whatever it was he was trying to cover up. The Sheriff didn't have a clue what was going on. The obvious connection was the school Bus Depot, that wasn't good for anyone. Danville knew both men had ties to Elliott, but he was never too sure what exactly those ties entailed.

Chad Danville was an Officer of the Law, but truth was, for the past eleven years he had really been an Officer of Donovan Elliott. That seemed to be the norm in town, but Danville was beginning to have his doubts. If Elliott really had nothing to do with the murders there was something new going on. There were always two sides to the Vandal run town. It was just the Vandals were on the side that accepted no challengers. The other side was happy to oblige the bikers, and just go on about their quiet little lives happy that the MC didn't bother them. The Police Chief's newest question was personal-Which side was he on?

Danville wasn't going to keep Cammy a second longer than Elliott questioned her. His original thought for murder was a lover's quarrel between Cammy and Sam. He knew this was a long shot. Cammy's fiancé, and father of her unborn child, was serving his second tour in Afghanistan. Danville thought the Counselor might have grown lonely over time. His instincts told him this wasn't the case. Sam had the type of looks that needed a dynamic personality to land a woman like Cameron Hart, and Sam's personality was well below dynamic. Danville had always thought the man was bland, boring, and lacked any personality. The main problem with the whole scenario was his gut; it told him she didn't kill Sam Montero.

This led to the fiasco with Donovan. What black book did Cammy have of Sam's, and what was the MC up to. Was he running a prostitution ring out of the bus depot? His guess from the conversation between the counselor and MC President was Sam started to figure this out. He started keeping tabs on the drivers, girls, and whatever else he was in the process of discovering. Danville had always known Elliott influenced some of the hires of the bus drivers.

The excuse was to get them a regular paying job to appease their PO, who was no doubt also in Elliott's pocket. Did Sam figure out who was all paid off? One thing was for sure, Sam Montero seemed to be more of a Detective than Danville had ever been.

The Prostitution ring with underage teens made the most sense to Danville. It made sense for the bus drivers too, they were perfect scouts to research new talent. Danville had one problem with this. Donovan Elliott was THE drug dealer in town. He knew what girls were hooked. He knew what those girls would be willing to do- or had to do. Was it forced prostitution? Why risk involving the school when you got every resource available?

Danville thought to himself as he dropped his head on the desk. When he returned home after failing as a college quarterback the shame kept him in his parent's basement for six months. When he finally left, the local taverns were his only place of existence for the next year. He flashbacked to those days, they were the lowest point of his life, until now. Chad Danville finally realized why Elliott would try to get away with running a prostitution ring out of the school bus depot. He had the Chief of Police in his pocket.

Chapter 76

The campground was a converted farm that backed up to the used half of the farm. I was pretty sure by the looks of the dirt campsites and smell the farmer alternated the cow pasture and campground every few years. We drove in at sunrise, a fog hovered over the grounds that hid the last half of the park from the gate. It would work just long enough for us to get our wits and figure out what we were going to do. Angel pulled up to the unmanned guard shack and dropped twelve bucks into the cash box. We didn't need anyone coming to collect and start asking questions. An old green six- man tent was in one of the first sights. The tent was accompanied by a rusty powder blue Suburban, whoever was in the tent would be our only company. They wouldn't even know we were there for the next hour, if they were up by then. Scattered beer cans and a smoking fire pit told me they had had a long night, we knew we'd be good for a bit. Angel drove all the way to the last sight. It backed to the barbed wire fence that separated the cows from the campers. I tossed my cigarette, and closed the window. The smell of cow shit was unbearable.

"We gotta make the deal," said Angel. I closed my eyes for a second, a thousand thoughts ran through my head. "It's the only way we get out of here and they don't follow us for the rest of our lives."

"I can't," I said. I knew what he was asking me to do, but I couldn't. I didn't want to be one of them. I wasn't a killer, I'm not a murderer.

"You have a better idea? Listen, I'm in this mess because of you," he said. He leaned close enough I could smell the cigarette off his breathe. "You talked me into this."

"You wanted to do this, it was your idea."

"You started fucking me puta," he said. That pissed me off. I did know puta meant whore, or maybe bitch.

"So you get a piece you do whatever the girl says?" I asked, but more yelled it at him. In all reality, I was madder at myself for getting into this situation in the first place. I should have been smart enough to just get out of town the last time. Now I was left with little to bargain. I added with heavy sarcasm, "I hope the bitch who sucked your dick doesn't go asking for nothin'."

Angel took a deep breath. I hate to admit he was actually the more rational of the two of us at the time. My every thought was clouded with what I had to do. I was focused on getting what I needed and getting gone. In the end I had one goal: poof- Disappear.

"What are you going to do?" I asked. He was right, we had to make a deal. We didn't have much, but I had one chip in my hand. I felt bad but had to do it. It was her or me.

"I'm going to go call Vampire Eddy," he said. He lit a cigarette. "Hopefully he can get to Donovan and convince him we don't have shit to do with this. This has to be one of their guys going rogue or something. Maybe some chick who just woke up pissed about everything or something."

"You think that's gonna fly?" I asked. Angel had been affiliated with the club when we got into this mess. I was his assignment. His only job was to keep tabs on me. I had told Miss Hart we had met a couple years ago, but that was a lie. I had never seen Angel in my life until after I got knocked up the first time. "I don't know if I'd bring up the phrase going rogue," I said. Angel shrugged, then nodded. He grabbed his phone from the middle counsel and got out of the car. I looked toward the farm, through the fog I could see a cow chewing the grass. She just stood there and chewed her grass and stared into the nothingness of the misty farm. She was oblivious she would soon be slaughtered for someone's personal enjoyment- survival.

Chapter 77

Donovan Elliott took a swig from the tequila bottle. He pushed the bottle back toward the young kid working the bar. The kid took the bottle and put it back on the shelf of the clubhouse bar. The roided up kid looked to be about twenty. He wore a white wife beater, under his black sleeveless leather vest. The back of the vest only said *Prospect* across the bottom. The kid outweighed Elliott by about fifty pounds, but it didn't show in their interaction. He almost dropped the bottle when he took it from Donovan he was such a nervous wreck. Elliott was not in a good mood, and he didn't try to hide it either.

"Get lost," he said to the kid. The kid was out the front door before Elliott's cigarette was lit. He turned to his number one enforcer, Vampire Eddy. They were alone in the clubhouse. "Fuck, Eddy, this ain't good," he said. Eddy sat silent, waited for his clue to give his two cents. "Big man called, pissed as a fucking snake on ice."

Vampire Eddy cleared his throat, he had a plan, an option at least. "Well, um, what's he think? Who's knocking 'em off?"

"He don't know, he don't care either. Wants us to take care of everyone," Elliott said. He took a long drag on his smoke and turned to Eddy. "Everyone."

"The girl?" he asked.

Donovan nodded. "Counselor too, doesn't give a shit about the money or nothing. All this shit lately got him acting funny, situation in all. He just wants it over with."

"We gonna do it?"

"You're gonna take care of your boy, and you're going to get it done right. This list is building, and it ain't a list you want to be added to, got it? Big man ain't happy about Fat Taco, wants to know where he came from, who backed him," Elliott said before a brief pause to let the enormity of the situation set in for Eddy. Fat Taco was Elliott's name for Angel, a name he gave him when Eddy first introduced Angel to the club.

"I hear ya," Eddy mumbled.

"I told him I'd take care of the situation. You're my guy Eddy. I got yer back, but you gotta come through for me. This is a big fuck up."

Eddy nodded and looked at the ground. The situation was more serious than he suspected. Was he on the list already? "I'll take care of it, the fat fuck gonna be begging to die," he said. He waited for a response. Elliott stared at the rows of bottles behind the bar deep in thought about something other than what Eddy had said. "Listen, what about the counselor? We can still get it done, ya know, a redemption."

Elliott sat silent for a moment. "That bitch is off her chain, what was she thinking?" he said. His face contorted as he tried to control his anger. "You tell that bitch she is on ultra fucking high alert. If she pisses me off in the slightest again the closest thing she'll ever be to a mother is singing Twinkle the fucking star with the god damned worms, you got it?"

Eddy didn't say anything until he was sure his boss was done, then he slowly looked up with a nod.

Elliott looked at Eddy and held out his fist. He slowly bumped it and got up even slower. He headed for the door.

"You want the girl back here?"

Elliott stared out the window as if he didn't hear Eddy. He took another drag, shook his head no, then let out a deep breath. "Just get her, I'll deal with all that."

Chapter 78

The McDonald's was as crowded a public place you could find in Franklin on a Tuesday at 9 in the morning. Cammy knew it would be, always was. Kids screamed and ran throughout the restaurant. The parents just watched in a trance. They looked like they were either up all night with their screaming children, or hung over from the relief they found once the kids had finally fallen asleep. Cammy watched the zombie parents more than the spastic children, and smiled to herself. Not because she enjoyed the earsplitting atmosphere, she didn't at all. She smiled because she told herself she was more qualified to be a parent than these people. A kid would be fortunate to be raised by her, even blessed she believed.

The bell on the door rang again when it opened. This time it wasn't one of these crumb snatching kids trying to escape their stone faced parents. Pete Wellman had finally showed up.

Cammy walked a half mile from the police station and went into the McDonald's. She could have just walked to school, but wanted to clean herself up before. Her apartment was too far to walk. She wasn't ready to go back home yet anyway. Cammy told Pete where a spare key was in a flowerpot on her back porch. Pete went to the apartment and got some clothes. She had Pete take her to his house so she could shower and change. Not much was said on the drive over. Pete was either in shock of her appearance, or afraid of what her answer might be if he asked what happened. She quickly showered at his place, and they headed back to school.

Pete drove a couple blocks, but in the end the suspense got the better of him. "What is going on?" Pete asked. He looked in her eyes for the first time since he first saw her face. Her cheek was red and swollen enough to notice. "Cammy, what happened to your beautiful face?"

"I need a favor?" she asked.

"Anything you need, what is going on?" he asked.

"I need your car, just for a couple days. You can use mine if-"

"No, no, don't worry, not like Shelly leaves the house. You saw her, that's what she does, sits on the couch watching daytime TV- all day. I'll use hers," he said. Cammy knew she would never be back in Franklin County, probably not even Missouri after she left. She liked Pete, felt bad if she stole his car. Then again, he just told her to take it. "Are you going to tell me what's going on?" he asked. Pete took her hands to console her. She pulled them back.

"Do you really want to know what happened? I mean what's really happening?" she asked.

Pete hesitated before he shook his head, "I don't know."

"Well, our school buses, or bus drivers have been scoping out, or keeping tabs on some of the students."

"Scoping out?"

"I think they're recruiting the girls to be prostitutes. Or they are and these guys are just there to keep tabs on them."

"I don't think, how, that doesn't make sense," he said.

"I can't really prove it yet, I have to talk to Macie. I might get her to tell me more."

"How? There's no way."

"Why not, these people can do anything they want in this town. They're getting these girls hooked and then when they can't pay, they work it off."

"Um, I don't know. How many girls, how? Is it Elliott?" he asked as he pulled into his parking spot. "And why high school girls? There's plenty of crack whores in this town who would love to trade rock for cock."

"You said it- crack whores. Come on Pete, even you know what guys really want. They're sick, twisted bastards. A trucker stopping in the middle of Missouri isn't going to pass up one of these sixteen or seventeen year olds for one hour then be long gone the next. Sure they pay big bucks too."

"Elliott?"

Cammy took a deep breath and looked at Pete. Cammy shook her head, "I don't think so, I don't know much yet. Listen, you probably should forget all about this anyway. Sorry. I kind of wanted to throw it out there to see how you reacted. You don't think it's impossible, that's good enough."

"Maybe you should go to Danville with this," he said. The chuckle she let out let him know she wasn't sure the Sheriff wasn't in on the whole set up.

"I have to go Pete. Keys?" she asked. Pete nodded and reached into his pocket, he handed her the keys. Cammy opened the door and was halfway out of the car when he called to her.

"Cammy?" he asked.

"It's for your own safety Pete. You have a wife and kids, or well whatever it is, you're best left in the dark. Sorry I told you this much."

He looked away from her and nodded in agreement. She knew he wouldn't go any further when safety was brought in to the picture. He could tell himself and her he was better being an observer for his family's protection. They both knew why he didn't want to know anymore. He was born and raised in Franklin County. Smiling and waving was the way he was brought up. No reason to get involved with other people's problems, you might end up involved. "Mm hmm," he said. He watched her walk toward the school. He shook his head, possibly disgusted with himself.

Chapter 79

"Not a chance in hell," Angel didn't hesitate in shooting down my plan. I didn't care. I had two things I needed then I was gone. In reality I didn't care if Donovan chased me down for the rest of my life. It was probably not a solid plan on how to live out my days, but I was sixteen, pregnant, and raised in Franklin County foster homes. Rational thinking had left town years ahead of me.

"You want me to go through with your plan, get him off our back? You follow me through on this and I'll go with you on your end."

"What good is any of this if we're fugitives?" he asked.

"What's the difference? Your plan is to lead someone to death."

"No one's dying," he said.

"You don't know that. Jesse Henderson was in a coma for Christ sakes."

"That little slut got jumped and raped," he said. Jesse had been one of the biggest sluts in school. She told me she got pregnant in a Vandal three way, ended up getting jumped and left for dead right before her due date. They told her she had lost the baby, that was really all I knew about it. She claimed amnesia once she came to, and would never talk about any of it again with me, and I don't think anyone else had ever asked. Whoever got to her scared her right good.

"Sometimes it's just easier to not remember. Think I know a bit more on the subject. Either way, there ain't no difference, ya know it. Now are you in?"

"Makes no sense," he said.

"Then get out," I said. When Angel had called Vampire Eddy I got into the driver's seat. I knew he was going to shit when I told him what we were about to do, so I had to take control of the situation. I pulled the gun out from my purse and pointed it at his stomach, keeping it low in case the cows were watching. "I'm doing this one way or another. I don't really give a shit if you help me or not. Now Angel, are you in?"

"You fucking crazy puta," he said.

"In or out?" I asked a final time. He shook his head then turned from me and leaned his forehead against the passenger window.

"I should just let you shoot me," he mumbled. "It'll be faster."

I looked at him, but didn't say anything. I rested the gun on my lap, keeping it pointed in his direction. I wanted to tell him we'd be alright, everything would be ok. I couldn't. Somewhere I knew it wouldn't work, not everything. I never thought I'd use a gun, point it at someone and actually be ready to use it. I was pretty sure I could, but I didn't want to murder anyone or anything. I was going to have my baby, and didn't care what I had to do to get us out of here safe. I turned the radio on and messed with the station till I found a song I'd never heard before. Country music hollered from the speakers, new beginnings I guessed. I sent Angel a forced a smile. It would be OK I continued to tell myself. I said it again to him, I was pretty sure it fell on deaf ears. Angel just shrunk further in his seat.

Chapter 80

The last decade had seen a complete swing in the make- up of what was once a candidate for *Best Small Town in America* lists. A town the rest of small town Missouri looked up to. The lumber industry had thrived due to the booming real estate market. Family businesses couldn't get by on just family employees. Two new motels were built. If you had an extra room, or even a decent unattached garage a renter would answer your call before the ink in the classifieds was dry. Then something happened.

Chad Danville sat in his office wondering where it all went wrong, why? Was the answer the reflection he hardly recognized anymore? There was a time when the sky was the limit to Danville. He wanted to make something of his life, and put his town on the map. When Franklin County was finally sprawled across the top of the city paper in bold, black letters it wasn't because of his athletic feats or criminal crackdown. No, Franklin County was known as the United States Meth Capital. No county in America exported more crystal meth, saw more explosions of cook houses, or more overdoses than Franklin County, Missouri.

Danville stared at that very article he had kept stashed away in a bottom file cabinet in his office. There was a time this was a great place to live, then it came crumbling down. He could tell himself it was the financial crisis, the housing market crumbling, but he knew the downfall of Franklin County was well before the rest of the country felt any hardships. When J.C. Jennings died from what appeared to be a crystal overdose it was thought that the white trash teens in the trailer parks were the only users. Then the explosions started. Once heroin entered the picture the mortuary business was the trade to get into; funerals for teens, burnouts, twenty to thirty year olds, and before Danville knew what was going on it seemed like anyone was a possibility. He just opened his eyes one day and recreational drugs seemed to have transformed into a full blown epidemic. Danville could have stepped in, could have stood up to the Lion. He didn't. Macie had told him that night in her trailer he would never help her because he was a local. The Franklin County way was to smile and wave, and that was the extent anyone would get involved. No one ever helped, not when it really mattered. Maybe she was right. No one ever did anything to stop the downward slide of Franklin, especially him. He had turned a blind eye, and soon it was a place where more pockets were full of drugs or drug money than a pack of gum.

Chapter 81

Cammy had to find Macie before it was too late. She knew the girl well enough by now to know what she was thinking- her best option was running. Cammy had to find her before she was gone.

She pulled up Macie's file on her computer to follow the trail of foster homes after the death of her sister. The death of her sister left her with absolutely no family the state could contact. There was an uncle, but he made a home in the state pen serving 25 to 30. Macie actually had one of those dirty creepy uncles who had a taste for little boys. The only other family on record was her mother; deceased.

In 2004 Jaclyn Christine was found dead on the banks of the River from an apparent drug overdose. At the time she was raising ten year - old Macie, due to her mother's explosive death. Lucky for Macie her sister knew what her mother was doing, and tried like hell to get her to stop. When she refused J.C. told her they were leaving. Their mother watched them, but put up no fight. On the fateful night in August of '01 they were at J.C's boyfriend's house. Cammy had to read the last line twice. She wanted to know for sure where J.C. took Macie.

Chapter 82

Danville sat in his office. The office was five tiles long ways, and six tiles wide. That made it twenty by twelve feet, not a bad office. Was it worth what he had done over the last decade? He looked around the bare office. He had his Associates Degree framed, but no awards. What had he been doing all this time? He closed his eyes, his mind rewound the last ten years. Was this twenty by twelve foot office with an Associate's Degree worth- to be more precise- everything he hadn't done?

Danville took a deep breath and opened a bottom drawer. He reached in the drawer and dug through a couple folders. He came up with a cigarette and lighter. He lit the cigarette and took a long drag. Chad Danville opened his eyes as he exhaled.

Danville got up and walked to the corner of his office, taking another long drag on his way. He pulled out his keys and unlocked a file cabinet. His fingers danced along the files till he found what he was looking for, Jennings, Jaclyn Christine.

Chapter 83

The kept the music loud, but the silence was deafening in the small car. Angel stopped talking to me once I told him our new plan. I can't say I didn't blame him since I had pulled a gun on him, but I didn't care either. He had nothing to say I wanted to hear. I drove the ninety minute drive south east back toward Franklin County. We got off Highway 61 shortly after passing Hannibal and took the back roads the rest of the way. I knew where we were going from the map in the back of my notebook. Of course, I had to give it to Angel to let him know I wasn't making the whole thing up.   He continued to read on our way to town. Well, he read what I had given him. Some things are on a need to know, and Angel didn't need to know shit about the last few pages. I did give him the bulk of it though. I had to let him know why I had no choice and had to go through with this. It only took about ten minutes of reading, which by his standards is a couple pages, to agree to the plan. He didn't like it, I don't think he wanted to be any part of it really. Yet, he agreed to come along. He would drive once we got there, I had to agree to that. If I had to describe his reaction while reading it would have to be shock. Disturbed would have qualified as well. Life ain't fair all the time, and in Franklin County, it ain't even fair all that much.

Chapter 84

My dear girl you must understand we were just kids, ignorant, uneducated teenagers. That's not an excuse for what we'd done though. It was actually quite the opposite. J.C. hated herself for it, but knew the reality of our lives. She knew what she could and could not handle. She didn't see it as a business venture that was for damn sure. This was just enough money to survive on, and when I say survive on I mean to get you new clothes and proper meals and care. Now don't think I am saying she did this because she was raising you either. That was not the case. She was messed up when everything first went down, we both were. We weren't ready to be parents to anyone, but she would give anything in the world to have you close to her. She wanted you so she could make sure you got your education, stayed clean, and turned into everything she did not. Always remember that.

How much you really remember of me I can't say for sure, but I was a shit role model. I made money illegally, and when I could I drank and used. Your sister would get mad at me, but then join me in our excesses. It was her escape from the pain of failing to be a mother.

You were her redemption. Every time she lost her baby the only thing that kept her going was that she had you. She would cry at night that they might take you too. Her true fear, only fear, was she was going to fail you. She would fight to get clean, and stay clean. I never helped. Not at first at least. I only hurt her chances by coming home high or drunk. If she were smarter she would have taken you, and ditched me and this damn town the first time she had a chance. She didn't. Soon enough it happened again. She would be too high or drunk and start missing her pills. I've heard the phrase 'History Repeats Itself,' every time I been in front of the board in here. It was a phrase I knew a long time before this place though. J.C. got knocked up again. This time was going to be different she had told me, and she was right.

Your sister was clean and sober the entire pregnancy. Stopped cold turkey and never looked back. Life was starting to look up then two things happened. You were old enough I guess to realize she was having a baby. When we found out it was going to be a little girl I'd never seen you two so happy, so excited. It triggered something in me too. The smiles on your faces sobered me up, and I been sober ever since.

The second thing that happened was you weren't the only person to realize your sister was pregnant again. That's when everything got a little dicey. Up until now I have made three decisions in my life that I can be proud of. I fell in love with your sister, got cleaned up for your sister, and finally became a man for your sister.

I wasn't with her that night she passed. I hadn't seen her since morning when I left to work on the farm. We had been trying to fix it in time to move all of us in before the baby. One thing I am certain of was she was murdered. There was no way she would have been high, I'd stake everything on that fact. She wouldn't touch the stuff again in a million years. This much you must know. This much is fact.

They killed her and took our baby. Again.

Chapter 85

The office door flung open as it always did when someone would run by Roberta and into Cammy's office.

"Son, you know you need an appointment," Cammy said. She was so into the article on the computer she didn't even turn to the boy.

"I need to see my records, my file," he said. Cammy told him again he needed to make an appointment, still engrossed in the computer. She was trying to read the police report on the death of J.C. Jennings that she had finally found. The boy continued talking, she didn't hear what he had said when she finally stood up and looked out the window at Roberta. The Secretary was sitting at her computer, completely oblivious to Cammy and her unwanted guest.

"Roberta," she called.

"Please," the boy pleaded. "Can't you just tell me if I was adopted?"

"Huh," Cammy said. It was really all she could say when she looked at him.

"I been texting my parents, or I mean, well I guess my parents, but they aren't answering," he said. Cammy stared at the boy in disbelief. Roberta was now in the doorway.

"Is everything alright in here Miss Hart?" she asked.

"Please," the boy pleaded. Cammy ignored him and just nodded to Roberta. She walked to the door and closed it before the Secretary could turn away.

"Sit down," she said. Cammy walked to the blinds and closed them. "Now tell me again, or what is your question?" she asked. Cammy only heard bits and pieces of what he was saying and she stared at the boy's eyes. She caught that his name was Lawrence Lynch, but everyone called him Larry. Cammy didn't really care about his name because she was pretty sure it wasn't who he was. Lawrence, or Larry, Lynch was a spitting image of the whore drug addicted pedophile, as it was put by Danville, Katherine Siebert. The woman who just a couple weeks earlier had been dragged out of this very office by Danville after claiming her boy was here, but she didn't know his name. The boy continued to talk as Cammy looked up Katherine Siebert on the Franklin County Case Net.

Case Net was a website with local police records, warrants, etc. It was a valuable tool the school used from anything to looking up parents when a kid seemed out of sort to a quick background on an applicant's name when hiring for various positions before an interview, and an extended background check. Cammy had used Case Net at least once a week since she had started at Franklin, the most common reason was to look up a parent of a student. When a kid came in to tell her he hadn't eaten in days, or sometimes just from his or her appearance and stench Cammy would look up the parents. Usually her instincts were right; the student came from a broken home where one or both parents had spent some time in state facilities.

More often than not it was meth, but lately heroin was behind the parents fall from grace.

Cammy couldn't remember why she didn't think to run Katherine Siebert through Case Net that day she came in demanding to see her son. It could have been the woman's appearance or state of mind. Cammy reminded herself that Katherine didn't know her son's name, or what he looked like. In less than a year on the job Cammy had no reason to believe the story Danville told her wasn't true. If it wasn't true about Siebert, Cammy knew it to be true ten other times.

Six mug shots of Katherine Siebert popped up on the screen. The top photo was the most recent taken just a few weeks earlier when Danville took her in from the school.

"So I'm just walking into the lot and the van door opens, she comes running at me," the boy said. Cammy looked up, she did want to hear what he said about the confrontation. The rap sheet was stealing most of her attention. Most of it was drugs, or drug related until the statutory rape charge.

"I mean I thought she was going to attack me or something," he continued. Cammy looked up to focus on the boy. "Her face and how fast she was running, then she grabbed me like this," he said. He held up his hands like he was grabbing someone by the head.

"Did she say anything?" Cammy asked.

"I'm your mother."

"Well," Cammy said and nodded. "You know this town has a fair share of you know, some people are a little out there."

"No, no she wasn't. I mean, yeah she was a little," he said and stopped. He stared off out the window, Cammy watched him replay the incident in his head again, and again.

Cammy saw on the screen Katherine's statement the night she was arrested and charged with Statutory Rape of the fifteen year- old boy. She claimed to have never seen the boy before, even that night. She had snorted three lines of crystal with the boy's older brother. Not him.

"The thing is Ms. Hart," he said.

"I don't think she was crazy. I mean what if-," he said then looked off again for a moment.

"Go on," she said.

"What if she is my mother?"

Cammy looked in the boy's eyes. If it was true or not Cammy knew one thing for certain, he believed it was.

"Well, we can look into some history here if you'd like," she said. She quickly continued to read the victim's statement in the Katherine Siebert Statutory Rape case. The boy claimed he didn't remember the woman. He told police he was stoned on marijuana and drunk on whiskey. The brother had called the police when he found Katherine naked and passed out in his younger brother's bed. The fifteen year-old was passed out in only his t-shirt when police arrived. Cammy skimmed through until she saw the older brother's name was Edward Van Pearson. She knew exactly who he was, but like most people in town she knew him by his street name- Vampire Eddy. Cammy quickly closed out the screen and looked at the boy.

"She didn't want to give me up she said, she had no choice," he said. Cammy looked at him, she wasn't sure what to say. Her mind was spinning. "She tried to get me back or get in contact she said. No one would tell her where I was, or even who I was."

Katherine Siebert was set up. Cammy listened to Larry, but couldn't hear anything when she read the last line. *All Charges Dropped- No Court Date.* Why would they set her up, and not pursue the charges? Was it to scare her, or was it to remind her what they were capable of?

Chapter 86

There was a time when a twenty- five year- old male was expected to be a man. You were married, had children, and a career by your early twenties. Those days were long gone. Danville thought back to when he was that age. He wanted to be a man, acted like it. He was the youngest officer in Franklin County back then. He had the walk and talk down to act like the Chief, the ultimate goal he had been promised would be his, if he could follow the rules of the County. He thought back to those early days, and knew he was far from a man. He was doubtful he was much of a man after a decade on the job, the last five as Police Chief. He had been fooling them all, but he knew, he had been fooling himself most of all. He had to consistently remind himself he was the man in charge. Danville told himself this, but always knew he was nothing more than a scared boy doing what he was told.

Danville looked over the police report he had written when he was just a young officer. Something about the death of J.C. Jennings had always bothered him. That was why he kept it after all these years. He sat for a moment and realized something else. Something else he had lied to himself about for all these years.

Danville often found himself checking in on Macie Jennings for the last six years. "The apple don't fall far from the tree boys," he would tell other officers. He would always remind them the mother killed herself cooking, and the sister overdosed. That was his excuse if someone mentioned how he would harass the girl if she was out with friends, always search her car and belongings. He would tell himself she was a bad apple, but he knew the real reason he watched her- Guilt.

When J.C. Jennings was finally found she had been missing for ten days. Her boyfriend reported the teen missing immediately, claimed she was kidnapped or worse. Danville read through the report, but all the boyfriend's statements were omitted. The missing persons report didn't contain a name either. This was all missing because Danville was the Officer responsible for going back and rewriting the final reports. He was just following orders from his Boss, not the Boss with the badge either. No, this was the same Boss who gave Danville the gun to plant on the same boyfriend. The gun that put him away for the next six years.

The decomposed body had been eaten by coyotes when she was finally found. Danville grimaced at the memory. It was far and away the worst body he had encountered in all his years. He had nightmares about it for the next six months until he finally turned to three shots of Southern before bed, for comfort.

The county declined to perform an Autopsy at the request of the former Police Chief. He had reported the girl was a known drug addict with a history of arrest. Of course, the boyfriend claimed she had been clean for eight and a half months. That statement was ignored and omitted as well. Danville just stared at the rest of the file, he knew any kind of answers he was looking for would have been deleted six years ago. He sat there looking at all the names in hopes that something would point him in the right direction. He stared at all the names, death, drugs. It was the same movie, same ending all the time. Jaclyn Christie Jennings was a drug addict, her boyfriend was a drug addict. The previous police reports confirmed all this, and she came from a lineage as bad and rotten as the corpse she had left behind. The Chief confirmed everything.

The Police Chief, Danville thought to himself. He had said it was so, so it was fact to the young officer back then. He had his doubts, but those were kept in his private vault, and filed. Just like the gun he planted on the boyfriend. How could he have been so naïve for all these years? He didn't know if he was more upset others were on the payroll, or he was too stupid to realize it.

"Damnit Chad," he yelled. He knocked the file off the desk. "What makes you so damn special," he said to himself. The thing that got him the most was not that there were other dirty cops, but how many and how dirty. Danville had always felt bad about the gun, and told Elliott he wouldn't go that far again. Never again would he intentionally ruin a life. The boyfriend was a piece of shit who probably gave J.C. the lethal hit, the Chief had told him. Danville had come to believe this as fact, but now he had his doubts. Up until three months ago his town was quiet. They had their problems, but it was kept on the outskirts among the outcasts. Now he had a kidnapping and two murders within city limits.

Broken Lullabies

Danville knew he had to find a way to put an end to all of it, and for him it started with getting all the facts behind the murder of J.C. Jennings.

Chapter 87

He asked if I would do the unthinkable. Would I be willing to risk someone's life, an innocent life? I continued to justify everything by telling myself it was to save a life, but it was much more selfish than that. I told Angel I was on board with his plan if he would follow me through with mine.

The young mother stared off into nothing. Was she watching clouds? Was she watching the other moms at the park? I couldn't tell what she was doing, or what she was on.

We sat in the car in silence, just watched the kids play in the park. A lot of the moms sat on benches staring into the talisman in the palm of their hands, their cell phones. It's magical powers distracted the mothers enough that a kid fell off a swing and laid crying for three minutes before any adult walked up to the crowd of children that was already taking care of the little five year- old boy. He looked to be fine, but that wasn't the point. They had no idea who was sitting on the other benches watching their children play or in a car across the street.

Angel still wasn't talking to me. I couldn't tell if he was going to have a change of heart, or just pissed, maybe nervous the plan wouldn't work. I didn't care what he thought really, and after reading the letter he knew this. This was going to happen with or without him; his only decision was if he was along for the ride. Like I said, I didn't tell him everything about the plan and escape. Truthfully, I still hadn't made up my mind I wanted him to be part of it.

Chapter 88

The right eye lid of the tied up drug dealer drooped as if fishing weights were pulling his eye shut. His other eye, which didn't look that good, was swollen shut from the repeated meetings with Vampire Eddy's giant silver ring and the studded 'V' on the ring.

"You know, I've heard of a few of these little labs like yours going ba- boom before," Eddy said. He smiled at the dealer. They were in the trailer of a small time meth maker and dealer named Spanish. The dealer was actually Mexican by blood, but for some reason he became Spanish in Franklin County. Angel had once told Eddy it was because his light skin combined with the Spanish accent that gave most locals the impression he was from Spain originally, rather than his native Mexico. Angel had met the dealer a few years earlier and formed a small little partnership.

Spanish opened his mouth, but only blood dribbled down his chin. He took a deep breath and whispered, "I'm telling you the truth." Eddy started to turn then came back with another right to the left eye of Spanish. The dealer's head jolted to the side, a string of blood connected his bottom lip to his shirt before it fell onto his chin.

"Then tell me this Mexican," said Eddy. Eddy lit a cigarette and took a long hit. He pulled the cigarette out of his mouth and held it to the eye that the dealer had already destroyed in a meth cooking session gone wrong. The cigarette inched closer to the white filmed eye. "Will you feel this?" asked Eddy.

"Please, please what do you want, I don't know nothing," Spanish screamed now. He kicked his feet in a terrified frenzy. The chair tipped back till the Prospect behind him stepped up and held him from falling.

"Well, I guess that answer's that," Eddy said and laughed. He flicked the cigarette at Spanish's eye. Spanish shook his head and thrust his body when the Marlboro landed on his lap before falling to the floor.

Eddy's phone rang twice before he took it out of his pocket. "Shit," he mumbled. Eddy looked at the Prospect, "Fucking Elliot." He answered the phone, but held it further than normal due to his past experiences that it could be loud on the other end. "Hey boss," he said.

"We found the girl," said Elliott. Eddy smiled and nodded to the Prospect, then gave a thumbs up to Spanish.

"That's good, eh?" he asked. Elliott was silent on the other end. Eddy heard him take a deep breath.

"No," he said. Elliott was still calm which confused Eddy, maybe he didn't hear him correctly.

"Did you say no? It's not good we got her?"

"I didn't say we got her," said Elliott. He was silent again.

"She dead?" asked Eddy.

"Worse," Elliott responded. "We didn't find her, Tater did."

"Oh," he answered. Eddy didn't know where this was going so he figured his best bet was to wait for Donovan to fill him in.

"She was sitting at a park, watching kids with Fat Taco. A specific kid," he said and paused. Eddy knew who he was talking about but kept silent. "You told me this tub of shit was cool Eddy, what the fuck am I supposed to do now?" Elliot asked. His voice got louder; Eddy knew he was pissed as all hell.

"I don't," said Eddy. He turned from Spanish and Prospect. Eddy got quiet and took a long breath, "He was cool, man." Eddy waited, but all he heard was silence. He knew the situation, he knew where Donovan stood at that moment. Eddy had vouched for Angel, he would have been a good, great addition to the club. Soon the Big Man would know about everything, he would want to know where Angel came from. Eddy was in trouble and he knew it. "I'm telling you the guy is cool Boss, I guess, you know," Eddy paused. "We got it under control, he's on board."

"Yeah? This little plan of yours is starting to run out of steam."

"Donovan, it's cool."

"It better be. I'm starting to think the pussy is starting to fuck with all y'all."

"We're good. All's good Boss, I swear."

"You better hope so and make this right. You with the tweaker still?"

"Yeah."

"Does he know we're looking for the girl?" Donovan asked.

Eddy nodded to himself, "One sec Boss," he said.

"Where's he taking the fucking girl Spanish?" asked Vampire Eddy.

"What man, what girl?"

"You know what girl, the girl. His little whorito."

"Macie man? He's not with her, she kicked him out," Spanish said. Eddy watched, he believed Spanish was telling him what he thought was the truth. The tears down the dealers face told him this much. His lip quivered, and his legs tap danced a frightened jig. "I think he gots someone new, I swear brother." Eddy ignored Spanish and went back to his phone.

"Yeah, he knows we're looking for the girl."

"Then take care of that, then get the fuck up there and take care of this shit. It's your fucking ass now," said Elliott.

"I'm making this all right, ok." Eddy was more asking Elliott to save is ass than anything. He waited for an answer. Elliott was silent. Eddy thought he heard an 'mm hmm,' before the dial tone. Vampire Eddy wasn't a religious man, but said a quick prayer that his plan was still going to work.

"He said he's tagging some teacher or something man, I'm for real," Spanish pleaded on last time.

Vampire Eddy reached behind his back and pulled up his gun. The barrel pressed against Spanish's forehead. Without any pause or time for Spanish to protest the back of his skull exploded from his head. "And I ain't no fucking Mexican, Mexican. So I'm sure as shit not your brother."

"Jesus Christ," cried the Prospect. Eddy looked up at the blood covered biker and gave a little chuckle. "What the fuck man, look at me."

Eddy stared for a moment and the chuckle escalated to a hearty laugh. Eddy bent over to catch his breath as he viewed the entire scene. He stood up and pointed at the Prospect. He tried to talk, but just shook his head.

"What the fuck am I supposed to do Eddy?" the Prospect asked. "Who knows what the fuck this guy has," he said. He threw his jacket and shirt off and grabbed a towel that was sitting on the counter. He started wiping the blood and bits off his face, his mouth. "You just shot fucking AIDS all over my face and my mouth ass hole, or whatever this dude has. Shit!"

"Clean up, I'll be in the car," Eddy said as he walked out. The Prospect stood there staring at Eddy, then pointed to the dead Spanish in the chair. "Yeah I know, that's why I said hurry the fuck up. I'm torching this shit hole in 30 seconds. You might want to get out cuz he's got enough shit in here that this place is going to go up like Saga- fucking- naki."

Eddy walked out. "I think you mean Nagasaki, or even Hiroshima," yelled the Prospect. "You god damn psycho," he said much quieter.

Chapter 89

The crowd at the park left too many witnesses so we followed them instead of doing anything stupid. It wasn't like they would go far. These types of moms have to be home before Daddy so she could have him a hot dinner on the table when he walked through the door. I didn't mind the wait so much, gave me more time to think everything through. The only setback really, was it just gave Angel more time to try to talk me out of it.

I kept two cars between me and the beat up brown Saturn. The last thing I could risk was to get spotted, it'd put me right back where I was before any of this started.

"We don't need to do this, there's other ways Macie," Angel said. I ignored him at first. His conversation bordered begging, which can be really annoying when you are about to commit your first felony. I pulled up to a stoplight. I took a deep breath and looked his way as I exhaled. I hoped my look told him to give up- this was going to happen whether he liked it or not. He just leaned in close, "I made a deal baby. We can get out of here," he said. He put his hand on my stomach and looked me in the eye. "All of us."

"If you want to bail, you can bail. No hard feelings. I don't have a choice," I told him. "I have to do this, and you know it. I'm going to do this. I know you're scared, I understand. For some reason, I am not," I lied. My heart raced. I tried to hide my sweaty palms from Angel by acting like I was fiddling with the windows or radio when I would wipe them on my pants. I was terrified like none other, but I was calm. I sat up and knew what I would do, had to do, and it calmed me.

Angel leaned back and sulked down in his seat. He mumbled something again about this being suicide while he rubbed his face with both hands.

I followed the Saturn and turned right. I tried to look at Angel, but noticed the dark green truck. It turned when I turned, again. I noticed it left the park when we did, here it was again. Were we being followed? I didn't say anything to Angel. He looked like he was about to lose his lunch, no reason to make him shit his pants too.

Chapter 90

"I have a problem," said Donovan Elliott. "You see, someone's been taking out some of my," he paused, "associates." He stared at the frail creature slumped over holding her head while resting her elbows on her knees.

"Just tell," she said. She struggled to lift her head. Her eyes remained closed when she managed to ask, "Why don't you tell me what you want?" asked Katherine Siebert. She was worse than ever. It was her third day riding the meth train, this was usually when she finally crashed for thirty or so hours. Donovan shook his head. He was certain she didn't remember confronting the Lynch boy earlier that morning, but he wanted to be sure.

"And someone confront-" he stopped, "Assaulted a student at Franklin High this morning." He waited, she didn't respond. "Told him all kinds of bullshit about being his mom and what not. Hear about any of that?" he asked. Her head dropped again, this time further down till it hung between her knees. Her mangy hair reached all the way to the filthy carpet. To add to the overall grime of the trailer it looked like someone had spilled a bag of cat food that had been kicked all over the place since it was dumped. The smell of cat food was only slightly stronger than the stench of garbage and shit.

Donovan walked to a cabinet. He opened and searched the bare shelves, a stack of blue

Solo cups laid on its side on the top shelf. He took the stack down and pulled it apart. Donovan took a cup from the middle of the stack and filled it with tap water. He took a long drink and refilled the cup. He walked the cup over to Katherine. Donovan grabbed a fistful of her hair and pulled her head up and back. He slowly poured the water down her face. One thing about Donovan was he was always up on his current events, especially military and all the different little wars going on in the world. His favorite story to follow of recent times was the 'Guantanamo Prison shit,' as he referred to it. The torture tactics used on suspected terrorists was an all- time favorite. Something he read all he could on, mainly to get ideas how to torture those he needed to torture. Waterboarding was his number one move. He didn't want to water board Katherine Siebert as much as he just wanted to get her to comprehend anything he said. She finally opened her eyes.

Katherine looked at Donovan standing above her head. "You holding?"

"Are you serious woman?" he asked. She looked over her left shoulder and up at him. Her biggest challenge seemed to be staying focused on the biker.

"Donovan?" she asked. Did she just again realize he was standing in front of her? "Funny thing you're here," she said. "What you need?" she asked. He gave her a puzzled look. She put her hands on his belt, more to hold herself up. "Want me suck your dick?" she asked. Frustrated, Donovan threw the remainder of the water on her, right between the eyes.

"You're out of your mind woman," he said. She looked up at him, her head wobbled till her forehead landed on his belt buckle. He backed up and she fell to her knees. "Look at you, no kid would want to be yours even if he was."

Katherine lunged toward Donovan. She landed at his feet. She laid there for a second before he realized she was sobbing. He turned around and walked away. Katherine managed enough strength to get up and jump onto his back. She hit him once with her fist before he leaned forward and flipped her off. She landed on her back and cried.

"You, look what you did. This is on you," she sobbed. Donovan ignored her and walked over to the couch. He took a pillow off the couch and walked back toward the sobbing meth head. "You're a fucking monster, you did this. Look what you did to me."

Donovan pulled a chair out and sat down so he was hovering over her head. He talked much quieter, "You shouldn't have gone to the kid woman," he said. He reached around his back while he talked. "You've risked everything, you're so fucked up you could ruin it all. This whole town would be fucked, everyone done for," he said. He pulled out a joint and lit it. He took two quick hits to make sure it was burning, then leaned down and placed it between her lips. She inhaled with her eyes closed.

"Just do it you cock sucker," she said before she took one more hit. She held the joint with her bony fingers between her lips when the pillow came smashing down. The rolled joint shot down into her mouth, Donovan couldn't tell if she choked on the joint or if it was the pillow he held down on her face with all his force. He pulled the gun out of his belt and shot once into the pillow. Her body shuttered from the gunshot, then nothing. He removed the pillow and looked at her face, frozen in shock with a lone bullet hole between the eyes. He dug his fingers into her mouth for a moment, then pulled out the crumpled bloody joint. He walked into the bathroom, flushed the red mess he fished out of her mouth, and left.

Chapter 91

The blinds were closed and door was locked in Cammy's office. She sat staring at her desk. The computer beeped, she bent down and shut it off. On her desk was her purse and bag, both were zipped up, all folders and binders she needed were packed. She picked up the phone and dialed.

Cammy waited a couple seconds, finally someone picked up on the other line. "I have something to tell you," said Cammy. "It's not good news."

She listened to the other line for a couple seconds before interrupting, "I know, I know too. This though, this news is urgent." Cammy explained her newest discovery and waited to hear the response. "I think you better," she said. She took a deep breath, "He is here today, second floor, Room 212." Cammy stood up and threw her purse over one shoulder she held the bag with her free hand. "Uh huh, just hurry, I will, I'm locking the doors now." Cammy hung up. She gave the room a quick double take, and walked out.

Chapter 92

My heart was faster than the Daytona 500 as Angel raced the car back toward Franklin. Not that I was a NASCAR person or anything, but in Franklin County you couldn't get through a day without hearing about it from someone. I had never even seen a race to be honest, even so, the few people I talked with each day there was always one. One would have to tell me who won the Drunkface 500 or whatever race it was the day before. So from the bits and pieces I know about NASCAR, I could finally relate. The speedometer was pushing 90, and in this car, that felt closer to about 115 MPH. No one saw us as far as I could tell, and we definitely weren't being followed- yet.

It felt like my chest was about to explode, but I was calm. I had to be. Angel was a wreck in the front seat, couldn't stop screaming and banging the steering wheel. "What the fuck were we thinking? I'm a dead man, a god damn dead man. Why'd you do this to me Macie?"

"Will you calm down, relax would ya?" I said. I was sitting behind him in the back seat so I leaned forward to whisper in his ear, "You have to get your shit together."

"He's going to know, he's going to know it was us," he said. Angel turned around and looked at me. His head shook in disbelief, then he looked at her. She sat there in silence. I couldn't tell if she was scared or just confused.

Angel wouldn't stop looking at the girl. The little girl I had just grabbed from her front yard. The little girl I had just kidnapped. "Oh my god, oh my god what were we thinking?"

I tried to mouth but really whispered, "Shut the fuck up." He turned back around and drove even faster. I looked down and saw she started to get frightened, or maybe more frightened. "It's OK, I'm taking you somewhere safe."

I watched the little girl give me a half smile. I smiled back in hope of fooling her. Angel continued to dwell on our impending death. Somewhere inside it started to get to me-how was I going to pull this off? What the fuck WAS I thinking?

Chapter 93

"We are going on an anonymous tip here gentlemen, so we will be proceeding with extreme caution," Danville lied. He stood in front of five other police officers in the Sinclair Gas Station parking lot across from Franklin High. "I will enter the front doors and take a direct path to the classroom in question. Officer Monroe will be with me. Officers Cherington and Keegan will position approximately 100 feet from the school's east entrance. Victor and Gates at the west," Danville ordered. He continued to address the other men.

Danville was taking no risks with his current situation, but he also had his doubts. He didn't want to cause a big scene with his entire police force storming the high school in full SWAT gear. He wanted the whole operation as quiet as it possibly could be, if very quiet at all. He was taking Monroe with him because he was one of the officers Danville always had suspicions about. He knew they all hung out at The Tattooed Lady, but Monroe was the one he felt was closest to Elliott and his boys. Danville had questioned all his men and Elliott multiple times if anyone was on the take. The question never failed to get a resounding no. The story from Elliott was always the same; Danville was his only connection on the force. Danville never believed him, even when they were on good terms. Elliott was a businessman. The more pockets he filled the better his business did.

Danville hadn't spoken to the MC President since the murder of Sam Montero. He tried to contact him a couple days earlier with no luck. Danville knew Elliott had something to do with the missing Macie and Angel. He believed that he had them so scared they skipped town, at least that's what he hoped.

The student in question was on the second floor, Room 237, the Science Lab. Danville and Monroe marched down the empty hall side by side. They kept their weapons holstered, and hoped they would remain that way. The science lab had a door in the front and back of the classroom. Danville stopped when he got to the front door, Monroe continued to the back door. Danville nodded to Monroe and walked in the front door. Monroe stayed in the hallway.

The Biology teacher, Mr. Mix, was at the front of the classroom dissecting a fetal pig when Danville walked in. He stopped talking and looked to the officer, "Can I help you Officer Danville?"

"I need to speak with a student, Cooper Lawson," Danville said. He looked to Lawson who was hunched over his own dead pig, completely oblivious to the Officers entrance.

"Um, Mr. Lawson?" asked Mix. "Are you?" he gave up and walked to Cooper. "Cooper the officer needs you for a moment," Mr. Mix said. Cooper finally looked up, still holding his scalpel and tweezers.

Danville walked beside Mix toward Cooper. He watched the boy's face when he finally looked up. He wasn't frightened, more annoyed. Danville thought he seemed more annoyed about his dissection getting interrupted than having to talk with the Chief of Police.

"Lawson," said Danville. "Come with me, I got a couple questions." Cooper remained in his seat in absolutely no rush to get up. Danville looked to Mr. Mix and saw the teacher wasn't going to be much help. He then looked at the boy and waved toward the door. Cooper's eyes followed his hand, then back to Danville.

The Chief finally had enough, "So get your ass up boy." Danville immediately regretted his tone and language, but wasn't too concerned. He dealt with these local kids on a daily basis and had grown tired of the disrespect they showed him. The disrespect they showed everyone really. If he had his way he'd throw each and every one of them in the pen for a night to get them straightened out. That wasn't unheard of in Franklin County when he was growing up. Parents would come to the police to ask them to teach a kid a lesson, the request was rarely denied.

Cooper dragged his feet down the row of tables toward the door. "Lawson!" Danville nearly shouted. Now he had the boy's full attention. Danville had his hand on his hip, just above his holstered weapon. He nodded toward the boy's hand, which still held the small dissecting scalpel.

Cooper threw it on the table like a hot coal. "Sorry sir, really sorry," he said. The words were unsteady, shaky. He messed up, completely accidental, but he knew the cop wouldn't buy it. "I forgot sir."

"The hallway," said Danville. Danville gave a half a smile, and swiveled his head around the class to put them all at ease. He never really looked at any of them as he kept an eye on Cooper at all times.

Chapter 94

It had been almost a half hour since I had committed the unthinkable. I had kidnapped a completely innocent six year- old girl. We had followed the car from the park. I kept my distance as I followed the car, and it worked perfectly. I parked in front of a house four doors down from where the car pulled into the driveway. The old neighborhood street was narrow and had a bunch of cars on it. This was good, it meant our car wouldn't draw any unwanted attention. The canopy of old, tall trees made the street kind of dark too. The mother got out of the car and walked into the house. She said something to the straggling little girl, but I couldn't make it out. The way she pointed to the driveway told me it was something like don't leave this yard. I looked at Angel, he didn't say anything. He didn't move for a couple seconds, then just shook his head a little. I'm pretty sure he still couldn't believe what we were going to do- I was going to do. The little girl played alone in the yard. She'd kick a soccer ball from the driveway to the edge of the yard then back again. We sat and watched for around five minutes, never saying a word.

"Right now," I finally said to Angel. He gave a startled jump as he looked back at me. "We can do it right now."

"You crazy chica? It's broad daylight."

"You see that woman stumble in?" I asked him. I kind of shook my head and leaned toward Angel, "She's not coming back out anytime soon." Angel continued to protest, I didn't listen. "She's either asleep on her couch already or hitting whatever it is she hits." She looked like some kind of addict, although I don't think it was meth. Probably some kind of pill popper.

"Uh uh, no way, too risky," said Angel.

"Look at this neighborhood, ain't a soul around," I said. I opened the door and turned to Angel. "You gotta drive, follow me and don't go all the way to their house until I'm ready." I smiled and got out. I left the door open for Angel to come around.

If this didn't work it would end up one of two ways, with spending the next ten years in prison being the better of the two choices. I was pretty sure a torturous, painful death would precede our departure from this world if it wasn't the law who nabbed us. That was how Angel saw it, even though he was afraid to say it out loud out of fear of losing his shit. When I got to the sidewalk I froze for a moment. There was no turning back now. I walked ahead toward the little girl. I still could have turned around. That thought disappeared when I made eye contact with her. The soccer ball kept rolling, the little girl stood frozen.

My legs grew heavier as I got closer. I could tell I was slowing down until I realized I wasn't moving at all. She stood ten feet away from me. She was my first and most important part of getting out of Franklin. Neither of us moved, our eyes were locked on each other's. I opened my mouth, but the only sound made reminded me of a tiny puppy fighting to get fed. I forced a smile, my eyes swelled up till a tear fell to the grass. The tiny little person watched me. Her head cocked to the side, and she walked toward me. She stopped a couple of feet in front of me in the only ray of sunshine coming through the treetops. The little girl's blond hair had such a white electric look I just wanted to reach out and touch it. I didn't because I was afraid of scaring her. I could feel I was shaking as it was, but I was pretty sure I hid it from her. I took a deep breath. I took a quick second to re-commit myself to the crime I was about to commit.

"Are you going to take me?" she asked. I didn't move for a brief second. I started to give a quick shake of my head, but stopped. I didn't want to lie to her, ever. I gave a slow nod. The girl looked older than six, like she was forced to be older than any six year old ever should. Her eyes were dark from the lack of quality food and sleep. She looked to her house, and back to me. "Can I go say bye?"

I knelt down so I could look into her eyes. "We gotta go."

The little girl smiled such an infectious smile it nearly broke me up. Was it a nervous smile?

"I promise though, I'm here to help you," I said. I wasn't sure what else to say. I didn't want to freak her out. I was terrified she'd start screaming and I'd have to grab her. Or would I just run?

"I know you are," she said. Then she reached up between my shirt collars and held my medallion of St. Nicholas that hung on a chain around my neck. "I'm not afraid." She smiled and put her hand to her chest. She reached into her t-shirt and pulled out a matching medallion. Hannah Cross looked into my eyes and gave me another one of those smiles.

Chapter 95

The school hallway was empty except for Danville, Assistant Principal Savard, Cooper, and Officer Monroe. Cooper watched as the Officer emptied all contents of his locker into a plastic container marked evidence. From the little bit Danville had seen of the locker it didn't seem he had anything any other fifteen year- old boy might have.

"Have you contacted Ms. Hart yet?" Danville asked Ms. Savard.

"No one has heard from her since she left due to illness," she responded.

"She left?" asked Danville. "Can you tell me what time?"

"Roberta said it was some time ago, at least an hour," she said. Danville stood still for a moment, then walked away.

From what Danville could tell Cameron Hart's office was empty of any personal belongings. He went through desk drawers and cabinets. Everything was gone but pens, pencils, and school issued books. Danville couldn't say he'd blame her if she took off and left Franklin for good. Why though, would she make up a story about an innocent student? Why would she say Cooper wrote a letter threatening to shoot a teacher?

Chapter 96

We drove to an abandoned farm to meet Vampire Eddie. Angel had worked out a deal with Eddie and the Vandals. We were going to meet Eddie so he could witness me call Miss Hart and tell her I needed to see her. Then I would be done with Franklin County forever. I told myself I would do anything in the world to save my baby, but how far would I go? I was starting to have second thoughts as we drove down Highway J.

"I can't do it Angel," I said. He looked at me, then back at the road. "I'm for real, I can't kill anyone."

"Good, cuz you ain't."

"We are. There's no fucking difference," I said. "Turn around. I'm not doing it."

"Too late Mace," he said. He didn't look at me this time as he turned the car into the gravel driveway. He rarely called me Mace. It was a name he used when he was pissed, same way a mother would use her kid's middle name with the first.

"This isn't the farm," I said. I watched as we passed a rusted out bus. Then we came up on an old decrepit farm house with a wraparound porch that no longer wrapped around the whole house. I saw the police tape near the barn. The half painted car was still sitting in front of the barn, still streaked with blood stains. The blood stains of Milton Hawkins. We were at his farm where police killed him just a couple months earlier. "What's going on Angel?"

Angel stopped the car in front of the barn. He turned off the ignition and removed the keys. "Get out."

"Why are we here? What's going on?" I asked again. He ignored me and looked at his phone. He told me again to get out of the car, I didn't move. The side door on the barn opened. Vampire Eddy, who we were supposed to be meeting at a warehouse two miles away, did not walk out. I watched in complete shock and disbelief when I saw who walked out; she walked toward the driver's side door. Angel got out.

Miss Hart walked up to Angel, they stood face to face, then she kissed him. He wrapped his arms around her and kissed her back. What was going on? I jumped out of the car and walked a few steps toward them. "What the fuck?" I yelled. Miss Hart looked at me, but it wasn't her. I mean it was her, but not the helpful Counselor I had known. She didn't have that caring, nurturing look. I could feel a cold rush over me as she stared through my eyes and down to my stomach. I looked at Angel hoping for some kind of answer. He didn't even look in my direction. "You called Eddy. Didn't you make a deal with Eddy?" I asked Angel. He just looked at her.

A blast from a gun filled the air. The birds scattered from the trees. My ears immediately started to ring from the roar of the cannon. It felt like it was only a few feet away, then Angel fell. I looked to Miss Hart, she was holding the gun. Smoke slowly rose as Angel's face hit the gravel. His body lay still.

"Angel," I screamed. I think. I don't know why. He had clearly set me up, if she didn't kill him I might have done it myself. I was on the ground trying to back away from her. I had fallen when she shot Angel. "What are you doing?" I screamed. Miss Hart walked toward me. I held back from becoming hysterical, but I screamed as loud as I could. I didn't scream for Angel, but I didn't want him dead. It was the first time I had ever seen anyone murdered. He had cheated on me with my counselor, set me up, lied to me for who knows how long so I didn't care he was dead. "Someone please help me!" I cared about my baby, and myself.

"Sweetie," said Miss Hart. She shook her head at me; she seemed to be oblivious to my terror. "Eddy wouldn't make a deal for something that doesn't exist," she said. She reached behind her back and started to mess under her shirt. Her hands came around and pulled at her under shirt.

My heart landed somewhere in the pit of my stomach.

What the fuck just happened?

Miss Hart pulled off a prosthetic baby bump. She threw the fake stomach and breast piece on the gravel driveway. "See, your plan wouldn't have worked," she said.

She wasn't pregnant. "You're not-" I started to say but stopped. My mind raced. Was she in on it the whole time? Was Angel?

"They'd never find anyone to adopt that," she said. She pointed to the pregnant belly girdle or whatever it was laying on the ground. My eyes were locked on it, the deceit and abandonment of everything in my life. I felt like

I was paralyzed in a dream. I couldn't move or speak. My nightmare took another step toward me, and smiled.

"What are you planning-?"

"Well," she said. She smiled some kind of sick and twisted smile. "I was planning on doing this on my own, you know, getting a baby." She stopped and looked at me. It was the same look she gave me when she slapped the cigarette out of my mouth in the diner. "All you girls seem to get pregnant every time one of these boys pulls out a pecker, and none of you are fit to be mothers. When I started digging through this whole mess with you and Ray I figured out what Donovan and them have been doing."

"You're not going to get away with this, they won't let you," I said.

"No, no, you got it all wrong," she said. She took a couple more steps and was right over me. "I made the deal with Eddy," she said. She nodded to my stomach. "That baby up for adoption, well, I'm the one adopting it," she said. She covered her hands with her mouth like she just discovered a great piece of gossip. If she didn't have the gun I would have attacked her right there. I was having a hard time holding myself back even with the gun. "Donovan had twenty thousand on Angel's head. I used what I got," she said. She spread her arms out to fully show her body. She looked like she hadn't been pregnant for some time. "Now I got what I need."

She held the gun up toward my chest. Miss Hart bent down and put her head to my stomach. My body froze as her hand slid under my shirt and began to rub my stomach. "I will finally have my baby."

I could feel the hot tears streaking down my face, and tried to control them, get them to stop. "I, I thought you were my friend?" I asked. She talked to my stomach, completely oblivious to my question. She stopped rubbing and brought her face up to mine.

"Just imagine what Angel thought," she said. She nodded toward his dead corpse. "For the record he was against the pictures. I knew you'd love 'em," she said. Her head tilted and she slowly slid her fingers down the side of my face. "I knew you'd come to find someone you could confide in. Someone you could talk to."

"How could you? How could you do this?"

She smiled, "It's very easy, you just give the guy what he wants and he'll pretty much do anything." Miss Hart licked her lips, then puckered them to make a popping sound. "You're still young, but one day you'll learn how to keep a man. Maybe, if you can be a good listener now," she said with a smile. She stood up and held out a hand. I ignored her hand and slowly got up by myself. I wanted to knock the bitch out, and thought about how to make my move. I would have to get my shit together in a big way. Get control of myself. Then I could get the gun from her because I was pretty sure I couldn't get to mine in my purse. When I finally stood up I was light headed and my knees shook I could have passed out, but I don't think I did. I'm pretty sure someone hit me in the back of the head. Everything went black.

Chapter 97

This was now a missing person's case in Danville's mind. Macie and Angel had been gone for three days.

He left Cammy's apartment and started to drive. The options were starting to dwindle, all leads came up empty. He racked his brain to think of something Cammy could have said that he missed. Something he saw in the apartment he missed. He had nothing.

The officer's who went to Cooper's trailer found nothing illegal. They didn't even find any legal, registered weapons. "That's odd in Franklin County," the relaying Officer told Danville.

Cooper Lawson was Macie's neighbor, and not much more than that, no matter what he liked to claim. The kid said they were good friends, but hadn't spoken to her in over a week. He really only talked to her in passing or their Art class. He didn't know where she was, and hadn't seen anyone at her trailer in days. He said he always kept a close watch out for her too because he didn't like Angel or his company. Danville figured Macie must have mentioned his name to Cammy once and that's why she chose him. Whatever was going on Danville had come to the conclusion that the counselor might not be what she had made herself out to be. Not good for Macie, he had to find her fast.

Danville passed by The Vandals clubhouse on the way back to the station. Passers- by wouldn't even know it was home to the notorious Vandals, it was such a basic looking building. Elliott tried to act like he wanted the club to have a low profile, but rarely hesitated wearing his patch, even in public buildings. The clubhouse looked abandoned as he passed. There wasn't a single vehicle or bike in the parking lot.

Danville drove in a daze. His mind had gone blank. He needed something to point him in a direction, any direction. He parked the car and stared at the police station. He could see the reflection of the setting sun in the glass doors. Danville squinted at the doors and made out a figure in the setting sun. Danville recognized the man on the steps. It was Jake Hood, a town drunk. He was beyond inebriated, barely able to stand. Danville shook his head as he watched the drunk, then reached for his cuffs. Hood watched Danville get out of his squad car and waved to the Sheriff with his free hand. The other hand was preoccupied holding the man's junk as he took a long piss all over the steps to the Franklin County Police Station. Danville didn't know it, but the drunk pisser was about to give the Sheriff the answer he'd been looking for.

Chapter 98

"Macie listen to me, Macie wake up," someone whispered. I was lying down, trying to open my eyes. I could hear talking, not sure what was being said. Was I still dreaming? Was it all a dream? "Sweetie, wake up."

My eyes opened, but my nightmare continued. The smiling counselor was leaning over me. I could see her mouth moving. What was she saying?

"It's me Macie, your friend Miss Hart," she said. She wiped my face with a wet rag. "I'm the one who saved you."

"Huh?" I asked. My head cleared and everything came back to me. I wanted to go back to sleep. I wanted to be anywhere else.

"Saved me?"

She smiled and leaned close to me, "Angel, he was planning on killing you. I'm going to help you, you can have your life back."

"You're not getting my baby."

"Macie, who do you think took care of Ray and Sam for you?" she asked. For me? I held back from saying it aloud. "Ray was a pervert doper who would tell the MC as soon as you girls got knocked up. He's the one who told Elliott you were pregnant again."

"No, what, what are you talking about?"

"Sam was a fucking patsy, did whatever he was told. He kept Elliott's men on all of you. Let'em get away with anything Donovan wanted.

They can't hurt you anymore," she said. She smiled and nodded to me like I owed her for a favor.

"You," I said, "Will not get my baby."

"Macie, I am going to get your baby, and I'm going to give it an amazing life. Something you would never be able to do."

I shook my head, my stomach tightened as I tried to break free. My arms were tied to a hospital bed, my legs were too. My eyes filled up with tears, but I refused to cry for that bitch. I let out a scream, she didn't flinch, just sat and watched me.

"You knew Elliott was going to take your baby, think of the good news. You'll know your baby is safe being raised by me, not some random couple you never met. You don't have to worry, you'll get your cut still. You can leave now, and I'll get what I always dreamed of. It's what we both wanted." She smiled, then giggled like she was one of the naïve girls at school, "I'm gonna be a mommy."

"No, no, let me out of here, I'll kill you," I screamed. I tried like hell to kick and fight my way out of the restraints. It was no surprise my results were the same as before.

"Want to know my most favorite part of all of it Macie?" she asked. I stopped kicking and stared at the ceiling. I heard her, but wasn't going to give her the satisfaction of looking at her again. She leaned close so only I could hear, "You gave me the idea. You told me where to find my baby when you came to me that first time. You looked for help, you wanted someone to help you. Macie, you asked me to do this."

She was out of her mind. I watched her eyes as she told me this. She tried to look warm and loving, but there was that look in her eyes. She was prepared to kill me, and anyone else in her way. I began to wonder how I'd defend myself if I could get loose. I was not a killer. I wasn't a criminal of any sort. My only goal for the last two years had been to leave all those elements in my life behind me, to escape the people I had been surrounded by who lived that lifestyle. I guess life and other circumstances often change us as people. After all, that is life. Isn't it? We adapt to the situation at hand if we want to survive. Kidnapping was a crime that had never spent any time as a thought in my head. Now I was technically a kidnapper. If I had to, for the sake of my child, I would be a killer too.

Chapter 99

The drunk stumbled away from the Sheriff, completely oblivious to the fact he was getting off easy. Normally the man would have been thrown into a cell head first, literally. Danville didn't have time to deal with a drunk at the moment, he finally had a breakthrough. He hoped.

He raced through the front office, barely acknowledging Officer Dean's presence at the front desk. Danville went into the lab and shut the door. He began digging through the cabinet labeled H-J until he pulled out a file on Cameron Hart.

Somewhere in his subconscious Danville knew what had been going on. There were rumors, of course, that The Vandals had a hand in sex trafficking and even something with black market adoption. He thought back to J.C. Jennings and Macie, who always told him her sister had been pregnant. He had never listened to the little girl, or J.C's boyfriend. Danville realized at that moment he hadn't ignored them because of J.C. had been an addict. He ignored them because he was a coward. He was told the death had been an overdose and her body got tore up by coyotes and other wild animals. It made sense, and it allowed him to clean his hands of the situation. There was always the guilt though; he knew the girl had been clean. He was forced to frame her boyfriend to put him away. That's why he always kept an eye on Macie, guilt can be the most addictive drug.

Danville dug through the file until he finally found what he was looking for. When Cammy was brought in and questioned in the death of Sam Montero she would have been looked up on the national database. He looked at the screen, and fell back into his chair. Danville stared at the screen. His arm dropped the mouse that held the weight of his entire failure as a police officer. He could feel the pit of his stomach hollow out, a lump formed in his throat. He stared at Cameron Hart's life before Franklin, his whole world locked in on the box next to marital status. Now he had no choice, he couldn't ignore Franklin any longer. He had said he was going to start anew, be an honest cop. Now he had to decide how to do that, and where to begin.

Chapter 100

The red pick-up truck drove on a gravel road through a wooded are. Donovan pulled out his phone and dialed a number. "We're here," he said when someone picked up the other line, "In back." He hung up and turned to the two men in the front seat with him. He gave them a smile that wasn't returned. The man in the middle was middle aged and professional looking. He stared straight ahead, barely acknowledging the MC President. The older, rougher looking man in the passenger seat mumbled something Donovan couldn't make out. He couldn't make out his expression through the hat pulled down covering the top of his face so he figured he was better off just ignoring the comment all together.

A garage bay door opened. Vampire Eddy walked out of the bus depot's side door. He unlocked the gate, and opened it enough for the truck to pull in the lot. Eddy was sure to close and re- lock the gate. The truck pulled into the opened bay door. Eddy followed, and closed the bay door. He led the men to a six foot tall metal cabinet. Eddy opened the cabinet door, it was empty besides one of Kurtz's coats hanging off to the side. Eddy reached in and pushed the back wall of the cabinet. The back of the cabinet popped open to reveal a spiral staircase.

"Follow me, Gentlemen," Eddy smiled. Elliott gave him a look that told him the niceties wouldn't be needed, or encouraged. The four men walked down the staircase.

The basement was nothing like the two men Elliott had brought with him expected. The room was 20' x 30' and had been completely refinished to resemble an operating room. The floor was tiled and the walls were freshly painted. A row of stainless steel cabinets lined the far wall. A table and chairs were set up to the left of the door to act as a waiting room. There were two mobile monitors near the center of the room. A large, overhead operating light hung from the ceiling. There was a hospital bed below the light. In the bed was a young girl, her arms and legs had been strapped to the bed. The girl was unconscious.

"She was getting out of hand," said Vampire Eddy. The younger of the two men, the professional looking one, looked at Eddy and shook his head. He walked over to one of the monitors.

"So you cracked her?" Donovan asked. He didn't yell, but his tone told Eddy he wasn't happy. Eddy shook his head, he tried to say something to cover his ass.

"I did," said Cammy. "She saw Kurtz," Cammy said. She nodded to the far corner of the basement hospital room. Kurtz had been Sam Montero's replacement as Transportation Coordinator, a position that was becoming one of the more dangerous jobs to have in Franklin County. Eddy had sat him up in the chair, but made no attempt to hide the bullet hole in his forehead. Donovan walked over and threw a sheet over the dead man.

"She's ok. Why would you do this?" asked the professional man.

"She freaked out when she saw him," Cammy responded.

He set the black bag he had been holding on a small table near the girl. He started pulling out different operating tools. The man gave Elliott a look of disapproval. This had been discussed previously, and would be the only mistake. If he was going to be the doctor in charge he would make all decisions that concerned the girl. Elliott nodded to let him know he understood. He gave Eddy a look that said 'No more fuck- ups.'

"What kind of time frame we looking at Doc?" Elliott asked. The Doctor brushed him off as he spread a clear gel on the girl's stomach. He moved a monitor closer to him and turned it on. He took the wand attached to the monitor and rubbed it in the gel on the girl's pregnant belly. When he seemed to have found what he was looking for he took a seat on a stool while he continued with the ultrasound. The girl started to move, her eyes opened.

"She's thirty- six weeks pregnant," he said. He turned to Elliott, "We can take the baby."

Elliott nodded his approval.

Chapter 101

The rush of energy came from my chest and fired through all my limbs. I felt the warmth in my arm where the IV was inserted, where the medicine came from. There were voices, I couldn't make them out at first. I opened my eyes. The voices faded off, I heard them but didn't know what they said. My attention was stolen.

I watched him for the first time. I saw my baby. I watched his leg kick, the kick I could feel just a second earlier. I had never seen an ultrasound before, not in person anyway, and definitely not of a child inside me. I just watched him kick and move his arms around. I heard the voices, people argued about something, but I tuned it all out. I knew they were going to try a C-Section so this might be the only time I ever got to see him. I laid there watching until I couldn't take the Doctor's gaze any longer. I tried to wipe my eyes, but was quickly reminded that I was tied down. I closed them for a long second before I finally looked at the Doctor.

"He's sucking his thumb," he said. I smiled briefly, then reality kicked me in the stomach. This man was here to take my baby and give it to Donovan who was going to sell him on the black market. He was going to sell it to some rich couple who didn't want to have to wait to go through all the state adoption bullshit, or couldn't. No he wasn't. I remembered now, Miss Hart was taking my boy.

"Fuck you," I said. I turned to Donovan, Miss Hart, Vampire Eddy, and then I saw him. The man responsible for killing my sister sat on a chair along the back of the room. I could barely see his eyes below the rim of his Vietnam Veteran baseball cap. I looked right at him and lost whatever control I had over my mental state. I started to kick and scream like I'd never kicked and screamed before. I wanted to bust right out of the restraints. I gave it all I had. "Fuck you!" I screamed. "You piece of shit, fuck you!"

Donovan jumped up and grabbed my shoulders. I could feel someone else jump on my legs. Whoever it was got whatever I could muster from my knees, it was a solid hit to someone's forehead. It wasn't enough though. I threw my head from side to side, and screamed louder than I ever had. Then I felt the warmth start in my forearm and quickly spread through my body. I couldn't move or talk. I remember Donovan's face only inches from mine.

"You little bitch, why are you all so God Damned stupid? I'm giving you a gift, a get of jail free. Huh, how do you think you got out of that hell last time? Who got you out of there? Me. You can't be a mother, none of you can. I'm helping you, I'm giving you more money you could ever dream..."

I heard him, but didn't listen. I just had one thought go through my head over and over again. I would kill him and Boone Cross if I lived. I would kill them both. Then it all went black.

Chapter 102

I was nine. My mother was there, in the hospital room. I was sitting in a chair next to the bed where my sister sat up, smiling. She held her newborn girl. The baby opened her eyes, beautiful ocean blue eyes. My sister's boyfriend commented how he had never seen a baby with such blue eyes. He'd swear it was my baby if he hadn't watched my sister give birth hours earlier. I smiled as he placed the baby in my waiting arms.

I smiled at the baby's father as his chest exploded. I listened to my sister scream as she absorbed gunfire from the assailant in the hospital doorway. I watched Boone Cross murder them then turn the weapon on me-

I woke up screaming to real gunfire. The dream was a life that was just that, a dream that never materialized. My sister never gave birth in a hospital. I couldn't tell you when my mother smiled at me last, but I know it was long before I was nine years old. None of that happened, except their death-at the hands of Boone Cross.

Chapter 103

Reality check- gunfire. I was surrounded by a hailstorm of bullets- strapped down to a hospital bed. The doctor who had been giving me an ultrasound before I lost consciousness was slumped down against the wall. His once white shirt was now splattered with red, shredded by the ammunition that did the same to his body. A red streak climbed up the wall from where he slid down to see his final living vision- me. A tied up teenage girl who's baby he was willing to help steal, for what? Money.

I could feel a hand tugging on my restraints, my hands were loose, then my feet. The gunfire continued. Vampire Eddy turned to my bed to pounce on me, but was interrupted with a blast that sent him flying into the doctor. An arm reached down and pulled me under the hospital bed. I fell under the bed and a body covered me. It was Miss Hart. I looked at my counselor and tried to fight through the sedation. What's going on? What had happened to Angel? Didn't she-

"Is my baby alright?" she asked. Everything raced back faster than the bullet that ripped into her ass. Her eyes grew wide as she let out a scream, "Shit!" The second shot knocked her clear off me as it tore into her ribcage. She landed on her back next to me. Miss Hart reached for me, "Please take care of my-"

Her hand landed on my stomach as she took her last breath. I swatted the hand off of my baby she would never know. Then everything stopped.

I could see Eddy's handgun just on the other side of Miss Hart. Without making a sound I leaned over and grabbed the gun. I hid it under the hospital gown and came back to rest where I was next to my dead counselor. I was pretty sedated and wasn't sure if I could move enough to get up. I took a deep breath, but froze when I heard the steps.

The slow heavy steps were only a few feet from me. My whole body froze. I looked to my right toward the door, where the steps were coming from. The bed sheet that had kept me hidden hung down to only a couple inches off the floor. The steps grew closer. He took another step and I saw the black boot right next to my bed.

I gripped the gun tight. This would be the one chance I'd have to kill Donovan Elliott. My hands were sweating, I was afraid the gun was going to slip out of my hands and fly across the room when I pulled the trigger. I tried to steady myself as I brought the gun up and aimed it toward his knees. If he leaned down to grab me I was going to take his head right off his body. I thought of my sister. This was for her.

"Ya' all right?" he asked. My mind raced to place the voice. It wasn't Donovan, but I knew the voice. Or did I? "Macie, I know you're down there. You ok?" he asked again. I took a slow breath, I did not know who was up there.

"I have a gun," I said. He took a deep breath, maybe a sigh of relief.

"Well hold on to it," he said. "I'm going to lift this sheet, alright."

"No," I said. I wasn't really sure why I blurted it out so quickly. Probably because I just woke up in a gunfight and someone I didn't know seemed to be the only one left standing. For all I knew he was one of Donovan's cronies.

"It's ok, I'm a friend of Mirko."

Chapter 104

Mirko was the only person in the world I still trusted. Not because he did anything to earn that trust really, well, before he sent this man to save me from getting my baby ripped from my stomach and sold to some crazy bitch. I trusted him more because he was the only one left who hadn't bulldozed my trust like an abandoned meth lab.

Mirko was The Bosnian. I met him, officially I guess, the day he was attacked by Cooper's dogs. That was when I knew I had to get out of Franklin. When I realized I had to leave before I ended up tied up to a gurney surrounded by Goons who were going to steal my baby. Or just ended up dead. I had gone looking for Angel, I needed him to help me out of there. I don't know why I didn't just leave. Probably because I was scared. I went everywhere I thought Angel might be, the last place I looked was The Tattooed Lady.

I had driven to The Lady and parked, my mind went back and forth if I should go in or not. I sat in my car for about twenty minutes before I came to a decision- the wrong one. Two Vandals I had never seen came right up to me. They were young, not much older than me really. The little scrawny one had a long greasy goatee to go with his dark hockey hair mullet. The other guy was average height but built. He had a rock solid body with a shaved head and a shit load of tattoos. He looked like he wanted to be a professional wrestler from his build. That dream and any dreams of climbing the ranks in The Vandals were surely held back by the baby face that got him carded every time he bought a pack of Camels. Apparently Donovan had already put a mark on Angel's head, and these two dirt bags were willing to do anything to get the attention of the mighty Donovan Elliott.

"Hey girlie," the little one said. I thought about running as soon as I saw them. "We need to ask you about your friend, you know the one."

I took two steps back before bumping into Stone Cold Dick Face. My heart raced when the little one started talking, my attention focused on trying to figure his intentions. I must have missed the other one get between me and the door.

"Funny," I said. I wanted to say that was what I was doing there too, looking for Angel. My mind blanked though. All I could think of was getting as far from these two as I could. The base pounded into my chest against my beating heart. It was a furious competition to break my body.

"What's so funny?" said the little guy. I just stared at him.

"I gotta go," I said. I turned and walked into Stone Cold, my head bounced right off his chest. I tried to scoot to my right to get past him. He shuffled his feet that way to block my path.

"Pardon me buddy," a voice said in broken English. All three of us looked behind Stone Cold right at the entrance. The Bosnian stood tall, he smiled and held his hand out to me. At first the two Vandals were in a state of shock

I think, that someone would interfere in their little shakedown. I took his hand and hopped around Stone Cold. I took cover between The Bosnian and the door.

"Who the fuck you?" asked the little Vandal.

"Her bro- der."

"Bro- what?" asked the little guy. "You don't even speak no English you foreign piece of shit."

The Bosnian smiled at the two bikers. I felt his hand on my stomach. He gently pushed me further back from him toward the door. Before I could grasp what was going on both his hands shot up into Stone Cold's chest. The crack from The Bosnian's head that smashed Stone Cold's nose was so loud the stripper almost fell off her pole. The little guy made a move for the gun strapped to his back, but was dropped by his flying biker brother.

The Bosnian grabbed me by the hand and pulled me out of The Tattooed Lady. He started to pull me toward his dark green pick up, but I pulled him toward my car. "I can't leave my car, they know it." He froze for half a second, then nodded. We got in my car and I peeled out of the parking lot. I ran the red light at the parking lot and gave a quick look back toward The Lady.

"It's ok," he said. "No one coming."

I got on the highway right away and headed north. After about thirty seconds I turned to The Bosnian. "Who the fuck are you?" I asked. Kind of yelled really, but he wasn't fazed.

"I am Mirko," he said. He said it as casually as you would meeting someone at a church fucking function.

"Mirko?" I yelled for real now. "I don't care what your damn name is. Who are you? Why do you keep showing up in my life?" I still yelled.

"Friend. I am friend for you," he said. I gave him a quick glance and shrugged my shoulders. His English may have sucked, but body language is universal. He figured he obviously hadn't given me the answer I was looking for. "Slow car, slow down, no police," he said. I slowed to sixty- five, then looked at him again for my answer. "I am best friend to Milton."

Chapter 105

Mirko began his story from the beginning. He had gone to prison for robbery. Once he stole twenty- five thousand dollars from a drug dealer in downtown St. Louis, killed five men in that robbery. That wasn't why he went to prison though, and he wasn't a thief. He wanted it clear he wasn't even a criminal, at least not by choice. Before going to prison he worked in a factory that made janitorial supplies. He worked as a mixer of industrial floor cleaner and made good money. Good enough compared to what he made before he escaped the war torn Bosnia only a couple years earlier.

The Bosnian population was quite large in St. Louis. The majority of these Bosnians had fled the country's Civil War back in the 1990's. This hadn't always been a popular settlement for Mirko's countrymen, just in the last ten or fifteen years.

Mirko avoided all criminal activities when he arrived in America. He came for a new beginning, there'd be no reason to leave much of his family and friends if he was going to turn to crime. He could have made quite a life as a criminal in Bosnia, so when he came to America he told himself he was going to be straight. The job as a mixer provided his 'American Dream.'

His dream came to an end after two years. It wasn't his fault, or anything he did. Unless you consider blind loyalty a fault, which in some cases it may be. In this case of family it was. Mirko had a brother who stayed back in Bosnia. Like Mirko he decided there'd be no reason to come to America to be a criminal if you could be a successful criminal back in the homeland. So Mirko's brother stayed back and began a life as a small time hood and shitty gambler. It was a foolproof plan until he tried to screw over the wrong person. That's when Mirko received a care package from the local Bosnian Gangsters. The package was a pair of severed thumbs, his brother's. Mirko had no choice but to start knocking off the dealers in the city. His brother had started selling drugs for some very dangerous people, but much of his product ended up in his nose. He was left with a debt he couldn't pay off. The Bosnian Mobsters already had control of everything in the homeland so they wanted to expand. Expansion in the drug trade meant expanding territory, which meant stealing some territory. Mirko became the point man in the Bosnian Drug Expansion in St. Louis.

The Bosnians knew Mirko had been a decorated soldier in his old life, stealing from some junky thugs was just a hunting expedition to him. He barely broke a sweat paying off his brother's debt. It took him six months to square up his brother with the Gangsters. He would go back to living the American Dream as Immigrant Factory Worker. There was one problem: Mirko was too damn good. They refused to release him of his duties, going back on their very word of his brother's freedom. Mirko refused to work for the Bosnians again. That's when he received the second package pertaining to his brother. There were no body parts in this package. Just photographs of Mirko's brother, his sister, and their parents. The Bosnians took everything from Mirko, every person he had ever loved.

The gangsters thought this would leave Mirko with little choice but to continue working for them. He refused in a way they had never experienced. Mirko began his revenge by taking out every Bosnian gangster he had ever been in contact with. His goal was to kill them all, and had almost completed his task when a city officer arrested him. The officer was on the gangster's payroll. Mirko was framed for an unsolved liquor store robbery, a robbery someone had an abundance of inside knowledge of. The lawyer's evidence was weak, but the judge didn't seem to care. Mirko went to prison for six and a half years.

Prison was as good as a death sentence to Mirko. The imprisoned Bosnian's were all part of the crime ring that Mirko had waged war against. He was as good as dead, until my sister's boyfriend saved his ass. Mirko never gave me many of the details except he was a kick or two away from blacking out in the showers when everyone stopped. J.C's boyfriend and some friends, if that's the word, stopped whatever was going on. They also had enough pull in the prison to get the beatings to stop. In the end, he just told me his newest debt was me. For the rest of Mirko's life he was to protect me, and all those who meant the world to me.

Chapter 106

"A friend of Mirko?" I asked. I didn't wait for an answer, "He didn't come here, did he?"

The man pulled up the sheet, then pulled me out from under the bed. I froze at first glance of the big biker. He was around forty, with long dark hair and a long dark beard. He looked overweight but I could tell by the lack of effort he used to lift me he was stronger than any boy I'd ever been with. "He's waiting for us, at the tree," he said. My mind was put at ease when he used our secret name for our meeting place if anything should get messed up, the tree. The man saw me staring at his black leather vest, he could tell I was a bit confused about whose side he was on. He chuckled to himself when he realized I thought he might have been a Vandal.

The man smiled big and shook his head no to reassure me. Then the back of his head shot a red spray behind him all over the red tiles. His mouth dropped open and froze. I tried to grab him but he fell to his knees before he toppled over onto his stomach. I started to shoot the gun behind me before I even looked to see where the shot came from. I stepped over the big biker, and ran out of the room away from the gunfire. The last thing I remembered in the room was looking at the man's back and saw the rocker on his vest was not Vandals. It read B.A.C.A.

I got out of the operating room and slammed the door shut behind me. I was in some kind of basement or boiler room. There were no windows. I didn't know where to go so I just ran from the door. I got about twenty feet around a wall and saw steps going up. I ran up the steps and opened the door at the top. I was in an office, but could see daylight coming from a door down the hall so that's where I ran. I was outside before I could gather in my surroundings. It was light outside. I couldn't tell what time of day, but it was snowing. I remembered I had heard on the radio it was going to snow tomorrow, which I guessed was now today. I looked around and realized where I was. In the distance I could see the football stadium, and my school was on the opposite side. I had been in the bus depot.

"Freeze," someone yelled. I knew the voice.

"Danville?" I yelled back. I couldn't see him, or tell where he was.

"Macie Jennings, drop the gun," he yelled. Danville walked out from behind the dumpster. He had his pointed at me, I raised my gun at him. "I said drop your weapon!"

"I can't," I said. He raised the gun. Listen, they're going to be right behind me."

"Who?" he asked. "Who's down there, what's going on?"

"I don't-" I stopped when the door swung open. I saw Danville swing his gun toward the door as I turned to face Donovan Elliott. Boone Cross came out behind Donovan. Elliott had a gun pointed at me before he realized Danville had him in his sights.

"Girl, you are starting to really piss me off," said Elliott. I aimed my gun at Donovan, he kept his aimed right at my head.

"Drop the weapon Donovan," yelled Danville. He took a few steps closer to Elliott and Boone Cross. Donovan didn't flinch.

"You done your job here Chad, time for you to," he said and stopped as he made a walking motion with his free hand.

"That's not going to happen."

"Don't be a dumb ass Chad, get the fuck out of here," Donovan said. He turned his gun from me to Danville. "Now," he said. He watched Danville set his sights right on the President patch on his vest.

"Not this time Donovan, this ain't the deal."

"Ain't the fucking deal?" Elliott yelled. "You don't get no fucking deals. You get your job and do what you are told. That's the fucking deal!"

"I know you been stealing these girl's babies. I know about Hannah, Boone. I know she was J.C's baby, and you killed that girl so you could take the baby," Danville yelled. I listened as all my fears, assumptions, and everything else inside was finally said aloud. Someone else knew the truth. They did kill my sister. They did take her baby. I was right, Milton was right. I watched as Boone started to walk toward Danville.

"You don't know shit. That's my girl. Hannah is my daughter, and Ezzy's."

"Ezzy?" Danville asked. "She was first wasn't she? You took her when you killed Theresa Rosa twenty five years ago."

"You're a dead man Danville," Boone yelled. He started to run toward Danville when two shots rang out and Boone crumpled into the snow. It took me a second to realize what was going on. Shots were being fired, I dove to the ground, and then there was silence. I looked at my hand in the snow. The gun was next to it, snow melted around it and condensation climbed the warm barrel. I had done it. I shot Boone Cross. I took a deep breath and turned my body to see Donovan lying in the snow on his back. Danville was on his stomach a few feet from where he had been standing. He army crawled in my direction. I could tell he was shot, but I only saw blood on his shoulder and arm.

"Macie, Macie are you ok?"

"Did you do it, did you kill him?" I asked. He looked in Elliott's direction, but didn't say anything. "Are you OK?"

He just gave a slight head nod. "I will be."

"Over here, help me. I need a doctor," Boone mumbled. I got up and walked over to the man who took everything I ever loved. I stood over him and aimed my gun at his head.

"Macie," Danville said. "Macie don't do it."

I heard him, but he knew I wasn't listening to anything at that moment. I had waited for six years for Boone Cross, I just never knew it until that moment.

"Please, please call an ambulance," Boone whispered now. The evil I've looked for since I was a girl personified. This was my chance to avenge the murder of my sister, the abduction of my niece, and all the girls who've had their babies stolen by this monster.

"Where's my baby?" I asked. Boone gave me a blank stare.

"I'll die, I need a doctor."

"Last December, Donovan took my child, where is he?"

"I don't know, don't know what you're talking about," he said. "That's all him, I don't know where they end up."

I watched the monster as he begged for his life. He pleaded with me to ignore all the pain he had caused me over the last six years of my life. I pulled back the hammer on the gun. I had it pressed to his temple. His face wedged between the snow covered gravel and the pistol in my hand. A trail of blood flew from his mouth into the snow. He coughed again, this time the blood shot further with the growing intensity of the cough as his lungs struggled to find air.

"Macie it's not worth it," Danville yelled. "You don't want to go to jail." My hand shook as I visualized the dream of my sister with her baby. She lived in the farmhouse with Milton and Hannah. They had a couple of dogs. Tears rolled down my cheek and landed in the snow.

"He took everything from me," I yelled.

"Not everything."

"He doesn't deserve to live."

"It's over now. You can't kill him," he said. "I know you have Hannah," he said. "Think about her, she needs someone."

I didn't say anything, but watched as Boone's breaths grew shorter and shorter. I released the trigger and let the gun drop to my side. I didn't have to shoot him again. The job was done, he would never see life outside of this parking lot. I knelt down and pressed my mouth to Boone's ear, "I want you to know this before you die," I whispered. "This was all for my sister and Milton." I watched as he approached his inevitable end. I smiled and looked in his eyes, "And Hannah will never step foot in Franklin County again. I pray you learn my pain, the torment you have left for all in your wake, and above all, I pray that you enjoy hell." Boone gave a last ditch effort to grab me, but it was really more of a tremor. His body shook with a grunt as he gave a weak blood soaked cough.

I turned away and walked toward Danville. He rolled onto his back so he could see me. His arm was covered in blood, his left leg had also been shot just above the knee. "How fast do you need an ambulance?" I asked.

He closed his eyes tight and grimaced, "I'd say pretty damn fast," he said.

"You're going to have to wait for your buddies to get here, they'll call an ambulance," I said. I knew he'd be pissed, but I had no choice.

"Get my radio," he said.

"I'm sorry Danville," I said. I knelt down next to him. "You know I have to leave, I can't stay here. If I call or even if you call right now I won't have time to get my things and leave. You gotta give me a head start."

"You have Hannah, don't you?" he asked. He looked me in the eyes and gave a half chuckle. "That's why Boone was here, why he showed his face."

"I don't know why he was here."

"Yeah ya do, he was the one running the show. We always suspected there was someone above Donovan, knew he wasn't smart enough to pull off some of the shit they did."

"I'll make sure someone is out here soon. I'm sorry Danville." I got up and walked past Boone to the dead Donovan Elliott. I smiled at the look of shock on the dead President's face. He thought he had everyone in his pocket, finally someone turned on him. Finally someone said enough is enough. I took the key ring off his belt and walked back to Danville. "Finally got the bad guy Chad," I said with a smile.

"Right place at the wrong time," he said. He took a deep breath. I knew his mind was racing. What would be the ramifications of killing Donovan Elliot? The good news was everyone at the top was dead in their chapter. Now everyone who was a no one had a shot at being someone. They would talk a big game about revenge for their boss's death, but nothing would ever happen. It was the life they had chosen. Each opening would be filled and eventually Donovan Elliott and Boone Cross would live again. In the end, Danville gave each of the living members the opportunity of a lifetime.

"I'm sorry," said Danville.

"For what?" I asked.

"Your sister, Milton, all this really. I mean, I knew Milton didn't kill her back then, should have believed him when he said J. C. was pregnant. Should have believed you when you said she was murdered."

"Yeah, you probably should have. Doesn't really matter now though does it?"

"I'm a shitty cop," he said. He was, I can't deny that. The past is the past though, and to be honest, he just saved my ass so I couldn't stay too pissed at him.

I knelt down by Danville again, this time I put my hand on his good shoulder. "Thank you," I said. "Thanks for being the good guy." I leaned down and kissed his forehead. He had given me enough shit over the years, but it was shit I deserved. I guess I kind of thought of him in some sort of big brother kind of way, well, maybe more like a second cousin or something. I walked toward Donovan's red truck when Danville called out. I turned back, "I really gotta get moving here. Tell you what, if you ever leave Franklin come find us."

"Where?" he asked.

I smiled, "I said find us, Detective."

Chapter 107

The Willow Tree was on a small island in the middle of the River. The snow covered branches looked like clouds reaching down from the heavens above. That's what I thought of at least when I pulled up in Donovan's truck. That's what it was to me, heaven reaching out and pulling me out of this mess I had been living in since J.C. passed.

I parked the truck next to Mirko's. I had given him my suitcase when I met him to drop off Hannah before the fictional meeting with Eddy. I never trusted the Vandals, and they never failed to earn that distrust. I got in his backseat and put on my jeans, a hoodie, and a pair of boots. When I was dressed I walked down to the river bank, "Mirko, Mirko you here?" I yelled.

A tiny poof of blonde hair popped up first from behind the tree on the other side of the island. I could hear her laughing. Then Mirko showed his big Bosnian mug, his hardened look faded when he saw me. We watched each other for a brief second, then both smiled. Her laugh made me laugh. It was my girl. The girl who started whatever this was Franklin had turned into over the past couple months. My sister and Milton had sacrificed everything for Hannah, and in the end, she was the one great thing they both left this world. The one great thing they both experienced in their short, turbulent lives.

Hannah ran across the island to the edge of the water. "Aren't you coming over?" she asked. "It's the most beautiful place I have ever seen."

My smile turned into a laugh as I stepped out off the snow covered bank and into the shallow river. Mirko started to protest, but gave up as I shook him off. He lifted Hannah high off the ground and sat her on one shoulder.

"Stay dry, we come to you," he said.

"Too late now."

"You crazy-" he started and stopped. He could see I wasn't stopping.

I wanted one more time out here, my heaven on earth. Willow Island, as it was known throughout town, was where my sister was found that morning. This was her gateway into heaven. I'll never know if she was murdered out here, or just left after the fact. This is why part of me found this to be a sad place, but so was a graveyard. None the less, this is where I was closest to her. It would always be our special spot.

The water sent ice- cold razors up my calves as I made my way to the island. The cold froze my body as I walked, slowing me more with every moment. It froze my final visit to the island in time. When I got to the island Hannah was at the river bank smiling. Mirko stood behind her a ways up closer to the tree.

"We were starting to get worried," she said. I knelt down and pulled her tight to me. I knew Mirko hadn't told her the truth about everything, I wasn't sure when I would either. It didn't matter, and I don't think she cared really. I hugged her tight. Hannah pulled her arms off to push me away, I thought. Then she squeezed me back. When I held her the weight of everything lifted from my body. I could feel my sister. I could feel Milton watching us, and smiling.

"You better go now," said Mirko. "They be looking for you."

"What are you going to do?" I asked. He shrugged his shoulders and looked around.

"I like town, I stay awhile."

"They'll figure it out, that you helped us."

"No, if they do," he shrugged. "They do, I will be ok," he said and smiled. I nodded, then looked down at Hannah. I didn't know what to say, or how to say what we were going to do. I didn't want her to think she was being kidnapped again. I don't know if she really thought she ever was though. I looked at her and bent down.

"Hannah, I have a lot to tell you," I said. I wasn't sure if that sounded right, what she was thinking. "Um, I have to leave and I really want you to come with me."

The little girl nodded and smiled. "I know, Monkey told me."

"Monkey?" I asked.

"She call me Monkey, I don't know," Mirko said. "I tell her my name Mirko."

"I like Monkey," said Hannah.

I smiled at her, "Well, what do you think?"

"Can I say bye to my mo-" she started and stopped. Did she know? "Say bye to Ezzy?" My face kind of scrunched up on a side and gave her a sympathetic shake of the head, no. She looked at me and her head tilted. "Poor Ezzy, maybe one day we can come back for her."

"Maybe, but I bet Monkey will watch her and always make sure she's safe," I said. I looked at Mirko and raised my eyebrows. "Huh, Monkey, will you do that for us?"

"Yes, always," he said. He then nodded to his car, "You go, now." He picked up Hannah and she let out a playful scream. He placed her back on his shoulder and walked through the river. I watched them cross then turned back to the giant Willow.

The only place in the world I had ever felt safe, and I would probably never be back again. I heard Hannah laughing up at the car and smiled. I used to come here to talk to J.C. I would sing a lullaby she taught me, *Watching the River Run.* I would sing and watch the beautiful river. I wanted to be the water running far from here. This was it, finally I would be on my river. The tree blurred through my water filled eyes, and I felt a tear roll down my right cheek. I tried to remember if the right cheek meant it was a happy tear or a sad tear. I had an idea, but at the moment it really could have been either.

"Take care of this place," I said. "Watch over all of us if you can, and watch out for each other," I said. The pit in my stomach grew heavy, I wiped my eyes really quick as if someone could have been watching. "I love you."

Chapter 108

Hannah and I drove away from Franklin County sometime before the sun set. Mirko gave us his dark green S- 10 so we could make it out of town. No one knew him, it was paid off, and he said he would never report it stolen. I had given Mirko the notebook/letter Milton had left me with instructions to send it to Danville. I also left a note for Danville about some girls who people assumed had run away over the past couple years. I was pretty sure some, if not all, had suffered a fate similar to my sister. Milton wouldn't accept me giving him a ride into town. He said he wanted to walk and enjoy the evening.

We were actually driving off into the sunset, it was the dream I had played in my head as long as I could remember. I never told Mirko where I was going. He must have an idea though because he sent me a text as soon as we crossed the state line. It was the first time in my life I had ever been out of Missouri. I left with no intentions of ever returning to reminisce about the good ol' days. I pulled over at the next rest stop in the bordering state. Which state you wonder? It doesn't matter really because we weren't going to stop. I didn't care where I was going, I just cared about going.

We got to the rest stop and the first thing I did was look at my phone. *Look behind seat. I could not save Milton, you and Hannah will do.* That was the text I had received from Mirko.

"Do you have to go potty or are you hungry?" I asked Hannah. She smiled and shook her head no. "OK, sit here for a second, I have to grab something. I got out of the truck and pulled the driver's seat up to see what was behind it. There was nothing back there except three old orange shoeboxes on the floor. I grabbed the first box and pushed the seat up. I jumped back into the heated car and shut the door. I sat the box in my lap and looked at Hannah before looking around to see if anyone in the lot was paying any sort of attention.

"What is it?" she asked. I shrugged my shoulders. "Then open it."

I started to lift the lid off the box and caught a glimpse of the contents. I slammed the top shut. My head started spinning. Still no one watching us, but I didn't care. I started the car and drove to an empty part of the lot. I tried to catch my breath, but was having sort of a hard time. I couldn't believe it, I couldn't believe what I had seen. I opened the box again.

"Wow," Hannah whispered. She looked at me with wide eyes, "Is it real?" I think I said yeah, but I might have just nodded as I stared in the box. A shoebox filled with stacks of One Hundred Dollar bills. There was a post- it note on the inside of the lid. *I never lie to you, but once. Be safe- Mirko.*

That lying son of a bitch stole the money from the gangbangers, and now he had left it for us. All of it. I didn't know what to do at first, I wasn't sure what I should do. This was dirty money, stolen money. This wasn't stolen from innocent Americans though. It was taken from drug dealers who got it from selling to drug addicts. Not to mention, the dealers Mirko took it from were now dead. If I wanted to return the money the only people I could really give it to would be the police. The same police and government who did nothing to protect me or my family when we needed to be protected. If I turned it into them what would Danville actually do with it? Sure, I felt he had changed his ways and would start a new life. He'd do his job the way he was supposed to do. I looked at Hannah and smiled. We were starting a new life too. I put the car in drive and looked into the sky in front of us. I stepped on the gas and drove for that sliver of sun.

Chapter 109

We arrived at our final destination, well, current destination just one week after leaving Franklin. To say we are in Paradise would be an understatement. Sure my old digs weren't much and anything would have been an improvement, but thanks to Mirko we've finally found our peace and tranquility. My sister once told me of a place she had read about, she described it as Heaven on Earth. She said many of the people who lived there had claimed a certain spot to be the gateway to Heaven. We haven't found that spot yet, but one day the three of us will look. Soon Hannah will have a cousin who will love her and look up to her like a big sister, and some day after that- we will find their other siblings.

One thing always comes to mind when I think back to this time- What will Hannah remember? I want to tell her everything I know, tell her everything about her parents that was so good. Tell her how much she meant to her mother even though she died before Hannah was born, she was with her, she carried her. There was a letter Milton had left that wasn't for me. In the middle of the notebook was a small sealed envelope with the letter H. I've thought about reading it, wanted to read it, but can't. It's not for me. Instead I have it hidden under the mattress Hannah and I sleep on. I like to think it brings her closer to Milton, being so close to some of his last words. One day I will give it to her, and maybe she will tell me what it says. When I close my eyes I often dream of the letter. I dream what he will say to Hannah one day, and what she will remember.

Chapter 110

Dearest Hannah,

You may remember me, but we didn't really know each other. I want you to know that I have thought of you every day of your life. The short time we had together was worth a thousand lifetimes, even just for a day. . .

"But I'll look like a boy," the girl protested. He smiled at her and shook his head no.

"You'll always look just like you," he said. Then he smiled, "A perfect Angel." He handed the little girl a Popsicle, and she crawled up on the bathroom sink in the hotel room. She sat with her feet in the sink and her back to him.

"OK, fine. Not too short," she said. She looked at him in the mirror standing behind her. He watched the girl for a moment, smiled, and began to cut her hair. He cautiously held her hair from her head with each cut. The two of them were silent for the short haircut. He finished and the two stared at each other in mirror. The little girl shrugged her shoulders then asked, "Can we dye mine too? Black cuz I ready got yellow hair."

"Sure," he said. "First I want to give you something," he said. He reached behind his head and pulled a chain hanging from his neck out from his t-shirt. He unclasped the chain and placed in on Hannah's neck. She smiled at him and held the medallion that now hung from her neck.

"Who is it?"

"St. Nicholas," said Milton. "As long as you keep this on he'll be watching out for you, protecting you."

Hannah smiled at the medallion, then up to Milton. "Who's St. Nicholas?" she asked.

"You know, like Santa?" he said. "He's the Saint who protects children. He'll protect you, when I can't."

"Are you leaving?"

Milton nodded, "Soon," he said. "But always wear this, and you'll be safe. Maybe you'll even remember where you got it. Maybe you'll remember me."

She was silent for a moment. She smiled to him. Hannah looked into the mirror and into Milton's eyes. "I'll remember you Milton, forever."

THE END

Ryan T. Smith previously produced an almost- award- winning chili. He lives in rural Missouri with his wife and three children. He has dabbled in the restaurant business, electrical work, and spent a month as a door- to- door steak salesman. *BROKEN LULLABIES* is his first novel.

Twitter: @RTSmith2

e- mail: brokenlullabies.rs@gmail.com

Broken Lullabies